MURDER INK

MURDER INK

Betty Hechtman

This first world edition published 2020
in Great Britain and 2021 in the USA by
SEVERN HOUSE PUBLISHERS LTD of
Eardley House, 4 Uxbridge Street, London W8 7SY.
Trade paperback edition first published
in Great Britain and the USA 2021 by
SEVERN HOUSE PUBLISHERS LTD.

British Library Cataloguing in Publication Data
A CIP catalogue record for this title is available from the British Library.

ISBN-13: 978-0-7278-9017-7 (cased)
ISBN-13: 978-1-78029-744-6 (trade paper)
ISBN-13: 978-1-4483-0472-1 (e-book)

All Severn House titles are printed on acid-free paper.

Severn House Publishers support the Forest Stewardship Council™ [FSC™],
the leading international forest certification organisation. All our titles that
are printed on FSC certified paper carry the FSC logo.

MIX
Paper from
responsible sources
FSC® C013056
www.fsc.org

Typeset by Palimpsest Book Production Ltd.,
Falkirk, Stirlingshire, Scotland.
Printed and bound in Great Britain by
TJ Books Limited, Padstow, Cornwall.

In memory of my parents Helen and Jacob Jacobson,
my brother David Jacobson and my dear friend Roberta Martia
You would have enjoyed this

ONE

As I pulled open the door, my smart watch vibrated reminding me it was time for the first of my two appointments. It took a moment for my eyes to adjust to the low light of the restaurant. It had an old-fashioned, lounge feel with the leatherette booths and white tablecloth and was the kind of place where people had martinis with lunch. No martinis for me. I was working.

Two guys were hanging around the host stand, eying everyone who came in. One was a hipster dressed in a T-shirt and a suit that looked like it came from the boys' department. He glanced at me with an open smile. The other one wore a slightly crooked bow tie and was wringing his hands. One guess which was there for me.

My name is Veronica Blackstone and I'm a writer for hire, my pen ever ready – though these days I suppose I should really say keyboard ever ready. The guy I was meeting had contacted me about writing some love letters for him. Not really *for* him, more like *as* him.

That's what I do. I write what anyone needs written. I've done love letters (a challenge, but my favorite, even though ironically my own love life is at zero), biographies, résumés, copy for business brochures, wedding vows, and tributes I call 'celebrations of life', which are mostly for funerals. I'll write just about anything – from a letter quitting someone's gym membership to ending an office lease – as long as it's legal. No ransom notes or letters threatening bodily harm. If this was an email or text, I'd probably add an LOL after the last comment to show I wasn't serious. It wasn't as if anybody had ever approached me to write either of those things anyway.

What qualifies me? you ask. I wrote the national bestseller *The Girl with the Golden Throat* about a singer who could hit a high note that shattered glass. Was it an accident or intentional when her voice shattered a glass ceiling and crushed the music critic beneath it? It was up to Detective Derek Streeter to find out. The trouble was, when it came to writing a sequel, I froze. The ten chapters I'd completed had been sitting on a shelf for months. I guess you could say I had no problem writing for others, just for myself.

I have to say it made for an interesting life, though. It put me right in middle of people's lives and privy to lots of secrets. Sometimes more than I wanted to know.

'Evan?' I said, addressing both men, though I was sure which one would nod. It was a very nervous nod at that, and when he reached out to shake my hand, he missed it and got my wrist instead.

'Then you're Veronica, right,' he said as he glanced around furtively. 'I'm glad you're here. She'll be here any minute.'

The *she* was Sally Rogers, his intended. There was no way I could write love letters as him or to her without having some idea who both people were. He'd given me some of the 4-1-1 on the phone, but it was not the same as seeing them in person. Evan got the host's attention and said we were ready for our table.

'Let's get our stories straight,' he said as he slid into the booth.

'You're going to tell her that I'm your neighbor who you ran into and that you invited me to join you. Then you're going to act like you got a phone call and excuse yourself, giving me time to get to know her.'

'Exactly,' he said glancing toward the front. I fought the urge to lean over and straighten the bow tie as I went over what I knew about him. His name was Evan Wilkerson and he was the head IT guy for the Bellingham Hotel. It was a luxury hotel located down the street on Michigan Avenue. They served high tea in the lobby and still required proper attire, and I don't just mean no tank tops or flip-flops. All I knew about his intended was her name and that he thought she was some kind of wonderful.

Evan had said that he found out about my services by word of mouth, which these days really meant social media. I had a website and a Facebook page, though I had to be discreet – no samples of my work, or testimonials from satisfied customers, since a lot of my work was really ghosting as someone else.

'Since we have a few minutes, why don't you fill me in on a little more. You were a little vague on the phone about where your relationship is. How long have you been dating?'

'Uh, we're not exactly dating. That's what I need you for,' he stammered. 'I tend to get nervous and I don't know what to say.' For the moment he seemed uncertain what to do with himself. As he fumbled around with his napkin, he managed to knock over a glass of water, across the white tablecloth. Thankfully, it soaked up the liquid before it drenched me.

'You do know her, though?' I said and he nodded.

'Yes, of course. She works at the hotel too. She's an assistant manager in charge of making arrangements for special events.'

Evan's head suddenly shot up and he tensed. I followed his gaze and saw that a woman had just walked up to the host stand. Evan stood up almost taking the tablecloth with him and waved at her, and all I could think was, boy, do I have my work cut out for me.

I know you're not supposed to judge people by outer appearances, but when I saw the beaming smile and the bright yellow suit, it was like sunshine had just walked in. Even her name, Sally, sounded sunny. I glanced back at Evan with slicked-down brown hair and the tense expression. She was so out of his league.

Just before she reached the table, he whispered, 'I probably should have mentioned that I want to marry her.'

If she hadn't been in earshot, I would have said what I was thinking. Was he serious? I wrote love letters, but I wasn't a magician.

She greeted Evan and glanced at me. Evan mumbled that I was his neighbor and she just flashed a smile my way. 'Sally Rogers,' she said holding out her hand. I shook it and gave her my name.

'Nice to meet you, Veronica,' she said then turned to Evan. 'I just don't know how to thank you,' she said as she slid in the booth. She pulled a slim computer out of her elegant tote bag and set it on the table. 'It is so nice of you to give up your lunch hour to help me with my computer issue.'

She turned to me and explained some problem she was having with a personal email account. 'Evan is so good with computers.'

He smiled sheepishly and seemed lost in the moment of praise. Then he remembered the plan.

He pulled out his cell phone as he got up. 'Sorry, I have to take this.' He glanced at Sally. 'I'm always on-call when there's computer trouble. Like an ER doctor,' he said. He gave me a nod before he walked off and almost as an afterthought put his cell phone to his ear.

'Evan is really something,' I said, deliberately leaving it hanging, hoping she'd say how she really felt about him. It wasn't my job to judge who belonged with who, but they seemed like such an unlikely couple. I had to believe there was some hope or I wouldn't take the job.

'He's kind of sweet,' she said, and I let out my breath in relief. At least she didn't see him as just a computer nerd. Even so I was still going to try to get him to lower his expectations and start with getting one date before he started looking at wedding venues.

Now my task was to find out who she really was. What she wanted out of life and what I could say as Evan to make her fall in love with him, or at least go on one date. And do it before he came back from his fake phone call.

I skipped right to the point and said I heard she had a stressful job at the hotel. I didn't really know it for a fact, but then who didn't think their job was stressful. She let out a sigh as if she was relieved that I understood.

Before she could launch into exactly what was so stressful about it, I made up some gibberish about reading a magazine article that detailed different things that executives did to get away from their work. I was about to ask her if she had any hobbies when she leaned in close.

'I bet they didn't list what I do.' The way she was whispering I got worried that she was going to say something weird, but what she said next caught me totally off guard. 'I have a real weakness for romantic comedies,' she said. 'I know they're just silly fluff, but all I have to do is pop in a DVD and let the movie take me away.' She started naming some of her favorite movies and I was about to comment on something – or really someone – they all had in common, but just then Evan rejoined us. He looked at me expectantly and I didn't know quite what to do.

Finally, I gave him a nod that I hoped made it look like I'd been successful.

The server showed up and began handing out menus. I looked at my watch. 'I had no idea it was so late.' I handed the menu back to the server as I got up. 'I have places to go and people to see,' I said airily.

'I'll talk to you later, then,' Evan said, as he stood next to the booth. 'That is, we'll talk when we pass each other in the hallway of our building.' He glanced toward Sally with a nervous expression. 'Since we're neighbors and we see each other in the hall all the time. When we get our mail or take trash down to the dumpster.'

I wanted to poke him. He was giving too many details, a sure sign that he was lying if anyone thought about it. Not that Sally seemed to be paying attention anyway. She was already looking down at her computer and was typing something while she glanced at the menu.

I ducked into the ladies' room to scribble down some notes about Evan and Sally before heading outside. No typing the words into a smartphone either. I always use a pen and soft-sided notebook. The cell phone might have been more efficient, but it wasn't the same as putting something on real paper. I'd once read that you used a different part of your brain when you hand wrote. And that part of my brain was much better with words.

What I'd said was actually true. I did have a place to go and people to see even though I dreaded it. 'You have to take the bitter with the sweet,' I muttered to myself as I went out the door.

TWO

The interior of the restaurant had been very dim, so it was a surprise when I walked out into the bright sun of the October afternoon. As soon as I turned onto Michigan Avenue a gust of wind sent my scarf flying into my face and I had to peel it away and secure it under my jacket. October was my favorite month in Chicago. The air felt crisp, but not really cold. It was ironic that it felt like everything was coming back to life after the languid days of summer, when actually the leaves were all dying off.

This area of Michigan Avenue was called the Magnificent Mile. The street was lined with nice shops and the sidewalks were wide with a landscaped strip cut into the cement. The trees were permanent, but the rest was seasonal. Right now there were rows of mums in yellows and rust, growing next to pumpkins and Indian corn. It continued on like that all the way almost to the river.

Normally I would have enjoyed the walk, but my next appointment weighed heavily on my mind.

The bridge shook as a bus rumbled past, which only added to my discomfort as I crossed the Chicago River. I glanced down at the murky water and saw that one of the architectural tour boats was just leaving. I caught a word here and there as the docent began his talk. Beyond the bridge, the wide street angled slightly to the left and sloped downward, reminding me that there was a level below. At Randolph Street, I looked longingly at the decorative hood over the stairs leading to the Metra station. I would have loved to have gone down them and just caught a train home.

But instead I turned and skirted Millennium Park which had been created out of thin air, well, sort of anyway. It had been built over the Metra tracks where there had once been just open air. A sign announced I was in the Lakeshore East neighborhood. It was a relatively new area and consisted mostly of modern high rises that appeared to be all glass. It was hard to see it as a real neighborhood though. All that concrete and glass felt too sterile.

It was easy to find the building. A little over a year ago, I'd made numerous trips there when Rachel Parker was preparing for her wedding. And now I was going there to discuss her funeral.

I kept thinking of how effervescent she'd been. How she thought she was the luckiest girl in the world to be marrying Luke. Some people might have thought he was the luckiest guy in the world marrying into the Parker family. Their name was everywhere – a wing of a hospital, a downtown office building and even a park had been named after them. Their money came from the shipping industry.

Rachel had shunned the trappings of her family's wealth and become a teacher at an inner-city school. She'd wanted a simple wedding but of course that would never have happened. Mrs Parker had coerced her into agreeing to the kind of grand affair that was expected of the family. It was as much a business event as it was about a marriage.

I came into the picture because Rachel wanted them to create their own vows, but Mrs Parker had not been happy with what the couple had come up with and would only agree to let them speak their personal vows if a professional gave them a polish. Well, it was more like a complete sanding.

There was a lot of haggling back and forth between Mrs Parker and Rachel as I made endless trips downtown to show them what I'd come up with. The Parkers were the kind of people who expected you to come to them. Luke had stayed in the background and, after the first things he'd scribbled down, didn't seem to care what happened to his words.

I'd gone to the wedding and it was a little strange to hear them recite the personal-sounding words I'd written. We'd come a long way from Rachel's original vows. She'd wanted something unconventional and had written that when they'd hooked up that first night, she'd been sure they were meant to be lifetime partners. There had been a few too many details of what exactly went on that first night and Mrs Parker had been appalled, which was probably why Rachel had done it. I didn't have to be a psychologist to realize that they were at odds with each other and were just using the vows as a battleground.

The final version of Rachel's vows was sweet and completely G-rated and the wedding was beyond elegant. After that I'd lost track of Rachel. Not that that was unusual. It seemed like as soon as I'd finished whatever I'd been contracted to write, most people wanted to forget that I existed. I'd been surprised to get the call from Camille Parker and more surprised to find out why she was calling.

After the call I'd checked around and found a small story about Rachel, which seemed odd considering how well known the family was. All it said was that she'd fallen from her balcony and died. The size of the story and lack of details made me believe there was a lot that had been purposely left out.

I turned off of Randolph and after a half a block reached the building called Lake View. The tall structures funneled the wind, and a gust of air pushed me toward the entrance. A doorman greeted me, and I had to wait while he called upstairs. The lobby was like that of a hotel, with comfortable seating and even coffee and tea. I was considering helping myself to a hot drink when the doorman pointed me to a door, which slid smoothly open. Several people took advantage of the open door and walked in with me before hurrying on ahead.

Rachel's parents had gifted her a condominium in the building when she started working. She very proudly had told me it was the only thing she had accepted from them and that when they wanted to give the couple a bigger place when they got married, she'd refused. Her parents had a place in the building as well, though theirs was really more of a pied-à-terre since they owned a mansion in Highland Park.

I wasn't sure which balcony Rachel had fallen from, though I suspected that it was the one attached to her apartment, and was therefore glad that Mrs Parker had said we'd meet at their place. I wondered how Luke managed to continue living there with the constant reminder of what had happened.

The elevator made a rapid ascent and I felt my stomach clench when I got off on the thirty-second floor and walked down the hall to the Parkers' apartment.

I'd written pieces for celebrations of life before, as I preferred to call them, but they had been for people who'd had full lives. There was sadness, but acceptance. There would be none of that for Rachel.

Mrs Parker answered the door. I knew her first name was Camille, but even in these days of informality, I couldn't imagine calling her anything but Mrs Parker. I gave her a once-over though I tried not to be too obvious. I couldn't help it – I was always observing people, thinking how I would describe them. I don't mean an autopsy description – height, weight, hair and eye color – you know, what writers are warned to avoid. I looked for something that gave a clue to who they were. So in Mrs Parker's case the fact she had brown hair with a lot of highlights that were probably painted in, wore designer jeans and an untucked white shirt, along with simple diamond stud earrings, wouldn't be what I was after. There was something brittle and cold about her. I'd noticed it when I'd met her before and now a pained tension about her eyes had been added.

She greeted me with a smile that stopped at her mouth and brought me inside. The living room wall was all windows and I had an instant view of the balcony and beyond to the southern part of the city. My first impulse was to look out at the view and see if I could see my neighborhood. But then reality hit, and I focused on the balcony. I sucked in my breath as I looked at the transparent barrier. It gave the illusion that the balcony was just hanging in space. I thought of Rachel's balcony and realized that it looked the same.

Mrs Parker noticed me looking at the patio and steered me toward a pair of off-white couches that formed a conversation area.

'Thank you for coming,' she said, offering me a seat.

There was a soft knock at the door, and she went to answer it. I saw Rachel's husband, Luke Ross, come in. The last time I'd seen him he was getting pelted with rose petals as he and Rachel headed off for their honeymoon. He'd definitely looked a lot happier then; now his mouth was set in a straight line. There was a casualness about his demeanor and his soft blue jeans with a navy sweater reflected it. I don't know why I looked at his feet, but his shoe choice was well broken-in tan ankle boots. As for the autopsy description, he was tall with a nice build, had dark blond hair and hazel eyes.

A look passed between Mrs Parker and Luke as she showed him to the couch. She tightened her mouth as if to tell him to stay quiet. There wasn't even a hint of a greeting smile between them and it seemed pretty clear that there hadn't been a big welcome to the family feeling after the wedding. I didn't know what Luke did for a living, but I'd gotten the impression that whatever it was didn't go along with the Parkers' reputation.

I began by offering my condolences to the pair and they both nodded in what seemed like a studied pose of sadness. There was no offer of a drink or even small talk. Mrs Parker made it clear from the start this was no social gathering and got right down to business.

'Mr Parker and I were pleased with the job you did on Rachel's wedding vows and we'd like you to write something for her memorial service,' she said.

'You mean something for the officiant to read?' I said, thinking of what I'd done before, but she shook her head.

'Actually, we want you to create something we can give out at the service. A biography that will show what her life was like and hopefully divert attention from how it ended.' Luke threw her a sharp look and she returned it. 'For now, her cause of death is listed as inconclusive. I'd leave it that way, but Mr Parker wants it to be labeled as accidental.' She let out a heavy sigh. 'It will still be a black mark for the family. If she'd died from some disease it would be so much easier.' Her mouth retracted into an angry expression. 'Even in her death, Rachel always made it so difficult.'

Did she really say that? I held in my surprise at her comment. She'd lost her daughter and all she really seemed to be was angry. I knew something about loss. I searched through my old feelings looking for any signs that I'd been angry. No, I'd just been heartbroken and sad.

'The funeral was private, but we're planning a memorial service in three weeks for all of our friends and business associates.'

So, it would be the same crowd that had been at her wedding, which had included city officials and even the mayor. I started asking about specifics like how long they wanted the piece to be, what form it should be delivered in and lastly, the money.

Mrs Parker seemed clueless about the length and left it up to me. All she said about the style was tasteful. They would take care of the printing and binding as they wanted it to be an actual small book. When it came to the money, it was a repeat of what I'd gone through with the wedding vows. Rachel had wanted to be generous, but Mrs Parker, like so many rich people, seemed to think I should be so honored to do work for them, that I would work almost for free. Honor didn't pay bills. I stood my ground until she finally agreed on a fair amount. But of course, to be paid on delivery and any expenses I incurred were my responsibility.

She went to the counter that separated the living room from the kitchen and came back with a stack of photo albums. 'This should give you some background. And it would be good if you placed some photographs in the copy.' They seemed rather unwieldy and I asked if she had something I could use to carry them. Seeming a little put upon, she rummaged through the kitchen and came back with a reusable grocery bag from Trader Joe's. The way she looked at the print on it, I was sure she hadn't been the one who'd shopped there. She left me to load the albums into the bag.

'I may need to speak to you later,' I said. 'And you as well.' I turned to Luke who'd remained silent the whole time. 'And possibly Mr Parker.' Camille Parker shook her head.

'I suppose if you need some details, we can talk again. But leave Mr Parker out of it.' I thought she might give a reason, but she left it at that. I suspected she either was protecting him or she just wanted to run the show. She turned to Luke and told him to walk me out. Got it. Our visit was over.

He appeared relieved as he stood and guided me down the short hall to the door. We walked out together and headed to the bank of elevators. He pushed the down button for both of us.

He stayed silent until the elevator arrived and even as we rode down the few floors to his. Then as he started to get off, he leaned against the door, holding it open.

'Rachel treasured those vows you wrote for us,' he said. 'Almost every month we'd go out to the tip of Navy Pier and she'd have us read them to each other again.'

I could just see it in my head. The old pier had been a lot of things, but lately had been revitalized into a destination with restaurants and amusements. The tip offered a view of the skyline and the shore and was one of the most romantic spots in the city.

I thought he was going to leave it at that, but since he was still holding the door open there was clearly something else on his mind. He finally let out a sigh. 'It's too bad that Rachel and you didn't keep in touch. She could have really used a friend.'

Before I could answer, he'd stepped out onto the floor and the elevator door snapped shut before it began to descend. What did he mean by that?

THREE

I never tired of the view of the lake and cars moving along the Outer Drive and automatically took a seat on that side of the Metra train for my trip home. But if I looked out the window on the ride, none of it registered. I was still lost in thought about my two appointments. I wasn't sure what I was going to do with Evan and Sally. In the past, I had always had a relationship to build the letters on. But this time the letter was going to have to create a relationship.

And then there was Rachel. I couldn't get Luke's comment out of my head. If he'd intended to make me feel guilty, he'd succeeded. Was he trying to imply she'd still be alive if I hadn't lost touch with her? I wished I'd explained that I was usually a person non grata once I'd fulfilled my purpose. And why put it all on me? She had my phone number. Then I chided myself for even thinking of that last part.

The whole experience made me believe that Luke thought it wasn't an accident – that she'd propelled herself off the balcony. Could that be? How could Rachel have gone from a bubbling bride to such a dark place in a year?

As my surroundings came back into focus, I realized with a start that we'd reached my stop. The conductor was already calling all aboard. I made a run for it. The door slid shut behind me and the train began to pull away.

I followed the crowd down the platform and took the stairs down to the street. The sun drenched me in light when I came out from the viaduct. I took in the scene in front of me and thought of how different my neighborhood was from Lakeshore East. For one, Hyde Park was much older and to my way of thinking more of a real neighborhood.

Some people thought Hyde Park was almost like a small town within the city. Really a college town, as the main campus of the University of Chicago was located there.

There were a few high rises, but most of Hyde Park was made

up of three-story walk-ups and houses in assorted architectural styles. Rambling Victorians on the block ran along the Metra tracks, while elsewhere streets were lined with more modern box-like townhouses.

As usual there was plenty of foot traffic. Two women wearing U of C T-shirts jogged by me. I noticed several people outside Powell's Bookstore checking out the freebies. It was a neighborhood tradition to leave books there for anyone to take.

I crossed 57th Street and started down the block that had a mixture of residential and commercial with the stores and restaurants mainly on the ground floor and apartments above. A woman with a fresh crew cut was just coming out of the hair salon on the corner. I considered stopping at the small market, but I had the bag full of albums and decided to pass for now.

As soon as I turned onto my street the noise level went down. The leaves on the tall trees that lined the block had turned a bright yellow as if they'd swallowed the sun. A small gust of wind sent a shower of them around me.

I glanced up at my building, thinking of the glass tower where the Parkers lived. They were as different as night and day. The word vintage was thrown around when describing my building, which was a nice way of saying old – like over one hundred years old. Still, the butterscotch-colored bricks look bright and the white columns on either side of the front were freshly painted.

I went into the vestibule and checked the mail. There wasn't a doorman, just a locked glass door that was commonly called a buzz door, because a tenant could push a button in their apartment which released the lock with a buzz to let a guest in.

The three flights of stairs were good exercise, particularly since I spent so much time sitting. I was only slightly breathless when I opened my door and went inside. Sunlight was streaming in the living room window and the room felt uncomfortably warm. I opened the door to my front porch to let some air in. I looked out on it suddenly seeing it differently. I always thought of it as a porch, but wasn't it really a balcony? It was confirmed when I checked the dictionary. Yes, I had a paper one and still used it instead of checking online. It turns out that a porch is connected to the entrance to a building whereas a balcony was like this – an enclosed platform attached to a building.

I stepped out on it, thinking of Rachel and her much fancier building. My balcony was more spacious than hers and shared with the next-door neighbor. There was a low wrought-iron fence between my side and theirs, which didn't afford any privacy. For the moment it didn't matter. The apartment was up for sale and was vacant.

I felt a little queasy when I walked to the railing along the front. It barely reached past my waist. I stepped back rather than looking down to the street and went back inside leaving the door open.

I glanced around the living room that was as familiar as the back of my hand. I groaned inwardly at my mental use of a cliché. Writers were supposed to know better. This had been my family home until I moved out, and then when my father died, I inherited it and moved back in.

Sometimes I looked at the room and thought of all the events that had happened in the same space over the years. I could see myself dressed in frothy pink for my fifth birthday. Then it was Christmas Eve and we were having our usual gathering. I could almost smell the cardamom coffee cakes my mother always made for the holiday. Memories of seasons flew by. I imagined the radiators chugging as the snow fell outside the window and piled up on the balcony. Then it was summer with the languid air blowing in from outside.

I saw myself lugging in the small fragrant pine tree I'd gotten for the holidays at the shopping center. I was nine and had taken it upon myself to make sure we had something to decorate since everything had changed. Time went forward to spring and I saw myself hunched on the couch when my father broke the news that my mother had died. I sobbed into the scarf she had taught me how to crochet.

Then time fast-forwarded more years and I was dressed for my wedding. I stopped the mental movie right there and shook my head to get rid of the memories. I needed to deal with now.

I took the shopping bag of albums and went into my office, which was right off the living room. It had French doors that I left open so that it was almost like an extension of the living room.

A long hall ran from the living room back to the dining room and beyond there was the kitchen and a small bedroom and bath left from the days when it was common to have a live-in servant. I was still finding surprising things, like the pipes in the ceiling left from when there were gas lights (closed off now) and there was a bell in the dining-room floor meant to summon that live-in servant.

Other apartments in the building had been remodeled and updated, but mine was mostly original. I still had a claw foot bathtub and a decorative pedestal sink.

I pulled out the albums and put them on my desk along with my notes about Evan and Sally. I really wanted to get started on a letter for him, but I needed to talk to him first and find out exactly what he had in mind. Even then it was going to take my whole arsenal of inspirational devices to find the right words. But there was no reason I couldn't start on the piece about Rachel. I started to look through the albums but was overwhelmed by the volume of photographs. I'd never done a memorial booklet before. When I'd accepted the project I hadn't really thought about how I would do it. But now I was filled with concerns. Mrs Parker had talked about a biography illustrated with photographs. That seemed cold and dry and I thought there had to be another way. But it also had to be something that Mrs Parker would find acceptable. I decided to let it simmer in the back of my mind for a while. I put the albums back into the plastic grocery bag. When I looked out the window, it was getting dark.

I went around the apartment turning on the lights, realizing I'd forgotten about dinner and now it would have to wait because it was Tuesday, which meant the writing group would be meeting.

Originally, I'd had three groups a week meeting to work on their writing, but I had gotten it down to just one. I was not only a pen for hire, but I guess a writing coach for hire as well. I might be stuck on my own fiction, but I was great at helping other people with theirs.

I sighed when I glanced at my partial manuscript on my shelf. All those pages equaled ten chapters of book two of detective Derek Streeter's adventures. I pulled out the last page I'd written and read it over. It was half blank and I remembered that when I could think of anything for Derek to do or say, I'd started writing my feelings. *I'm starting to panic. I can't breathe and when I do it hurts. Every word seems to suck. The whole thing sucks. I'm finished. Done. What am I going to do?* I cringed as I read my words. Would I ever be able to write the rest of it?

I had briefly thought of showing it to the group and getting their opinion, but wised up before I did. If I let them critique my work, it kind of blew my position of authority, and whatever justification I had for charging them for my opinion. They put me on a pedestal and thought I knew the secret sauce to writing. Besides, there was always tomorrow. Maybe the words would start to flow again. A girl could dream. I shut off the desk lamp and went to the dining room to get ready for my group.

FOUR

Ed Grimaldi was the first arrival. He was always the first one there and was anxious to get started as usual. He was in his sixties, favored blue track pants and T-shirts. Like a lot of people in the neighborhood, he worked for the university. I didn't know exactly what he did, but it had to do with maintenance. He lived down the street and his wife had convinced him to join the group. I suspected it was mostly about getting him out of the house for a while. He was obsessed with reality shows where men and women got to pick mates or dates. His work in progress was fan fiction based on his favorite show, *The Singleton*. It was a competition where a bevy of women vied to be the one picked by the current bachelor. It was hardly all sweet romance either. There were options for the man to take one of the women to Getting to Know You Suite, which probably should have been called the Getting It On Suite. Whatever went on there was off camera, of course. Not so in Ed's version.

I suspected he based the man character on himself, or who he wished to be. And the women he had fantasies about. I rolled my eyes just thinking about them. He had gathered a group of famous women living and dead who were supposed to be vying for the man's affection. They went from Jackie Kennedy to Lady Gaga with a lot of stops in between.

He went right into the dining room and took a seat and then dropped his folder of sheets on the dark wood table. He'd brought along his usual commuter mug of something. He said it was tea, but I suspected it was something a little stronger.

I buzzed Tizzy Baxter in and opened the door as she came up the stairs. She also worked for the university at an office job in the business school. She was married with grown kids. Tizzy lived down the street and I'd known her before she joined the group. 'I've got some exciting stuff this week,' she said coming in the door. Enthusiastic wasn't a strong enough word to describe her. She was writing a time-travel romance, which took place in our neighborhood, but back when the 1893 World's Fair took place. She was enthralled by the history of the neighborhood and was always talking about what used to be where, whether anybody wanted to know or not. Like how many times did she have to tell everyone that Amelia Earhart went to the local high school? Her dark brown hair was cut so it swung when she moved her head and she always wore layers of clothes that seemed to flutter when she walked.

I heard her greet Ed as she went back to the dining room just as the bell rang again. I buzzed open the downstairs door for Daryl Sullivan and waited while she came up the stairs. She worked downtown managing a clothing store that catered to young women. Though she dressed in a more of a classic style, she knew all of the trends. Her head was bowed when she came in and she glanced up with a weak smile. Her eyes looked tense and her breath sounded shallow and nervous. It would only get worse when we got to her work in progress. She was writing a sweet romance but didn't do well with any criticism.

Ben Monroe arrived with a knock at the door. He muttered a greeting and handed me a dish of something covered in wax paper. 'Sara sent this for you. She said all you have to do is heat it.'

Sara Wright was my downstairs neighbor and his older sister. She was also the reason he was here. Ben was a cop in one of the suburbs and he'd taken the neutral expression called 'cop face' to extreme. Bottled up was an understatement about him. Sara had gifted him with three months of workshop sessions. She hadn't said anything to me about it, but I was pretty sure she'd imagined he'd write something that expressed his inner feelings. Ha! He was writing about a hard-boiled detective and acted as if there was a penalty for using too many words. I'd call his style staccato. I kept trying to get him to explore the detective's inner thoughts, but Ben said they didn't matter to the plot.

Sara was married with a two-year-old son and in a much different place in her life than I was, but we'd become friends anyway. She was also intent on fixing my life. She was concerned that I was a vegetarian and not getting proper protein, hence the dish of food. Not that I was complaining. She was a great cook and, as she figured, I hadn't even thought about dinner yet.

I led the way back to the dining room and Ben joined the others, while I checked what was under the wax paper. It was a personal-size casserole dish of rice, beans and veggies with a sprinkling of cheese.

I suspected she was hoping that the weekly dinners and play time with his nephew before the workshops would also help loosen Ben up. I'd never seen him in action with Mikey and I wondered if the cute little boy was enough to coax a smile out of his uncle.

I think that both Ben and I were looking forward to the end of his gifted sessions.

When I joined the group at my dining room table, they were all thumbing through the pages they'd brought in. I knew they were all tense about going public with what they'd written and tried to loosen them all up with a little social time first.

'Anyone have anything exciting to report?' I asked, looking in Ben's direction since he'd seemed the most likely to have been in the middle of something interesting. I watched his even features for some kind of reaction. I guess he'd be considered good-looking, but his looks didn't do much for me. I'd rather have someone with a snaggletooth if it came with some personality.

He just shrugged and nodded toward the others as if to give them the floor.

They all looked back to me. They were awed that I was a professional writer and fascinated by what I did.

'What do you have going this week?' Ed asked. 'Anyone hire you to write some steamy missives?' He wiggled his eyebrows and I wasn't sure if he was joking or serious. I never used names, so it seemed OK to talk about my work.

'Actually, someone did, though I'd say more romantic than steamy,' I said, before describing Evan.

Ed shook his head. 'I never had to do anything like that. Back in the day, the ladies were always running after me.'

'Obviously this guy doesn't have your abilities,' Tizzy said, with a touch of sarcasm. 'He sounds kind of sweet and old-fashioned, but I don't know what you could say to get that woman to want to go out with him.'

Daryl shrugged. 'I'm glad it's you that has to come up with

something. I wouldn't have a clue.' There was a pause and Ed started gathering his pages, as if we were going to get started.

'Wait,' Tizzy said. 'There's something more, isn't there?' She was studying my face. 'You look like I feel when there's something I have to do, but don't want to.'

I was surprised at how on the money she was. I mentally chided myself for the cliché. Simply put, I didn't like them and avoided them whenever possible. I thought it was better to find a more original way of saying whatever. The writers' group knew all about it. Mentally, I changed the thought to how accurate Tizzy was. It was easy to talk about Evan's situation, but a whole other story talking about Rachel. 'There is this other assignment.' I left out the details that might have hinted who it was since Rachel's family was so prominent, but I explained I'd been commissioned to write something to give out at a memorial service. 'She was young and there's some debate about how she died.'

'What do you mean, "debate"?' Ed asked.

'Right now, it is being considered inconclusive, but it seems like some members of the family want it to be considered an accident and another seems to believe it might have been deliberate.'

'You mean like suicide?' Tizzy said. Hearing the word was jarring, but I nodded.

'What else do you know about her?' Daryl asked. She shuddered when I mentioned Rachel's age, which was right around Daryl's. Ed's interest was piqued when I added she'd been married just over a year and that I'd helped write her wedding vows.

'Sounds like her happily ever after might not have been,' he said.

'How exactly did she die?' Tizzy asked. She realized her question sounded a little blunt and tried to soften it. 'Sorry, I didn't think. If you wrote her wedding vows, you must have gotten to know her pretty well.'

I nodded. 'For a short time, it was pretty intense. Wedding vows are about as personal as you can get. Though I didn't really get to know her husband.' I swallowed, once again transitioning in my mind from Rachel the bride-to-be to Rachel the dead. I explained the balcony without giving any more details. 'The last time I saw her was at her wedding as she was leaving for her honeymoon. She appeared blissfully happy.' I gestured to Ed to pass out the copies of his pages. 'I suppose I'll find out more about what led up to her death as I work on the piece.'

'Who decides if it was an accident or a suicide?' Daryl asked. She turned to Ben. 'You must know about all that.' Though he was in street clothes and never talked about it, they all knew he was a cop.

'The coroner is the one who determines the cause of death,' he answered in a matter-of-fact tone. 'There is something besides inconclusive, accidental or suicide.' He let it hang in the air a moment before he continued. 'There's also homicide.' It was the most he'd said during our social time and I looked at him with surprise.

'Murder?' I said. 'I don't think so.' I shook my head vehemently, thinking again of the pretty bride.

Ben's expression stayed the same – both his tone and his eyes were flat as he continued. 'I'm just saying that it wouldn't be the first time someone tried to cover up a murder by making it look like a suicide or an accident.'

The other three were looking at me intently. 'So, what are you going to do?' Tizzy asked.

'I'm not really sure. I do feel kind of guilty about not getting in touch with her after the wedding.' I explained that generally that was the way clients wanted it. 'I just assumed she was the same, but then her husband said she could have used a friend. And I did write a mystery, so I know a little about investigating.' I hadn't meant to say all of that. I'd never opened up as much to the group before and it was making me a little uncomfortable. I glanced around the table anxious to change the subject. 'OK, who's going to read Ed's work?'

The way we worked was that someone other than the writer read the work out loud and then everyone commented with me giving the final word. My opinion carried more weight since, as I mentioned, they thought I knew all the answers.

Whoever read Ed's work usually ended up blushing since it seemed like his characters were always in the Getting to Know You Suite and it was pretty graphic. There were always some chuckles too because all the who-did-what-to-who along with the euphemisms came across as funny when read out loud. When no one volunteered, I pointed to Ben. He was the only one who could read Ed's work with a straight face. It always sounded like he was reading a police report, which distressed Ed because he insisted it took away from the drama.

Everyone gave their comments at the end and then I added mine. I said what I always did – that he might want to consider concentrating more on the characters' personalities and less on their body parts.

Tizzy read Ben's pages. He was compulsive about giving accurate details of what kind of gun and caliber of bullets the bad guy had used. But the characters had the personality of a paper doll. I did my best to nicely suggest that he add some details to the bad guy. 'He must have some life besides robbing a bank. Maybe if you think what his favorite food is or what his fifth birthday was like, you can give him a little juice.' Ben listened and then acknowledged he'd heard what I'd said, but he gave no indication if he planned to change anything.

When Ed finished reading Daryl's work, everyone sucked in their breath waiting for the onslaught. None of them offered a comment and it was all on me. Who could blame them? She never took even the mildest criticism well. Daryl had a particular problem in her writing. She wrote like she was writing some kind of manual and included every step along the way. Tonight, her pages were about a couple going to a party. The couple stopped for the traffic light and pushed the button to make it change. They watched the light across the street waiting for the walk sign to appear. When it did change, they crossed, holding hands. They stepped up on the curb on the other side of the street before beginning to walk down the block. You get the idea. I did my best explaining that it was too much information. She seemed OK for a moment, but then exploded.

'You don't understand. I was setting up the scene so the reader could have a mental picture with all the details.' She went on for a few more minutes defending what she'd written, her eyes flashing with anger. Finally, she grabbed the papers back and shoved them in her folder. As always, she calmed down after that and smiled as she thanked me for the help.

Tizzy's work was never a problem. She was almost at the end

of a rewrite of her time-travel novel and it was just polishing now. There were just some grammar corrections and suggestions for a change of words. When we finished with her work, everyone began to pack up.

'When are we going to have an extra session,' Ed asked. Once a month or so we met at a public place and just like art students had sketch classes out in the world, they had a writing experience using what they heard or saw. The point was to write something short like a scene, a piece of flash fiction, or merely a description. We talked it over and decided on the following week. We'd go to a restaurant down the street.

Ben seemed to be taking longer to gather up his pages and he was just coming down the hall when the others had already left.

'I hope the comments were useful,' I said. He responded with a half-nod.

'I got the impression that you might be planning on doing your own investigating while you're writing that thing – what did you call it?'

'A celebration of life,' I said.

'Right, a celebration of life,' he repeated. 'Forget what I said about homicide. I'm sure it wasn't. And it shouldn't matter to you whether it was an accident or a suicide. The best thing you can do is to write your piece and leave it at that.' He looked at me with almost an expression on his face that could best be described as stern. 'Leave it to the professionals. Cops don't like it when civilians muck around in their business.'

I considered arguing with him, but decided it was pointless, so I nodded as though I agreed with him, though inside I was thinking no way was I dropping anything. The hunt for the truth was on.

FIVE

I think the group imagined that I just sat down at the computer and words started falling off my fingertips.

I wish.

In the morning, I took my coffee and the notes I'd written after meeting Evan and Sally. I planned to write something and email it to him. Then we'd discuss. But even after playing romantic piano music and lighting a rose-scented candle for inspiration, I was coming up empty. After an hour all I could manage was: *Hey, Sally, how about we go somewhere together and by the way, I want to marry you.*

I stared at the words on the computer screen and began to feel panicky. The unfinished manuscript on the shelf was a constant reminder of what could happen. The screen went dark as the computer went into sleep mode. Sitting there wasn't going to get me anywhere.

I went into the living room and found the bag with my crochet work. I settled on the black leather couch and began to move my hook through the purple yarn.

Crocheting reminded me of my mother and always helped me feel better. I mostly worked on squares using different yarns and different stitches. I had a cardboard template I used to make sure they were all the same size. When I had enough, I sewed them into blankets. I'd been doing it for as long as I could remember. I glanced up at the blanket on the back of the couch. It was the first one I'd made and was in shades of rust and orange with a black border. I'd given it to my father, and he'd kept it in his office at the university, telling anyone who would listen that I'd made it. He'd taught English Lit.

Bringing me up on his own after my mother died hadn't been easy. Well, I hadn't made it easy. He'd done the best he could and I'd brattily complained that his French toast wasn't like my mother's. He had the audacity to make it so that blobs of scrambled eggs hung off the side of the finished piece. The irony was that recently I'd seen French toast served that way with a new fancy name at a new fancy restaurant.

'I'm sorry for all the hassles, Dad,' I whispered to the heavens, as I worked on the purple square. I let out my breath as my anxiety receded. The crocheting had calmed me, but I wasn't any closer with what to put in the letter. The problem with writing was you couldn't grit your teeth and just try harder. If anything, trying harder just made it worse. I needed to step back and forget about it for a while. I knew my best bet was to go for a walk. Besides, it was a good antidote for all the sitting I did.

It was another sparkling October day. The sun was shining, and the sky was an electric blue. I left the shade of my tree-lined street and turned onto 57th. As usual, there was a fair amount of foot traffic. At this hour, it was mostly U of C students heading to the campus. I went the other way, going toward the lake.

I followed the curving sidewalk along the strip of Jackson Park. The grass was still green, but the leaves were turning colors and the slight breeze was sending more of them floating to the ground. A lone kid was being pushed on a swing in the playground. I thought of Tizzy and her time-travel story as I looked across to the imposing Museum of Science and Industry. The domed building was actually a leftover from the 1893 World's Fair. I loved the design, particularly the columns that were actually stern-looking women wrapped in what looked like concrete togas. It had been the Palace of Fine Art building and built sturdier than the other buildings in the fair, which is why it was still standing while the others were all gone. Of course, a lot of refurbishing had gone on as well. Instead of being filled with paintings and sculptures, the museum had all kinds of interesting interactive exhibits. Old planes hung from the ceiling and there was a replica of a coal mine so real that it seemed as if you really were underground instead of just in the basement of the building.

Tizzy used a huge old steam engine on the main floor of the museum as the portal spot where her character moved back and forth through time. Thinking of Tizzy made me start thinking about writing again and much as I tried not to, I went right back to thinking about Evan and Sally.

She was definitely out of his league, though there had been

something in the way that she'd said he was sweet that made me believe there was some hope. But what could I say that would sound like Evan to convince her to go out with him, let alone anything more?

I took the underpass under the traffic on Lake Shore Drive. As soon as I got to the other side, I joined the sprinkling of walkers and joggers on the path that paralleled the water.

Some people thought Lake Michigan was more like a fresh-water sea. It was shaped like a finger, was very deep and could be treacherous. Today the water seemed calm and reflected the deep blue of the sky. There were only ripples on the surface and soft waves coming onto the 57th Street Beach.

My destination was Promontory Point, or the Point as everyone called it. It was a man-made peninsula and was a major hang out spot in the summer. It was park-like with grass and benches and the perimeter was lined with several layers of blocks of limestone going down to the water. The views were amazing. On one side, the curve of the lake was visible, outlined by industrial buildings in Indiana. The other side looked toward the downtown skyline all the way to Navy Pier. As soon as I noticed the building on the tip, my thoughts went to Rachel. I pictured her hair blowing in the wind as she looked lovingly at Luke and repeated the vows I'd helped her write.

For a moment I thought back on my meeting the previous day. The whole thing confused me. Camille Parker seemed more angry than sad. Luke had just been quiet. It was impossible to read his emotions. He'd stayed out of the whole vow-writing episode. Thinking back, it was obvious that it must have been Rachel's idea and he seemed to have gone along with it without much concern. Maybe he was like Ben and kept everything locked inside.

The wind changed, coming down from the north, and instantly there was an icy edge to it. The sharp breeze cut right through my jacket. I turned to head back, picking up the pace in the hope that it would build up some body heat.

All that worry about being cold seemed to work some kind of magic and as I hustled on my way home something popped in my head from my few minutes I'd had with Sally. I suddenly knew how to write the letter.

As soon as I got home, I dropped my jacket, went right to my computer and started typing. An hour later I emailed Evan a draft of a letter. I'd barely hit send when my cell phone rang.

No surprise it was Evan. 'So what do you think?' I asked. Then before he had a chance to answer I explained the plan to use a letter to score a first date.

'I don't know,' he muttered, and then he read the letter out loud to me.

> *Dear Sally,*
>
> *I know that you are out of my league. You're beautiful, talented, smart – I could go on and on, but it would just make more of a point of how out of my league you are. That was supposed to be a joke, but you might have noticed I'm not that good at being funny.*
>
> *I really like being in your company. Just seeing you brightens my day. But so far all of our interchanges have been connected to work. Do you suppose we could spend some time together that was just social? Like maybe this Sunday afternoon at Lincoln Park Zoo with a coffee stop afterwards?*

There was a moment of silence on his end. 'I don't know about saying she's out of my league. I mean, I get that she is, but should we really remind her? I'm not sure about the zoo thing either. Maybe she'll think I'm cheap.'

I let him finish before I started to talk. 'You weren't at the table when she told me how much she liked romantic comedies. And it occurred to me that you're a sort of Hugh Grant type. He plays characters whose endearing charm is that they're self-deprecating and a little bumbling. The zoo on Sunday afternoon comes across as romantic, but also not too much too soon.'

'Oh,' he said. 'I'm afraid I don't know anything about Hugh Grant. I'm more of a *Mission: Impossible*, *Star Wars* type.'

'It would help if you watched some of his movies. Particularly, *Notting Hill*.' I explained the plot – shy bookstore owner meets a movie star. There was some debate on how he could access the movie and he asked if I owned it. I offered to lend it to him, but he suggested in the interest of time that he watch it at my place.

'Then I'll be able to OK the letter,' he said. I agreed and he said he would come by in the evening.

With that taken care of, I turned my attention to Rachel's piece. The bag of photo albums was sitting next to my computer where I'd left them. I suddenly had a thought of how to do the booklet. Rather than some narrative with dates and details of when she was born, where she went to school etc., I would collect anecdotes and illustrate them with photographs. It would capture the essence of who she was. I thought it was a great plan, but it was pointless to go ahead with it without getting an OK on it. I debated whether to call Mrs Parker or Luke. In the end, I called them both.

'Yes, I suppose that would be acceptable – as long as it's tasteful and it reflects well on the family reputation,' Mrs Parker said. There was something rushed in her voice and she cut me off when I mentioned wanting a story about Rachel from her.

'I can't deal with that now. I have a luncheon to get to.' The phone clicked off before I could even ask for a better time to call. Her behavior continued to confuse me. I decided that either she was so devastated that she was trying to shove away every-thing connected with her daughter's death. Or she was angry at Rachel for what she did and upset she had to deal with the whole situation.

I was relieved that Luke was friendlier on the phone. I would have liked to ask him a whole lot of questions about Rachel, but it didn't seem like the right time, so I simply told him my plan for the memorial book. 'I like that idea,' he said, as soon as I'd finished explaining. I could hear noise in the background and wondered where I'd gotten him. With cell phones you never knew.

'I'm glad you agree,' I said. 'I haven't caught you at a bad time, have I?' I was hoping he would tell me where he was. It almost sounded like he was at a party. 'It would be great if you could give me a story to include. Some special moment you had with Rachel.'

'I'll have to think about it,' he said. There was a slight impatience to his voice, and I thought I heard a woman in the background calling him honey and complaining about being forgotten.

'I thought I'd start with talking to some of her co-workers,' I said, continuing undaunted.

'Good idea,' he said curtly. 'I'm kind of busy right now.'

'If you could just tell me where she taught.' I spoke quickly before he could end the call.

'Oakenwald Elementary,' he said, and then with a click he was gone. I sat looking at my phone for a moment wondering what was really going on with him.

SIX

Now that I had the go-ahead, I contacted the principal of the school where Rachel had taught. I knew from the time I'd spent with her that she'd loved her teaching job. I wanted to see her old room and meet with some of her colleagues. Mrs Jones suggested I come at lunchtime which meant that I had to hurry. I considered taking an Uber, but economy won out and I took the bus.

It let me off several blocks from the school on a sad-looking commercial street. I passed empty stores with boarded-up fronts and the few storefronts that were open had grating across the windows. It seemed as if the street cleaners had missed the area as there were food wrappers and drink cups littering the gutter.

The high rises here were red-brick public housing instead of the glass towers where Rachel had lived.

The day had turned gloomy which only made the brown-brick school look more desolate. I passed a schoolyard filled with kids letting off steam during their lunch break as I looked for the entrance. The interior was utilitarian with lockers lining the beige walls. I found the principal's office and introduced myself to the school secretary.

Mrs Jones came out to meet me. She seemed harried and I felt bad interrupting her lunch.

'Thank you for doing this,' I said, following the lanky woman as she led me down the hallway.

'No problem. I'm used to interruptions during lunch. We're all still in shock about Rachel,' she said, opening the door to one of the classrooms. 'We've had to bring in a replacement, but the room is still mostly as she left it.'

I walked around looking at the rows of student desks and the teacher's desk at the front. I could see why they'd left it as Rachel had arranged it. She had turned the impersonal schoolroom into an inviting space. It even smelled nicer than the hall with the faint scent of cinnamon.

Orange and yellow translucent colored paper cut into the shape of autumn leaves decorated the windows. The bulletin board had more autumn leaves along with cutouts of pumpkins and Indian corn and featured students' artwork and Halloween stories they'd written. There was a library corner with a computer and a bookcase of books.

'And she left this,' Mrs Jones said, opening a supply cabinet. It was stocked with school supplies and extensive food items. One of the shelves had a stack of computer tablets.

'Not only that, but she was always getting companies to donate stuff to the school. I'm hoping they keep it up in her memory.' The principal stopped. 'You know she could have taught anywhere, but insisted she liked working here the best. We sure miss her and not just from all the wonderful things she brought in. She was a gifted teacher. She made learning exciting for her class. It was amazing. All the kids showed up every day. And there were hardly any discipline problems.' She stopped talking and swallowed back her emotion before she continued. 'She loved the kids and they all knew it.'

I asked if it was OK if I took some photos with my phone and explained what I was going to use them for. 'Take all the pictures you want,' she said. 'It sounds like you're going to create a wonderful tribute to her.'

When I'd gotten enough shots, she took me down the hall to the teachers' lounge. She hadn't asked any questions about how Rachel died, and I wondered what she knew about it. It was not comfortable to bring it up, so I let it be.

The teachers' lounge had a few comfortable chairs and an old wood library table in the middle. There was a kitchenette set up with a refrigerator, a microwave and a coffee pot that was just filling with a fresh brew.

'This is Veronica Blackstone and she'd like to talk to you about Rachel,' Mrs Jones said, before introducing the three women in the room as Kanesha Wilson, Jean Lee and Mercedes Phillips.

'Sit, sit,' Kanesha said. 'How about some coffee?' She was on her feet pouring me a cup before I'd even settled. 'So what exactly do you want from us? Are you some undercover detective? What's that business about they don't know how she fell off that balcony?'

'I'm not a detective, undercover or otherwise,' I said, chuckling at the thought. 'I'm afraid I don't know any more of the details of what happened to her than you do.' Then I explained who I was and why I was there.

'My goodness, people actually hire you to write love letters. People actually send love letters,' Kanesha said with a laugh. She shook her head at the thought. 'But that's a righteous thing her family is doing. Better than some couple of paragraphs to tie up someone's whole life.'

'I was hoping you might have some stories about her that I could include.'

I drank some of the coffee and watched as the three women looked at each other. 'I've got a good one,' Kanesha said. 'The first day she came here, she showed up in some fancy clothes with a designer purse I assumed was a knock-off – completely out of place around here.' The curvy woman gestured with her finger. 'I figured it would be one day for her and she'd be gone. I thought she had princess written all over her forehead.' The woman rocked her head to display how wrong she'd been. 'But she came back the next day and kept showing up. After about a week, I pulled her aside and told her to ditch the purse. I was shocked when I found out it was real. I mean, who spends that kind of cash on a bag. I told her to ditch the fancy duds, too. I thought she might be offended, but nah. The very next day she showed up dressed for combat like the rest of us and replaced the fancy purse with a cloth tote.' Kanesha stopped talking and I saw her shoulders drop as her eyes began to well up. 'It's just not right that she's gone. She did so much for the kids in her class. Hell, for all of us.' She pointed at the coffee pot. 'Where do you think that came from?'

'She invited us all to her wedding,' Mercedes said. 'What an affair. My chance to see how the one half of one percent lives.'

'I was there, too,' I said. I was going to leave out why I'd been there, but there was no point hiding what I'd done for Rachel and so I told them about helping with the vows.

'If you ask me that husband of hers is kind of skunky,' Kanesha interjected. 'You should have heard Rachel go on about how lucky she was to get a guy like him. How she felt like she hit the jackpot when he put a ring on her finger. Her family is rich with a capital R. But she just kept going on about how she wanted to please him.'

I noticed that Jean was shaking her head. She seemed the most reserved of the three women. 'It's not my place to say it, but I think her husband was the one who put it in her head that she needed to lose weight.'

'Rachel went cuckoo. We curvy women are meant to be this way.' Kanesha did a flourish to show off her own soft shape. 'She must have been starving herself and then taking all those dance classes. I think that was what made everything go downhill.'

'What do you mean downhill?' I asked.

'She was just different when she came back in the fall. She got real nervous-looking and she seemed worried about her memory,' Mercedes said.

I asked her if she had any specific details. 'I can't remember exactly. There was something with her husband about texts she didn't remember sending,' Mercedes said with a shrug.

'She had circles under her eyes all the time lately. I even told her about some herb tea that might help her sleep. I'd say there was something on her mind,' Jean said. 'Maybe it wasn't the happily ever after she wanted. Like Kanesha said, Rachel was kind of a princess. Who knows what she expected?'

'At least I think she liked the dance classes. She talked about them all the time,' Mercedes said.

'Like what did she say?' I asked.

The older woman shrugged and sighed. 'Look, I have a husband who complains all the time and I've learned to tune out to survive. I'm afraid I wasn't really listening. I just remember something about line dancing or maybe it was belly dancing.'

'I don't have a husband who lectures me. Mine's the silent type,' Jean said with a chuckle. 'So I actually heard what she said to me about the classes. Mostly it was about a friend there.' I asked Jean for a name, but she smiled guiltily. 'Maybe I didn't listen as well as I thought. I think it was a nickname. Something like Dee. I'm not sure.'

Kanesha leaned closer. 'Did she push herself off that balcony?'

I debated what to say and Kanesha rushed ahead and took my silence as an affirmative answer.

'I thought so,' Kanesha said shaking her head with regret. 'I wish now I'd said something. But you know how it is, you don't want people to think you're sticking your nose where it shouldn't be. And every time anybody asked about Luke, she'd beam this smile and repeat how lucky she was.'

A bell rang somewhere and the three women stood up, saying they had to get back to their classrooms.

I gave them all my email address and they promised to think about it and would let me know if they came up with any more good stories. Just before we all walked out into the hall, Jean pulled me aside. 'You might be able to use this. She sold that fancy purse at an auction house and used the money to buy supplies for the whole school.'

Princess or not, it seemed Rachel had a heart of gold. I felt even more of a responsibility to find out what had happened to her.

SEVEN

I dropped off my notes about Rachel next to my computer. Then it was time to deal with the normal parts of living. I grabbed my pull cart and walked to the shopping center and loaded up on groceries. As I went back across the courtyard, I admired the display of pumpkins surrounding the graceful sycamore tree. All the stores in the center were independents except for Walgreens, though it almost didn't count as a chain since the very first Walgreens had been located almost in the neighborhood. I chuckled at the two kids who were trying to drag their father into the toy store. Even with the chill in the air, all the outdoor tables for the French bakery were full. I always checked out the window of the shoe store to see what they'd gotten in. It seemed like yesterday the display was all sandals and sneakers. Now it was boots and fuzzy slippers.

It was impossible to get out of the shopping center without running into someone I knew. As I said, Hyde Park was almost like a small town within the city. People often greeted each other on the street with at least a smile, even if they were strangers. The someone I ran into was the president of our condo association out buying some wood for his fireplace. I was jealous that his worked. Mine still had the chimney blocked. One of these days when I had some extra cash, I'd get it opened. How cozy it would be to sit in front of the fireplace and read.

I was still thinking about Rachel and what the teachers had said. I'd gotten at least a couple of good stories – Kanesha's about Rachel's first days at the school and Jean's story about the fate of the fancy purse. And I'd gotten another lead. The dance classes. They sounded positive and I was hopeful about picking up a story and maybe some pictures – though I had to find the place first. None of the three teachers knew the name of the place or even had a hint of where it was located. Maybe Luke would have more information.

The afternoon was fading into evening when I pulled the cart up the stairs to my place. I was thinking about writing up what I'd gotten at the school, but then I remembered that Evan was coming by to watch the Hugh Grant movie. I'd rushed out and left everything a mess and there was barely time to put away my purchases and do a little straightening.

He rang the doorbell at exactly seven. He was dressed in a white shirt, bow tie and tweed sport jacket. This time the bow tie was straight. I noticed him looking around the apartment as he came in. All the furniture was geared toward comfort and there were books everywhere. The wood floor was covered with oriental-style rugs in warm shades of red. He commented on the blanket hanging over the couch.

'I made it,' I said. I left out explaining that I'd learned to crochet from my mother and that crochet had been my first go-to when I'd been stuck trying to write his letter. I had an image to keep.

'So you have other talents besides writing letters for people like me.' He smiled a little sheepishly. 'Now why exactly am I watching this movie?' he asked, as I led him down the hall to the dining room.

'Sally seems to have a soft spot for romantic comedies and when she mentioned her favorites, I noticed Hugh Grant was in all of them. I'm not telling you to pretend to be like him, but I thought it would give you an idea of what she likes.'

He seemed thoughtful. 'I don't know about that. I have enough trouble being myself without trying to be someone else.'

'There, you got it before you even watched the movie,' I said with a laugh.

'Got what?' he asked clearly perplexed.

'Being vulnerable and a little self-deprecating with just a touch of humor.'

He bowed his head. 'I thought that was a bad thing. Aren't guys supposed to be powerful and in charge?'

'Says who? I'm not telling you to be anything other than who you are. I just noticed that you have a quality that I think Sally will find appealing,' I said.

'You're good. I would never have figured that was a plus. I'm glad I got over being embarrassed about needing help.' He sat down on the sofa against the wall and I handed him the remote.

'It's all cued up for you,' I said.

I went down the hall to my office. I'd printed up a copy of the letter and if he okayed it, we could talk about how to get it to Sally. I had an idea, but I wasn't sure he'd go for it.

There was a knock at the door. The fact it was a knock and not the bell meant it was probably a neighbor and I was pretty sure I knew which one. Sara was very neighborly. Being a stay-at-home mom with a toddler got to her and occasionally she needed an adult to converse with. Her husband was a pharmacist at the local Walgreens and since they were open twenty-four hours, he often worked odd shifts. And of course, Ben was her brother. I couldn't imagine him being much help in the conversation department.

'I know this sounds corny, but could I borrow a cup of sugar?' Sara said. 'I really am making something, and I ran out.' She had that frazzled mom look. There were some streaks of flour on her black leggings and, I suspected, on the oversized white T-shirt that proclaimed that she was Supermom.

'Quentin and Mikey are watching TV together. It's really sweet and it gave me a few minutes for myself,' she said, as I invited her in. She glanced down the hall at the sound of the movie drifting from the dining room. 'I didn't realize you had company,' she said. 'A date?'

'It's a client,' I said. 'And he's fine for now.'

'A client for what?' she asked. She was enthralled with what I did and particularly the love letters.

'Sort of love letters,' I said in a whisper and her face lit up. But her face fell when I added I couldn't talk while he was there. I offered her a seat and took the measuring cup. Evan was deep into the movie and I don't think he even noticed that I went through to the kitchen. When I returned with the sugar, she made no move to get up, so I sat down with her.

'So tell me how it's going with Ben?' she asked. I sighed, thinking of how he had sat through the Tuesday night gathering with his usual non-expression.

'To tell you the truth, he never seems like he wants to be here. I think he's only coming because you paid for the sessions. I don't usually do this, but I'd be happy to give you a refund since it seems so uncomfortable for him to be here.'

She shook her head vehemently. 'No way. He might not show it, but I do think he likes coming to the group. I know my brother and if he didn't like it, gift or not, he simply wouldn't show up. He doesn't tell me much and as far as I can tell his social life seems to be drinking beer with other cops. All they do is tell horrible dark stories they think are funny.' She made a face of distaste. 'Ben wouldn't want me to tell you anything about him, but I'm going to anyway. He got a divorce last year. I never got any details. He was married and then he wasn't. After that it seemed like he shut down emotionally.' She hesitated and looked down at the sparkly white sugar granules in the measuring cup for a moment and then looked at me. 'You're single and he's single.' She shrugged helplessly. 'I thought maybe there'd be something. Maybe he'd become teacher's pet.'

I rolled my eyes and she laughed. 'For someone who writes love letters, your own social life seems kind of barren.'

I held my finger to my lips to shush her. It wasn't something I'd want Evan to hear. But of course she was right. There was a reason I'd stopped my mental movie with the shot of me in my wedding attire. I didn't want to think about what came after. I'd been just twenty-one and, in hindsight, an idiot. I'd actually thought that if Larry and I got married somehow everything would just work out. Ha! It had only got worse. He'd felt trapped and spent all his time hanging out with his friends. And I'd found out that one person couldn't make a relationship work and we got a divorce. There had been some boyfriends since then, but after what happened with Larry, I'd been a little gun-shy about getting involved in anything serious.

'If that's why you pushed him to come, I'll give you a check right now.' I got up to get my checkbook, but she gestured for me to sit down.

'The real reason I gave him the sessions was because I thought he'd like them. I was just hoping there'd be some kind of bonus in it for both of you. Being a cop probably isn't the best job for him. Things just roll off some of them, I guess. Not Ben.' She stopped abruptly. 'That's all I can say. If he knew I even told you about the divorce he'd never talk to me again.' She shrugged. 'He barely tells me anything as it is. Whatever I hear comes from his partner.'

'As long as you understand that's not going to happen,' I said, easing back into the chair.

She nodded as if she agreed, but something in her expression made me think she wasn't giving up. 'Then tell me what else you're working on. My days are filled with everything Mikey. When Quentin comes home, he's wiped out and mostly wants to crash in front of TV. I need to hear about the outside world.'

Without revealing any names, I told her about Rachel and what had happened to her. 'I started collecting stories for the piece I'm going to write. From the outside, it seems like she had it all.'

'Wow, that's really sad. A newlywed with a job she loved and a fabulous apartment. It would seem she had everything to live for. You really think it was suicide?'

'I've thought about it a lot and, honestly, I'm not completely sure, but it seems like that's what her husband thinks and could be why her mother is trying to cover it up.'

'You have to wonder what would make her feel so desperate.'

'That's what I intend to find out,' I said. 'Her husband made a comment to me that it was too bad that I hadn't stayed in touch with her after the wedding – that she could have used a friend.'

'Ouch,' Sara said. 'So you feel guilty, huh?' I nodded, and she tried to reassure me it wasn't my fault. I heard her phone *bing* and she read a text, making a face. 'Quentin said Mikey's diaper needs changing. Men,' she said with a groan as she stood. 'But speaking of men, in another way. I'm sure Ben would be glad to offer any cop help with your investigation. I keep telling him he ought to do whatever he has to, to become a detective. He really has a natural talent.' Then she laughed at herself. 'OK, I'll stop trying to push you two together. And just hope that nature takes its course.' She winked at me before she went out the door.

'Do you really think I'm like Hugh Grant,' Evan said when the movie was done.

I looked him over. 'Your teeth are definitely better.' I smiled and he realized it was a joke. 'I think there's a chance that Sally will find the qualities you share with the characters Hugh plays endearing.'

'You just *think* it? I thought you were sure,' he said suddenly worried.

'Nothing is ever one hundred percent, but I have a good feeling about it.' I held up the copy of the letter. 'So then it's a go with the letter?'

He sucked in his breath, and when he let it out, he said, 'OK, let's do it.' There were a few more steps involved. Did he want to handwrite it? We could print it up. I could also do calligraphy. We went back and forth and finally decided to print it up and he would sign it.

'Then you can leave it on her desk with a rose,' I said.

'Do you think that might be too much?' he asked, seeming uncertain. 'What would the Hugh Grant character in *Notting Hill* do?' He started discussing the movie and how Julia Roberts had made the first move by kissing Hugh. Should he expect Sally to do something similar?

'I didn't mean for you to take the movie literally. He's a sweet, unassuming guy and even though she's a gorgeous, seemingly unattainable woman, underneath it she's just a girl looking for someone to love.' I gave it a moment to sink in. 'He'd leave the flower and then chuckle uncomfortably when the recipient commented on it.'

'I guess that sounds like me,' he said. 'I'll go with the flower.' He prepared to leave but before he went out the door, he added, 'I'll let you know if she accepts. Then I'll give you the details so you can swing by.'

'What? You want me to go on your date with you?' I asked incredulous.

'No, no. You can just view us from a distance and see how it's going. Hugh's character had his friends to help him. It'll give you something to put in the next letter.'

'Oh. I thought this was going to be a one-and-done,' I said.

'I never do things halfway. I'll need you to compose letters until it's time for you to write a proposal.'

EIGHT

't worked!' an excited male voice said into the phone. Usually I was good at identifying voices, but I was just waking up. 'Who is this? And what worked?' I asked holding in a yawn. My type of work meant I could make my own hours which meant I rarely got up before eight. I glanced toward the window and saw that the light was still low. At this time of year before the clocks went back to standard time, the sun didn't even come up until almost seven. I guessed it was close to eight. It was lucky for my caller that I slept with my phone next to the bed.

'It's me, Evan,' the voice chirped. 'Sally said yes.' He sounded so happy he almost sang the words. 'I left it with a flower just like you said. Only I went with a sunflower and I'm afraid some of the petals fell off, but she didn't care. She sent me a note back. It was pretty basic and didn't have any of the pizzazz mine did. All hers said was yes. Well, and she asked for the details. What do I do? Should I tell her to call you?'

I had sat up by now, knowing that my voice sounded different when I was lying down. I don't know why I cared whether Evan knew I'd been sleeping. I guess it was an automatic reaction. It was something about wanting to seem like Superwoman with a pen, ready twenty-four-seven to fulfill your every writing need. I wrapped the comforter around me for warmth. The temperature outside was still too high for the heat in the building to come on which left the interior with a chill.

'No,' I said with a laugh. 'I write love letters, but I'm not a match-maker. You could call her and tell her when to meet you and where.'

'I don't know about calling her. What do I say?' An *oh, no* was going off in my head. If he was concerned about talking to her on the phone what was he going to do when they were together in person. While I was having my mental moment, he came up with an option. 'Maybe I'll text her and I could send her an e-vite for her calendar.'

It seemed a little cold to me, but then it was his date. 'I'm sure that would work,' I said. 'Well, then, I guess it's mission accomplished.' I got ready to end the call. I hoped he'd forgotten he'd said something about wanting me to spy on his date.

'I better send you an e-vite, too,' he said. I could feel my face fall. So, he hadn't changed his mind. This was a first since I'd started writing relationship notes. And I wasn't so sure about it. Maybe if I mentioned charging him for my time, he'd rethink it.

'Of course,' he said when I brought up a fee. 'This is an investment in my happiness.' There was a sweetness in his tone, and I melted. I really wanted this to work out for him now and was glad to do anything that helped. We discussed the logistics for meeting up on Sunday, before ending the call.

The window in my bedroom looked out on the brick wall of the next building. I craned my neck to get a look at the sky and was glad to see it was blue. I dropped the comforter back onto the bed. It was time to get going on my day. After a shower, I pulled on a comfortable pair of jeans and a sweatshirt and headed to the kitchen. I put on the coffee as I thought about what lay ahead of me. I needed to get down to business and start working on Rachel's memory book. For a moment I regretted taking the project. Helping Evan with his romance was fun and would hopefully lead to a happy ending. The memory book was another story. There was no room for fun or humor in the writing. The best I could hope for was touching. And a happy ending . . . not a chance. I was confused by Mrs Parker's attitude about the whole thing. Was she keeping up appearances or was she simply not that broken up about Rachel's death? But then relationships came in all sizes and shapes. I thought back to when I'd been helping with Rachel's vows. Camille Parker had seemed involved with the wedding as an event, but not involved with the bride.

Maybe it was because I'd lost my mother when I was so young, but I'd always had a romanticized image of how mothers and daughters got along. I was sure that if my mother had still been around we'd be best buddies.

I took my coffee into the living room and went to open the door to the balcony to have a better look at the weather. I was surprised to feel that the air coming in from outside was warmer than inside. But not warm enough that I wanted to sit out there.

My touch with nature was watching the three mourning doves sit on the branches of the tree out front. The taupe-color birds were regular visitors and often made trips to my balcony. It was a pleasure to have leafy branches to look out into again. My street had once been lined with tall old elm trees and it had been like being in a tree house. But one by one the elms had gotten diseased and had to be removed.

The tree out front had begun as a spindly replacement that barely reached the first floor. But over the years, the small tree had filled out and grown taller and now reached all the way to the roof of the building. A breeze passed through the branches sending a flutter of the yellow-tinged leaves to the ground. Soon the branches would be naked, and snow would gather on them.

Now that I'd checked out the day, I went into my office. Like in my bedroom, the one window in my office looked out toward a brick wall, making the room rather dim. I turned on the brass student lamp with the yellow glass shades on my desk and took the bag of albums to the burgundy wing chair. This time I was determined to go through them and pick the photographs I would use. The first album started with a birth announcement and moved through Rachel's first year. The last page had photos of her taking her first steps. I chose one that seemed to illustrate the pride she felt at her accomplishment. She was older in the second album and it covered a much longer time span. I found a photograph that I liked of her in her school uniform with a group of her friends all striking a pose. It seemed to capture a happy time in her life. There was another I liked of her on a small sailboat from her time at summer camp. She had on a T-shirt that said *Boats are in My Blood*. The last album was white and covered in silk. Before I even opened it, I knew it had the wedding photos. I thought about using a picture of Rachel and Luke, but instead chose one of Rachel alone. She was wearing her wedding dress and looking directly into the camera. The white silk dress was elegant and simple, cut on the bias so it seemed fluid. Her expression was so full of hope and joy that I felt myself tearing up.

The common denominator in all of the pictures was that Rachel was always beaming. Her heart-shaped face was dominated by her smile and it was all you noticed. I went back through the wedding album and picked some additional photographs I thought I might need.

After I scanned the pictures into my computer, I packed up the albums. Mrs Parker hadn't said anything, but I assumed she'd want them back as soon as possible. Feeling on a roll, I began to write the biography that would begin the booklet. Between what I found out from an obituary that had appeared in the *Chicago Daily Times* and what I'd gotten from the albums, I wrote about her life up to her wedding. There wasn't a hint of darkness in it and I thought Mrs Parker would be happy with it.

I left the notes I'd taken when I met with the teachers to deal with another time. Looking through all the photographs and writing about her fairy tale life had left me drained. And confused. The teachers had said she seemed different when she came back in the fall. I wondered why.

Sunday turned out to be another beautiful fall day. The sky was a bright blue without a cloud. The temperature was just cool enough to require a sweater. Evan certainly had the weather on his side for his premier date. We'd talked two more times discussing the plan.

Thankfully, he didn't actually want me to go on the date with them. It was more like I was going to play detective doing surveillance. The plan was for me to blend in with the background so that Sally wouldn't notice me and then hang back and watch their interaction. I looked through my closet for something nondescript. I found a pair of jeans faded from years of wear and a white peasant blouse with an embroidered design along the yoke that seemed like a good choice. I threw on a charcoal gray sweater and a baseball cap and headed for Lincoln Park Zoo.

It was a small zoo, easy to get to on the bus, and was located just north of the downtown area, with a view of Lake Michigan and a harbor filled with pleasure boats. It was one of the few attractions in the city that had no entry fee. We'd agreed that I would wait for them in the rookery and then begin trailing them. The rookery, also known as the lily pond, was a perfect place to wait for them. The pond was surrounded by artfully arranged stacks of stone slabs, and lots of foliage. It attracted ducks, geese, and other birds looking for a place to hang out for a while.

I found a spot under a shady tree and checked out the area for my mark. I smiled thinking I sounded like my fictional detective, Derek Streeter. I wasn't sure what good watching them would do, but Evan seemed to want it and the client was always right.

I'd barely been there a few minutes when they arrived. Evan surveyed the area and gave me a nod when he saw me. Trying to be a good detective, I zeroed in on Sally and checked out her clothes. She was wearing jeans rolled up at the cuff and ballet flats. She finished the look with a red sweater. I was amazed at how different she seemed now that she was out of her business attire. It fascinated me how clothes defined the perception of people. When she'd been dressed in the yellow pencil skirt and suit jacket, she'd seemed full of authority. And the heels had made her walk differently.

From what I could see, Evan seemed nervous and Sally was too busy looking around at everything to notice. I chalked it up to first-date jitters. They hung out for a few minutes watching some ducks glide across the water. She pointed to the pathway out of the peaceful area and they were on the move. I kept my distance behind them. Their interaction had changed slightly. Evan didn't seem as nervous and she'd become very animated, doing all the talking and gesturing with her hands. I made a mental note that if he wanted me to write to her again to be sure and include something regarding what she'd talked about. I had the feeling that being listened to might be an aphrodisiac for her.

They glanced at the aviary and moved on. It continued on that way with them barely noticing what species they were passing. They never seemed to consider going into any of the buildings that had indoor housing for the animals. He continued hanging onto her every word and she continued throwing out a lot of them for him to hang onto. She seemed upbeat and I guessed that she wasn't complaining, but I wished I could hear what she was saying.

She was still talking when they exited the zoo. Evan stole a look back and when he saw me pointed across the strip of park to a coffee spot. Now that I knew where they were headed, I gave them a wide berth of space. I wasn't so sure about the next part. The plan was I'd happen to run into them, and Evan would invite me to join them. He'd offer to get me a drink and while he was getting it, I'd talk to Sally and see how it was going. As I crossed the street, I tried to remember how I was supposed to know Evan. I thought I'd claimed to be his neighbor. Now, I wished I'd asked him where he lived. It wouldn't do to break my cover. I laughed at myself, thinking I was getting carried away with playing the detective.

They went into a small coffee place and I watched from the outside until they'd gotten a table. Evan looked up as I walked in and then he came up to the counter, so we were standing next to each other as if we were each going to place an order.

'I think it's going great,' he said appearing enthused.

'Do you still want to stick to the plan?' I asked.

'The plan? What were we supposed to do?' he asked, seeming a little discombobulated.

I was about to remind him, when I sensed someone stop next to us. I looked up, and was surprised to see Luke Ross. His head was down as he unzipped his windbreaker and it wasn't until he got it open that he became aware of his surroundings. I smiled prepared to greet him, but he surprised me by talking to Evan.

'Hey, man,' Luke said, giving him a pat on the shoulder. 'You're my hero.' Then Luke caught sight of me. He nodded a greeting before glancing back at Evan and then at me probably trying to figure out if we were together. Just when I thought it couldn't get any more complicated, Sally joined us, seeming a little breathless.

She held up her phone. 'Don't get anything for me,' she said to Evan. 'I just got a call that there's a problem with the event I arranged at the hotel.' She appeared apologetic as her gaze moved over the group. 'Maybe you can all have coffee together another time.'

Evan's bright expression instantly faded, and his shoulders slumped. He caught my eye and seemed to be pleading with me to do something. I wasn't a matchmaker, but he seemed so desperate I felt like I had to do something. While Sally was checking something on her phone, I leaned close and surreptitiously whispered something in his ear.

He smiled and nodded before he took her hand. 'It's been a

pleasure,' he said, lifting her hand to his lips and giving it a gentle kiss.

Her face broke out in surprise and her eyes twinkled. 'You're so sweet,' she said. When he released her hand, she gave his cheek a pat and with a wave headed out the door. Evan watched helplessly as she hailed a cab.

'I guess I better go,' he said, not looking in my direction. I sensed he didn't want me to see his expression, which I imagined was crushed. I wasn't sure what had just happened. Was the work thing an excuse to cut things short or was it real? I thought I should say something to him, but honestly, I didn't have a clue what to say.

Evan made a move to leave as well. The way his shoulders were slumped, I assumed he was admitting defeat and it was the end of his plan to win her heart. But just as he opened the door, he seemed to stand a little taller and he said he'd call me later to talk about next steps.

NINE

'What was all that about?' Luke asked, glancing in the direction that Evan had gone. I hesitated for a moment while I considered what to say. It wasn't like I was a lawyer or anything and had to keep things confidential, but I also didn't think Evan would want me sharing that he needed help in the romance department, since he seemed to know Luke.

Finally, I just shrugged, and said, 'I'm not sure.' It was the truth. I really didn't know what had occurred other than it seemed like Evan wasn't going to give up. Luke seemed OK with the answer and I was relieved he didn't ask for any details like how I knew Evan.

I felt at a loose end with my mission suddenly aborted. I decided to get a coffee after all and ordered their special blend. Luke had already ordered his and we stood around the counter waiting for the drinks to be served while we made small talk about the different roasts of coffee. I didn't know that light roast had more caffeine.

Our drinks came up at the same time. 'Do you want to sit?' he asked, indicating the tables at the back. I hesitated, looking out at the waning afternoon.

'I'd like to but it's Sunday, which already means the buses run slow and as it gets later, they come even less often, and I have to transfer.'

He offered a sympathetic nod. 'Public transit, huh?' He went to grab his drink. 'I have my car here. I'd be glad to give you a ride home.'

I laughed. 'Pretty brave of you, since you don't know how far away I live. I could live way out someplace like Waukegan.'

'It sounded like you only have to transfer once,' he said, smiling. 'So I took a chance.'

'You're right. I live in Hyde Park,' I said.

He nodded with a smile. 'I think I can manage that.' He gestured toward the tables again. 'Shall we?'

My relationship with my clients was varied. I was probably too involved with Evan and I'd been mostly distant with Luke. I'd never really spent any time alone with him, even when I was writing his wedding vows. All I really knew about him was that Rachel had been crazy about him and Mrs Parker seemed to dismiss him. But now I saw that he had an easy charm that made me feel instantly comfortable. I started to mentally say that he was easy on the eyes, but stopped myself from even thinking the cliché. The phrase didn't do him justice, anyway. True, he looked like a model for men's cologne, but what struck me was the warmth behind his symmetrical features.

The comment he'd made about me not keeping in touch with Rachel had been weighing on me since he said it. I felt comfortable enough to bring it up while we had our drinks.

'What did you mean that Rachel could have used a friend?' I asked.

'I'm sorry I said that. It's just that dealing with Camille gets me riled. Rachel was having a rough time. It didn't help that Camille was always critical of her and telling me I should do something about the situation. I tried to talk to Rachel, but it seemed to make it worse. I guess in hindsight I thought if there was somebody she could open up to . . . She'd seemed comfortable with you.' He shrugged.

He'd opened the door on discussing Rachel's problems, so I felt it was OK to walk through it and ask for details. 'What was going on with her?' I asked.

He took a moment to collect his thoughts. 'It was as if she'd become delusional. Packages came with clothes and cooking supplies that she insisted she hadn't ordered. And yet when I checked the online account, the orders were there placed with her credit card. I'd get a text that she was stopping for groceries and then she'd come home empty-handed with no memory of sending me the text. It didn't help when I showed her her phone and the text was there. She was having a lot of trouble sleeping. She seemed worried all the time. I thought it might get better when the school term began, and she went back to work.' He stopped and seemed to be remembering something unpleasant. 'Camille insisted we go to a fundraiser at an estate in Glencoe at the end of August. It was filled with all the elite people the

Parkers mixed with and Rachel had a meltdown. She thought she'd lost a bracelet I'd given her and came unglued. Luckily, I was able to get her outside before anyone noticed, but the Parkers were embarrassed anyway. They pushed it on me to do something. But I couldn't say anything to Rachel about it without her falling apart. Her head was filled with nonsense. She thought I was going to leave her.' He paused and let out a heavy sigh. 'All the Parkers care about is keeping up an image of being this perfect family.' He let out a long sigh. 'Mr Parker managed to get the coroner to ignore the message on her cell phone.'

'What sort of message?' I asked.

'It just said, "I need help". The recipient wasn't typed in. It seemed like the modern version of a suicide note.' He shook his head as if to clear it. 'I had no idea it was that bad for her.'

'Then you weren't there when she, uh, fell,' I said, careful with my words.

'No. She was home alone. I was at work.' He let out his breath. 'Maybe the Parkers are right, though. Maybe it's better to leave it as inconclusive or accidental. What's the point of saying it was deliberate?' He turned to me. 'Just do the best you can honoring her memory.' He'd kept his voice low because we were in public, but he sounded intense.

'That's the plan with the little book,' I said. 'I already started collecting anecdotes. I went to her school and talked to some of the teachers.' I told him about their praise of her, but left out their concern about how she'd been acting. 'They mentioned she was taking some dance lessons she enjoyed,' I said.

'They were more like an obsession. She got in her head that she needed to lose weight and it seemed like she went to a class almost every day. I thought they'd be good for her. You know how they're always saying that exercise is good for mental health. She seemed to have someone she hung out with. But they weren't lessons. She corrected me when I called them that. She said it was a dance gym and they're members not students.'

'That might be something for the book. Do you know what kind of dance classes she took? I like to be specific,' I said. I didn't elaborate, since I doubted he was interested in hearing my thinking, but it was something I always told the writers' group. Being specific about something made it seem real. Instead of saying a tree-lined street, it was better to describe the old elm trees that shaded the street and had managed to survive all the years of bad weather and disease.

He shrugged. 'I don't know. I think she tried all different kinds of dancing. She seemed to have a lot of different kinds of shoes.' He toyed with his cup and then took a long sip.

'Do you happen to know the name of the place? Maybe I can get something for the book.'

The idea of the anecdotes was great, but I was beginning to realize that tracking them down was hard.

'She never mentioned the name. I think she was afraid I might show up and watch her dance or something.' He almost smiled. 'She kept making the point that it was for fun and exercise, not so she could try out for the Rockettes. It's somewhere in the Loop. It could be on Wabash Avenue because she mentioned the noise of the El trains.'

The Loop was what people called main downtown zone. It seemed that the name came from the fact that the subway and elevated trains looped around the area.

Luke let out another sigh. 'Can we talk about something else? I'm crushed by what happened, but I can't wallow in it. I hope that doesn't sound uncaring.'

'Of course, all of this has to be very difficult for you. I understand you need to keep going with your life,' I said. As I said it, I thought back to the background noise I'd heard when I'd called him. Hadn't there been a woman calling him honey? It made me wonder how quickly he was moving on.

I noticed that his dark blond hair looked windblown and put it together with the windbreaker he was wearing. It wasn't particularly windy outside, but he'd clearly been somewhere the wind was blowing. He sensed me looking at his hair and raked it with his fingers. I thought of the boats I'd seen bobbing in the nearby harbor. 'Were you out on a boat?' I asked, leading the way to a new topic.

His expression instantly brightened, and he smiled. 'Very good,' he said, sounding impressed. 'Rachel told me that you'd written a mystery. I guess you must have developed some detective skills along the way.' He looked at me expectantly. 'Can you tell me why, though?'

I thought for a moment. My first thought was fishing, but he didn't look the type. 'It was a beautiful day, so I'm thinking it was for pleasure.'

'Actually I was showing our boat to a potential buyer. It was a gift from the Parkers, but now it seems it was more of a loan. They're insisting I sell it and turn over the proceeds.' He took out his phone and thumbed through the pictures and then handed it to me. 'That's the boat, in case you know anybody in the market. The couple I took out today passed.'

I took the phone from him and checked out the boat mostly to be polite. I nodded and said it looked great, and then as I went to hand it back to him, I accidentally swiped the screen and another picture took over. I was about to ask who it was and then I realized it was Rachel. I tried to hide my shock. She looked nothing like the wedding picture I'd chosen for the memory book. She'd lost her soft curves and was a gaunt, muscly sort of thin that wasn't attractive. Her eyes were like dark haunted pools. Most unnerving was it was the first picture I'd seen of her where she didn't have a smile. No wonder the teachers said she'd seemed different. She looked like a ghost of the person I'd known.

I knew he didn't want to talk about her anymore, so I made no comment and tried to swipe the screen back to the boat.

I noticed that it had gotten dark. He drained his cup and saw that mine was empty. 'Shall we . . .?' he said, getting up.

His black Porsche was parked about a block away. I wasn't really surprised about the car. He seemed like somebody who'd have a sports car. I watched a bus go by, glad that I didn't have to deal with it. Getting into the car, I felt like I'd been offered a magic carpet ride compared to the trip home on a couple of buses that took a convoluted route and made a million stops. He took the Lake Shore Drive and I looked out the window. The streetlights had come on and it was hard to tell where the lake ended and the sky began. I gave him directions from the 57th Street exit and he double-parked in front of my building. 'I love these old brick buildings,' he said, gazing up at the white columns that bordered the front balconies.

I gave him the rundown on how old the building was and noted some of the charming details and not-so-charming one of having no elevator to carry me to the third floor.

'Once everything gets settled, I'm thinking of relocating away from downtown.' He glanced at the wrought-iron fencing that enclosed the planted area next to the entranceway porch. A sign hung on it noted that one of the units was for sale. 'Who knows, I could end up your neighbor.' His tone was light, and I knew he was just making conversation.

I thanked him for the ride and just before I got out, turned to him. 'The reason I didn't stay in touch with Rachel is that I assumed that she'd want me to disappear once the vows were done. I accept that it is part of my job that people usually want to forget I was ever there. Like disappearing ink,' I said with a smile. Then I bid him goodnight and got out of the car.

My landline was ringing when I unlocked the door. Having a landline was beginning to seem redundant to a lot of people since their cell phones had become practically an appendage. To be honest, I kept the landline mostly for sentimental reasons. It was the same number I'd had my whole life and it bothered me to think of somebody else having it. But it was a little strange to get sales calls asking for my father.

I rushed to get the phone and didn't bother to check the caller ID. I was pretty sure I knew who it was anyway. Still, to be on the safe side, I didn't add a name to my greeting until I was sure.

'Hey, Evan,' I said after he'd greeted me excitedly.

'So don't you think it went great? What do we do now?' he said, his words tripping over each other. I wasn't sure how to respond. It sounded like he might be doing wishful thinking. I doubted he'd considered the idea that her abrupt departure might have been her way of saying 'not interested'. Her reaction to the hand kissing could have just been polite.

'It's up to you,' I said. 'I just give you the words.' I knew he wanted to talk about his potential future with Sally, but I really wanted to know how he knew Luke. I also didn't particularly want to let on that I knew Luke, so I couldn't ask him directly. 'It was nice how your friend said you were his hero,' I said finally. 'What's the story on him?'

'You, too?' he said glumly. 'He's got it all. Charm and good looks. All the women fawn over him.'

'You misunderstood. I'm not interested in him. I thought the hero thing was something I could use in a note to Sally – that is if you're going to keep on going with your quest.'

'I'm not giving up,' Evan said. 'I don't think you could use what Luke said in a note to Sally. She already called me her hero for the same reason. It's really a stretch. It's not like I saved anybody's life, or anything. It's just because they don't understand computers. We all work at the same place – the Bellingham Hotel. He's the bartender at The Top of the Town. The name seems silly now. The building is dwarfed by the ones around it, but back in the day I guess it was considered to have the primo view. The register keeps freezing up and Luke thinks I'm amazing because I can fix it.' Evan stopped for a beat. 'I could show him how to fix it, but I like having a reason to go up there. Even now the view is pretty amazing.'

'Does Sally know him?' I asked. 'You all work in the same place.'

'I don't know – I don't think so. The bar is on the top of the hotel and her office is in the lobby.' I heard him suck in his breath. 'Is that what you think happened? Sally took one look at him and I was like yesterday's lunch in comparison.' He seemed to be almost talking to himself. 'He's single now, too.' Then it seemed he was back to directing his words at me. 'His wife died in some kind of accident. We all signed a card.' I heard him sigh. 'We just have to come up with something great for our next outing. I'm not sure Sally understood it was a date. Whatever I do next has to be more date like than a walk through the zoo.'

It was pretty clear that he was starting to have doubts how their date had gone. I felt for him knowing how much he seemed to like Sally. And I was sure if she got to know him, she'd appreciate his basic niceness. How common was that these days? He wanted a relationship. He wanted to get married. I just hoped she wasn't one of those women who loved bad boys who were indifferent to them. He was sunk if she did.

My job was just to write missives, so I let him talk on about potentials for a second date.

'I still want to do something during the day, so we can spend time getting to know each other. At least, I want her to get to know me better. I already know she's amazing. Do you think brunch would— no, that's too ordinary.' He lapsed into a nervous silence. 'What do you think?' he asked, when I hadn't said anything.

'Remember, I'm not a matchmaker. I just handle the message.'

'I know, but you're a woman and you know what women like, and I'd really like your advice and your words to carry it off.'

'OK,' I said slowly. I really didn't want to become his date planner, but he seemed a little panicky. 'We could work on a note saying how much you enjoyed her company and something about why you enjoyed it. We could say you feel happy when you're with her and then suggest another date. I think another daytime event is a good idea. It stands out. What about the Architectural Boat Tour?' It was still running for a few more weeks until the weather turned too cold. 'It goes down the Chicago River and there's a fun guide who points out interesting buildings and sites. Plus, there's a snack bar with wine.' And, I thought, she couldn't leave in the middle.

'I like it,' he said.

'And this time instead of a flower, you could leave a toy boat. It would make you seem playful and fun.'

'Do you think it would work? Would she believe I was playful and fun? It could be false advertising. Honestly, I don't have a clue how to be playful and fun.'

'Maybe that's not your strong suit,' I said. 'But from what I could tell, she certainly liked talking to you. I thought it would be good to put something about what she said in the next note – so she would know you really listened.'

'Listening to her was easy to do. I loved hearing her talk. It was mostly about work and the difficult people she encounters. It doesn't sound like anybody ever says she's their hero, more likely they're complaining that the hot appetizers were cold.'

'Was there anything else? Something that wasn't a complaint? Maybe something she liked.'

'That's right. She said she wanted to go on a cruise through the Panama Canal.' His voice lifted as he said it. 'Your idea of the Chicago River cruise is perfect. It's not the Panama Canal, but there is a lock that keeps the water from flowing into Lake Michigan,' he said.

'I don't think we need to mention the lock, but I could certainly come up with something that ties what she said into the plan for the boat tour. I'd put in something about how much you enjoyed her company. How everything seemed nicer when you were around her.'

Evan sounded all smiles by the time we hung up. I'd promised to email him the final note once it was ready. If it was acceptable, he'd print it up and deliver it to her office along with a toy boat.

I sat back after I hung up. Now I had an idea why Camille Parker had regarded Luke so coldly. It wasn't very impressive to have Rachel marry a bartender, even if the view was great.

TEN

I n addition to my paid gigs, I did some pro bono work for a downtown pet shop, the Pet Emporium. Instead of selling pedigreed dogs and fancy cats, all the animals in the shop were rescues and were available for adoption. They were brought in by local shelters and were generally the most adoptable they had. That meant small cute dogs and cats with a wow factor like being Siamese or Persian. My job was to use my way with words to write pieces for the cats and dogs they had up for adoption. Something that gave them personality and would tug at the heart strings. I never worked from pictures or online videos. It was all in person for me and I always spent some time with the animal I was writing about. So when I got a call from the pet shop manager Monday morning about a hard-to-adopt cat that really needed something compelling and quick to find him a home, I agreed to come to the shop that day. I was always glad for a reason to get out in the world.

After the phone call with Evan, I had made myself some dinner and thought about what I'd put in the next letter to Sally. It would be easier to write than the first one, but I was less sure of the outcome. I was still a little uncomfortable with her abrupt departure and unsure what it meant.

While I chewed on my salad my thoughts went to the time I'd spent with Luke. I couldn't shake seeing the photo of Rachel he'd had on his phone. She barely resembled the beaming woman in the wedding photo I'd chosen for the book. In his, she looked broken.

The time I'd spent having coffee with Luke had altered my opinion of him. When I'd been working on their vows he'd stayed in the background as he had when I met him at his mother-in-law's, and I'd viewed him as being kind of like a human Ken doll. Nice-looking with a bland personality. But after being on one with him, I found I liked him – not the way Evan thought, of course. It would have been totally unprofessional under the circumstances and, well, he was a little too perfect for me. I had a soft spot for flawed types.

I'd ended my Sunday evening by focusing on the writers' group. They'd all left pages with me for me to look over. I had been in their place and I knew how sensitive they were, so I was deliberately cautious in the comments I wrote on their pages after reading them. I went for the positive, though honestly it was sometimes difficult, particularly with Ed. His didn't have much story. They were really just sexual fantasies and way too graphic for my taste, though we'd all prevailed on him to stick to euphemisms. That ended up making it seem funny, particularly when Ben read them in his police report voice. How he didn't crack a smile when he said *throbbing member roiling in a wave of passion* out loud, I didn't know. All I could say was that I was glad that I didn't have to read Ed's work out loud when the group met.

There was no doubt that it was a weekday when I went outside to catch the Metra train downtown the next morning. 57th Street was clogged with traffic, all trying to get around a truck making a delivery to the small grocery store on the ground floor of a red-brick apartment building. I had to thread my way through groups of students on their way to campus. A gaggle of gazelle-like joggers went past me on their way to the lake-front path.

I got up to the platform just as I heard the clanging sound as the train announced its arrival. It was an express train and barely fifteen minutes later I was walking through Millennium Station past the Starbucks with its scent of fresh-brewed coffee and the popcorn shop touting their special Chicago blend of flavors.

The wind hit me as soon as I got outside, cutting right through the fabric of my jacket. It was lunchtime and the sidewalk was bustling with people. Despite all the tall buildings, there was an open feeling thanks to the extensive park area and then the lakefront.

I walked down Randolph Street thinking I'd stay on it to State Street, but at the last minute I turned on Wabash. It was a quicker route as there was a lot less foot traffic to deal with, but it was also less scenic. The El tracks hovered over the street, held up by giant metal legs that looked like they belonged to some prehistoric insect and cast the street in shadow. A train rumbled overhead and squeaked as it stopped at the station.

It made me think of something Luke had said about the possible location of the dance place Rachel had gone to. He'd thought it might be on Wabash because she'd mentioned the sound of the trains. I started checking the businesses with new interest as I passed by until I got to a big display window. At first I thought the place was vacant, since the interior appeared almost empty.

Then I noticed the sign over the doorway that said *Dance with Me* and a plastic holder with a stack of sheets. I grabbed one and saw that it was a schedule of classes. I peered through the window and after a moment noticed a dark-haired woman peering back at me. She motioned for me to come inside.

The doorway was quite grand. I suspected the space might have had an earlier incarnation as a high-end preppy clothing store. For now it was a mostly open space with mirrors on the side walls. The woman who'd waved me in came from behind a reception counter to greet me. She looked at the paper in my hand. 'If you want to dance, you've come to the right place.' She was dressed in a short wrap-around skirt over leotard and tights and bore a friendly smile.

'Actually, I'm looking for information on someone I think was a student here. She might have gone by Rachel Parker or Rachel Ross,' I said. The woman's smile waned a little.

'Are you some kind of investigator?' she asked. This time I smiled.

'Hardly, well, I wrote a mystery with a detective in it and I guess I did pick up a few tricks. You know, like if someone claims to have been inside all evening on a rainy night and their shoes are wet, I know they're lying,' I said in a fun tone. I let out a sigh as I got more serious. 'I'm working on something else right now. I'm putting together a memory book for Rachel, for her . . .' I faltered, and finally said, 'funeral, well really her memorial service.'

'Oh dear,' the woman said with a concerned look, 'let me check.' She went to her computer and typed something in.

'I have sort of a connection with her,' I said, feeling the need to make conversation. 'I helped write her wedding vows. I'm trying to capture who she was for the memory book with anecdotes and things she liked to do. I thought I could put something in about dance lessons she took. Rather than be generic, I'd like to know what kind of classes she took.'

'I think I've found her name. I didn't realize who you meant at first. She called herself Ray here.' She turned and pointed to a wall next to her that was covered in small photos. 'She must be here somewhere.' She turned to me. 'Do you see her picture?'

I scanned the wall of photos and was amazed how much alike all the women looked. I finally located her picture. She'd struck a pose pointing at her tap shoes and had a happy smile. It was eerie seeing her looking so lively and knowing she was gone.

'That's her,' said the woman, recognizing her face. 'What happened to her?'

'She fell from the balcony on one of the high rises near the lake.'

'Oh,' the woman said, taken aback. 'How terrible. I'd be glad to help anyway I can.' She moved away from the computer. 'Darcy Miller,' she said, reaching out her hand. 'I'm the owner along with my partner. You referred to her as a student. We're not a dancing school. I like to think of it as a dance gym. All the classes are just drop-in and it doesn't matter if you're a beginner or have been going here for a while. We have it all: tap, ballet. hip-hop, western line, the jitterbug – if there's moving to music, we do it here. It's all about having fun while you get some exercise.'

'What an interesting concept. I had no idea,' I said. I looked at the sheet in my hand. It just listed names of classes and times. 'It would be better if you had some more complete descriptions of the classes.' Her expression dipped and I realized I might have said the wrong thing. 'Sorry, but I write things like this for a living, so it's like second nature for me to notice when some things feel like there's something missing.'

'Really? Maybe you could do something for us. My partner and I wrote all the copy and we're not professionals.'

'With a place like this, the story is important. Who you and your partner are. What your mission is. And more colorful descriptions of the classes.'

'You're absolutely right. If we had some good press releases, we could post them online and get them to the local talks shows.'

I reached in my purse and pulled out a card to hand to her. She held it in her hand. 'Why wait,' she said. 'Yes, I'd like to hire you. But if you're going to write descriptions of the classes you really should take them or at least watch them.'

'I'll go with taking them. It's the best way to capture the experience. Plus, writers sit too much, so the exercise would be good.' I felt enthused at the prospect of an entertaining project. 'As a bonus, maybe I'll be able to pick up some color to add to the piece I'm doing for Rachel. I mean Ray.'

We agreed on a price and she said she'd throw in a membership, and we shook on it. It was the quickest I'd ever gotten a gig. 'Now that that's settled, let me give you the grand tour.' I took that as a joke, as it was really just a big empty room. There was a bathroom in the back and a small room for changing. She showed me a rack of hooks for coats, explaining that most of the members came dressed for class. 'The cubbies are here for phones and small stuff,' she said, showing me how they could be accessed from the back or the front.

'Ray's husband said she talked about hanging out with somebody a lot.'

'It could have been my partner, Debbie Alcoa. She teaches a lot of the classes. But it also could have been one of our members,' she said with a shrug as we got back to the alcove. 'Do you live downtown?'

'No,' I said. 'I live in Hyde Park, but I'm downtown a lot. It's, like, fifteen minutes on the Metra train line.' I explained meeting clients and told her about my work for the pet shop. We seemed to have an instant rapport.

'I take the El,' she said, pointing at the tracks that hung over the street. 'I almost forgot,' she said, grinning, 'there's always paperwork.' She handed me a membership form to fill out and a waiver to sign.

I filled in a standard form with my particulars and signed the waiver that absolved them of liability and handed it back to her. She looked them over, pushing back a strand of her dark wavy hair.

'I have a few minutes,' I said, as I pulled out my notebook and a pen. 'I might as well start getting some background information from you.' I saw her look at my tools, and I smiled.

'I know – it's old-fashioned but I like take real notes on real paper.' I held the pen poised. 'Why don't you give me a little background on yourself and how you came to open this place.'

'I don't know how much you want to put in about me.' She looked down at her outfit. 'This is mostly for show. Debbie's the real dancer of the two of us. I was going through some big changes in my life and I was looking to get a fresh start and reinvent myself. I've always liked to dance, and I thought the combination of exercise and fun would be good for people's heads.' She laughed as she added, 'Well, and the rent was right.' I glanced around the open space which I now remembered had been a high-end shop that had sold tailored clothes. 'We didn't have to do much to the place beyond put up the mirrors.'

I looked at my watch. 'I guess that's it for now. I have to get to the Pet Emporium to meet a cat,' I said, and explained my next task.

'That's really nice of you,' she said. 'If you want to stop back afterwards, we have a tap class starting in an hour.' I gave her a thumbs-up as I headed to the door.

Back on the street, I thought how life was full of surprises. I'd gone there hoping for information and left with a membership card and a gig.

ELEVEN

The Pet Emporium was on State Street. As always, the sidewalks were clogged with foot traffic and had a circus-like atmosphere as street musicians serenaded passersby and a preacher with a microphone warned people to repent before it was too late. When I was growing up, this part of downtown had been a shopping mecca and the center of business. You shopped, you worked and then you went home. No one lived in the area. Then things began to change. The department stores that had lined State Street kept closing until the only two left were Marshall Field's and Carson Pirie Scott. And then there was just one when Carson Pirie Scott closed. By then Macy's had taken over Marshall Field's and the only remnants of the elegant store were the iconic clocks on the outside corners and the Walnut Room restaurant on the seventh floor.

People still worked downtown, but more and more people had chosen to live there as high-rise housing popped up and some old commercial buildings were repurposed into lofts and condominiums. The number of colleges and universities that had vertical campuses in the heart of the city had grown and they'd built dormitories. There were still plenty of shops along State Street, but many of them had changed to cater to the residents' needs. The Pet Emporium was one of them.

I'd been writing the personality pieces for a while and according to Melissa, the manager, had helped place a lot of pets. She'd warned me that the cat I was coming to meet was what they considered hard to adopt and really needed my help in finding a forever home quickly. It was all rather ironic that I was so good at figuring out pet personalities since I'd never had a dog or cat myself. My father was allergic and after that it simply wasn't something I'd considered.

The large shop had originally been a grand shoe store with display windows that surrounded the entrance. Where there once had been boots and sandals, the tiered space in the windows featured cat and dog mannequins showing off an astonishing variety of pet accessories hinting at what was inside. Just before the entrance, a water fountain seemed to be enticing a gray tabby.

Inside it was like a supermarket of pet needs. Several people were creating their own mixture of goodies for their pets from the gourmet treat bar. Maybe it was just because I hadn't had lunch, but I thought they actually smelled quite good. The adoption area was in the back of the shop with separate rooms for cats and dogs. Inside the rooms, the animals were in generous-sized enclosures. I hated to call them cages, but essentially that is what they were. Each of the rooms had an open area in the middle for the pets to have some play time either with workers at the store or for meet-and-greets with potential adopters.

Melissa was talking to a woman in sweats standing near the front. She waved me over and introduced me as the writer who did wonders helping the resident pets find homes.

'Natalie walks dogs and trains them,' Melissa said, gesturing toward the woman. 'And is one of our best customers for the treat bar.' The woman smiled and said something about only the best for her charges. Melissa explained I was there to meet a cat and the two of us headed toward the pet enclosures in the back. She always started by thanking me for what I was doing. 'But you have your work cut out for you this time,' she said, opening the door to the cat room. It always amused me to note the difference in how the cats reacted to someone coming into their area than the dogs did. The dogs reacted with enthusiastic interest, barking or whining. The cats mostly had an 'oh, well,' attitude and rarely made a move. She pointed to an enclosure on the upper level. A large black-and-white cat was sitting at the front of his living space and I could feel that he was watching me.

'That's Rocky,' she said. 'They brought him over hoping it would help him find a home.' She dropped her voice. 'He's at the end of his stay.' She didn't elaborate on what that meant, but I knew she meant getting euthanized.

'The previous owner dropped him off at the shelter, saying they were moving.' She pursed her lips in disgust. 'As if cats

can't move somewhere. Anyway, the problem is that he's eight.'
She left it at that, and I knew what she was trying to say. People
wanted puppies and kittens or at the very least pets that were at
most a couple of years old.

She opened the gate on his enclosure and brought him into
the open area. He looked around, seeming to be glad to have
his freedom, before he hopped on the end of the bench I was
sitting on. He looked at me and I looked at him, trying to sense
his personality. I'd have to find a way to put a spin on his age,
so it seemed like a benefit. He got closer and sat down next to
me. After a moment, he launched one paw onto my neck
and then he lifted his other paw and the next thing I knew it
seemed like he was hugging me.

'What was that?' I asked Melissa, as the cat retreated.

'Some cats are huggers. You could put that in the piece and
be sure to say that he likes to cuddle.' As if to prove her right,
he came back and leaned in next to me. *Poor kitty*, I thought as
I reached out to pet him. He pushed his head against my hand,
and I heard the rumble of a purr.

Melissa was fascinated with what I did and always asked what
I was working on. I told her about Evan and the love letters,
without mentioning names of course. 'Although I wouldn't quite
call them love letters yet. They're really *like* letters so far.' I let
out a sigh as I thought about Rachel. 'My other job isn't quite
so fun,' I said. 'Someone I helped with her wedding vows died.'
I stopped and gave the cat a few more strokes as I tried to figure
out how to explain what I was doing without making it a long
story. It was easier to do that when I was writing because I could
go back and edit. But you couldn't do that when you were talking.
'She died recently and I'm putting together sort of a memory
book to be given out at her service.'

'You said you wrote her wedding vows. She must have been
young. What did she die from?' Melissa asked.

'Actually, I only helped with her vows. I just gave them a
polish. Yes, she was young. She fell from a balcony in one of
the buildings in Lakeshore East.'

Melissa's expression sharpened. 'I think I heard about that.' She
thought for a moment. 'It was Natalie. She works in that building
a lot. She was there the day it happened.'

'Really?' I said, interested. 'Is she still here?' I glanced through the large window of the enclosed area that looked out into the store.

'There she is. By the treat buffet,' Melissa said, pointing her out. I followed her gaze to the dark-haired woman I'd met when I came in who was dropping biscuits into a paper sack. I thought about trying to catch up with her, but she was already headed to the cashier. I shrugged it off, figuring she probably didn't know anything about Rachel's fall, anyway. Melissa seemed ready to wind things down.

'I can't imagine how you would create a book for her funeral,' Melissa said, getting up. 'But then, I can't imagine how you come up with what you write about the animals either.' She gave my shoulder a pat. 'I guess that's what makes you a writer and me not one.'

Someone knocked on the glass and Melissa winced. 'Got to get back to business.' She picked up the cat and put him back in the cage. I stayed behind for a few minutes, scribbling down a few notes before gathering up my things. I took a picture of Rocky with my phone for reference purposes. 'I hope I can help,' I said to the cat before I walked out of the room.

Then it was time to change gears. I checked my watch and saw that I just had time to get back to the dance place in time for the tap class. I liked it when I could dovetail things like this and work on two projects during one trip downtown.

Dance with Me looked a lot different when I returned. There were about twenty or so people loosely organized in two lines. There were a few men mixed in with the crowd. I checked out everyone's attire and compared it to my own. Darcy had said street clothes were fine, and I was wearing leggings with a loose top and walking shoes, but still I felt out of place. Most of them had on stylish exercise clothes and tap shoes.

I left my jacket on one of the hooks at the back and I tried to fit my bag into one of the cubbies, but it wouldn't fit. Finally I hung the bag with my jacket and just put my phone and wallet in the cubbies as the others seemed to have done.

I checked the two lines and found an empty space. Feeling a little self-conscious, I stepped into it. The women on either side of me gave me the once-over and both stared at my shoes. Darcy had assured me that tap shoes weren't required, but my walking shoes seemed all wrong.

'First timer,' I said. 'It was a last-minute decision to come.' I was relieved when they both smiled at me.

'That's OK, New Girl,' the one on my right said. 'But it is more fun with the shoes.' To demonstrate she did some kind of shuffle step that made a clatter. 'Kat,' she said introducing herself.

'Veronica,' I said, turning to both of them.

'I'm Kelly,' the other one said. 'Don't worry about the shoes, but Kat is right. It's good to be able to make noise.'

More people had come in and a third row was forming. It occurred to me that I should explain why I was there and see if I could get some useful information from them. Maybe even a quote. They were both about my age and would have looked almost like twins with their short dark hair and even features, but Kat had tinted her hair aqua. 'I'm here for a dual purpose: exercise, but also to gather some color to write up some publicity pieces for Dance with Me. Actually, it's a triple purpose: I came here looking for information about another project I'm working on. Did either of you know Rach— I mean Ray?' They both took a moment to think before nodding.

'She's a regular, though I haven't seen her for a while,' Kat said.

'That happens all the time,' Kelly said. 'People come religiously for a while and then we never see them again. I haven't missed a week since the place opened.'

'Then you don't know what happened to her?' I said.

'Something happened to her?' Kelly said, surprised.

I mentioned her fall and they both gasped.

'I had a feeling something was going on with her, but I had no idea it was that serious,' Kat said, and I realized she assumed it was suicide. I suddenly panicked not knowing who was overhearing our conversation. I didn't want it to get back to the Parkers that I was undermining their effort to make it seem Rachel's death was an accident. I quickly added that it had been an accident. Kat shrugged off my comment. 'She was all bubbly and excited when she first joined. She thought dancing would be fun and she wanted to lose a few pounds. She wasn't fat or anything, but somebody must have said something to her.'

'She said she was newly married. Maybe her husband was the someone who said something,' Kelly said. 'The last time I saw her I remember noticing that she didn't look well. I even asked her if anything was wrong.'

'What did she say?' I asked, trying not to appear as interested as I felt. One of the teachers had said something similar.

'Ray shrugged it off. I thought maybe she wasn't eating enough and exercising too much. But then we were just gym friends. You know, you talk before class – like this – so I let it go.'

Kat nodded. 'Ray and I talked about getting together outside of here, but we never did. Now I wish we had.'

I saw that the teacher had come in and quickly told them about the memory book and collecting stories about Rachel. 'Any chance you might have a memory about Ray that I could include. Like something she said about the dance classes or a fun moment.'

The two women looked at each other. Kelly shrugged, but Kat spoke. 'I have something you might be able to use. A woman came to a tap class with her special needs daughter. The girl had Down's syndrome and you could watch people giving them disparaging looks and moving away as they tried to find a place in the class. Ray saw what was going on and helped them find a spot and then stood next to the girl. She was friendly and helpful when the girl had trouble with the steps. She put us all to shame and I was determined to follow her lead the next time they came, but the mother and daughter never came again.'

'That's just the kind of story I'm looking for. Would it be OK if I attribute it to you? I'd just use your first name and say something like fellow tap dancer,' I said, and Kat nodded.

'I'll try to think of something, too,' Kelly said. 'Maybe next time we meet in a class. But now it's time to boogie with Debbie.' She pointed to the front of the room as music came up and the teacher began the warm-up.

They might have boogied, but I just tried to keep up. By the end of the class, I was beginning to figure it out. The most important thing seemed to be to move in the same direction everybody else was.

'The first time is always the hardest,' Kat said, as we all walked to the back to collect our things. I thanked her for the encouragement, then let everyone leave ahead of me.

I made a stop on one of the benches in front of the display windows. My excuse was I wanted to scribble down some notes about the class along with some about Rachel and the special needs girl, but I needed a few minutes to recuperate before I walked the few blocks to the train. I was glad I'd brought a bottle of water and power bar. It was shocking to realize how out of shape I was. And clumsy, too. More than once I'd almost stepped on Kelly's foot. Darcy saw me sitting there and came over.

'So, made it through,' she said with a friendly smile. Then she said basically the same thing Kat had about it getting easier with time. 'I forgot one important step in the membership process,' she said with a smile. 'We need to add your photo. Give me your phone so I can take one.' I hardly looked my best, but she assured me I had a glow from completing the dance class. I unlocked my phone and handed it to her. She snapped several shots and then handed it back to me. 'Pick the one you like best and then print it from your phone.' She held up a small photo printer.

I thought I looked awful in all of them, but picked the least bad one and a moment later it rolled out of the printer. She stuck it on the wall along with all the other faces.

'What did you think of the class?' she asked.

'I like the format and I really needed it,' I said. 'Writers sit too much.'

'And you probably spend a lot of time alone,' she said. 'I saw you talking to the women around you. It must have been nice to be around people.'

'Yes, having a computer being my significant other can be lonely and I did enjoy the company. They were very encouraging, and the bonus was that one of them had a story about Rachel.'

Darcy wanted to know the story and nodded with interest. From there, I somehow segued into talking about myself. I never did that with clients, but she seemed interested and was easy to talk to. By time I left, I felt like I'd told her my life story, including mentioning the manuscript lingering on the shelf. I ended by telling her that I'd be back for a ballet class the next day.

* * *

As I rode the train back to Hyde Park, my thoughts were on Rachel. It was thanks to her that I'd ended up at the dance gym and gotten the gig writing about it. I imagined she'd probably be happy about it since I'd heard how excited she'd been about the place. And I'd gotten another story for the book. It just reaffirmed what the teachers had said and what I'd seen in the short time I'd spent with her when I'd been working on her vows. She was a genuinely caring person. It made it even sadder to think she'd been having a rough time herself. I felt a pang of guilt thinking back to what Luke had said about her needing a friend. Could I have made a difference?

As soon as I got home, I took a hot bath in the claw-foot tub to ease my aching muscles and dressed in some comfortable sweats. I could have gone right to my computer and started work on everything, but I felt like I needed it all to simmer in my unconscious for a while first. It was getting dark when I went into the kitchen and made myself a cheese and mushroom omelet with a side of salad. Someday I'd get the kitchen brought up to modern standards with cabinets, counters and modern appliances, but it worked for now even if I did have to wash the dishes by hand. I took my food into the dining room and thought about what Darcy had said. She was right – I did spend a lot of time alone.

When I felt compelled to clean up everything before I went to my work, I realized I was stalling, hoping I'd build up steam and when I sat down at the computer that the words would explode from my fingers to the screen. My notes from what Kat had said about Rachel were pretty sketchy and I wanted to get them in the computer while the story was still fresh in my mind. Rocky was depending on me to come up with something so heart-wrenching it would get him his forever home. And I had to come through for Evan. The only piece that didn't seem too daunting was the description of the dance class.

My office felt cozy and inviting when I finally got in there. I turned on the student lamp and it illuminated my desk, the burgundy-colored wing chair and the old oriental rugs in shades of red covering the wood floor. I used one of the metalwork wall sconces to light up the perimeter of the room. I was pretty sure it dated from when the building had been constructed. The lamp itself was meant to look like a candle. Some people put in flame-shaped bulbs, but I used a regular bulb covered by a silky off-white lampshade. Outside the patter of raindrops began to hit the glass. It was a nice night to be inside.

Tap never goes out of style, I began writing. *Drop in any time to get your shuffle ball change on. No experience or shoes required, though it's more fun if you have tap shoes. You learn the steps to a fun routine and dance away the hour.* I wrote a note to myself that it might be a good idea to get some quotes from members about the different classes.

It turned out to be no problem typing up Kat's story about Rachel. I made sure to include how Rachel's behavior had inspired Kat. I moved on to the layout using placeholders for the photographs and a capsule of the copy that would go around them. I wrote out the basic story about the purse that Rachel had auctioned off and then used the money for school supplies, to get an idea of how much space it would take. I put in placeholders for the other stories I hoped to get from the Parkers and from Luke. There might be something more from the dance classes, and if need be, I could always put in some poetry. Then I set it aside since it wasn't as immediate as my other tasks. Evan needed his note so he could get it to Sally, and Rocky needed his story posted as soon as possible so he could get adopted.

I was on a roll now and started on to Evan's note. The challenge was to write something romantic, but in a tone that sounded like him.

Hi Sally,

I really enjoyed the time at the zoo with you. I'd really enjoy being anywhere with you. I'm so sorry you had to leave our date because of work. I was hoping for a raincheck and the chance to whisk you away on a cruise. It won't be to the Panama Canal, but the Chicago River is a lot closer. I thought we could spend the afternoon on the architectural cruise gliding along past tall buildings and interesting sights while we sip wine. You might not have noticed because I'm so serious at work, but I can be fun.

I called Evan and read it to him on the phone. He was still a little worried about having to live up to the fun part. I assured him he'd rise to the occasion. He was also worried about finding a toy boat that looked like the one they'd be taking. I convinced him that was an unnecessary detail and any boat would do. I emailed him a copy of the letter as we spoke.

'Let me know what happens,' I said. I heard him take a breath and I was afraid he was going to suggest that I go on the cruise to watch them from afar, but thankfully he didn't.

I let out a heavy sigh as I moved to my last assignment. I always wrote the piece from the animal's perspective. I did some research and found out that Rocky was what was called a tuxedo cat and that what Melissa said about some cats being huggers was true. It seemed that sometimes it was a sign of affection; at other times, it was the cat trying to grab onto its prey. I was sure that in this case Rocky's hug was affectionate because there were no claws involved. I also read something that said cats picked their human companions.

I started to write trying to put a spin on his age. *My name is Rocky and I'm looking for a forever home. I could lie about my age, but here it is – I'm eight, but I still have a lot of good years ahead of me. It also means I'm past the crazy kitten stage. If you take me home, I will show my appreciation forever. My specialty is giving hugs. You won't find many cats that do that.* I stopped to pull up the photo I'd taken before I said anything about his markings. When I looked at the picture I was stunned. His big yellowish eyes had a pleading quality and he was holding out one paw as if to say *take me with you.*

Did that mean he was choosing me?

I thought back to how he'd hugged me. Tears were rolling down my cheeks before I realized I was crying. There was no way I could let him down. Well, it looked like I'd succeeded at my assignment. I hadn't even finished writing the piece and Rocky had found his home.

TWELVE

I know it was crazy, but as soon as I decided to adopt Rocky, I was sure a hoard of people would show up at the Pet Emporium and want to give him a forever home. So I was on the phone when the pet store opened telling Melissa the cat would be coming home with me. She laughed. 'I knew you were a good writer,' she said. 'You sold yourself.' She promised that no matter what, she wouldn't let anyone else take the cat.

I'd barely hung up when the phone rang. It was Mrs Parker and I'd just gotten out a hello, when she started to speak. 'I need to see what you have so far for Rachel's memory book.'

'I could email something to you,' I said, thinking over what I had.

'No,' she said. 'It must be in person. Today. This morning.' It was a definite command.

I looked at my watch and tried to calculate when I could get there. 'Can we make it as late as possible?' I would have to get the train and walk to her place.

'I don't care what you have to do, but you'll have to get here by 11:30. I have a luncheon.' Her tone was curt and the message clear, I worked for her.

Now I was glad that I'd done the work on it the night before, but it was still in very rough form. It would give her an idea what it was going to look like, and I could tell her what else I planned to add. I hoped that was enough because there was nothing else I could do since she'd insisted on seeing it that morning. I threw on a pair of leggings and a loose T-shirt for the dance class, then covered it with a long black sweater that made it look more professional. I printed up what I had, packed up the albums in the bag and left for the train. I rushed to the station and got to the platform as the train was pulling in.

I was annoyed that I'd had to drop everything to meet with Mrs Parker, but she was the client. The grocery bag of albums weighed me down as I walked from the downtown station to their building. At least I'd only have them one way.

It wasn't a particularly cheerful day either. The sky was a mottled gray and the air felt sharp. The only positive was that it wasn't raining. I checked in with the doorman when I arrived in the lobby of their building. He called upstairs and got the OK before he opened an inner door and directed me to the elevator.

She was alone this time and attired to go somewhere fancy in a dress with a jacket and heels. Her dark hair looked as if it had been professionally blown out and her makeup was perfect. She seemed impatient as she brought me into the apartment. I held up the bag with the albums and she instructed me to put them down against the wall in the hall.

She brusquely told me to sit. 'Let me see what you have,' she said.

I took out a folder with the printout I'd brought. 'I wasn't expecting to have to show you anything today,' I said. 'It should give you an idea what I have in mind.'

She waved her hand as if to demand the pages and I gave them to her.

As she began to look through them, I explained what was going to go where. 'There will be more from the teachers that Rachel worked with.' I pointed to the placeholders and then to the rough idea of the purse story. 'This is just a sample of the type of anecdotes I intend to include.'

'She gave away a Victor Luis purse! Do you know what those things cost? I don't know about using that story. It makes her sound a little crazy.'

'Or someone with a good heart,' I said. Mrs Parker glared at me.

'She was taking tap classes?' Mrs Parker said as she read down the page. 'That makes her sound sane at least.' She shook her head and let out a sigh.

I explained about the dance gym, omitting that I'd gotten a gig writing copy for them, figuring she'd probably think I should give her a discount since I'd been at the gym to find out about Rachel when I'd gotten the job.

'I want to get a story from Luke to include,' I said, pointing to a spot on the page where I planned to put it.

'You better run it by me before you put it in. Who knows what he'll say?'

'But he was her husband and she seemed crazy about him.'

'That might have been another sign of her bad judgment. I don't know what's up with him.' She sounded perturbed. 'Rachel was clearly going through something. Mr Parker and I thought she might need to be hospitalized, but Luke said that it was all because she was having trouble sleeping and that he was sure if she got some good nights of rest everything would straighten out.' She was silent for a moment and was clearly thinking something over. 'What I meant to say was that we thought she needed to be hospitalized because she seemed so exhausted. That's probably why she fell.' She seemed anxious to change the subject and looked over the pages again. She pointed to the biography. 'There's a mistake here,' she said. 'Rachel's mother's name is Candace.'

'You're not her mother,' I said, surprised. 'But you never said anything when I was helping with her vows.'

She looked at me coldly. 'There wasn't any reason to tell you. It had nothing to do with what you were hired for.'

I felt my face grow hot as I realized that I must have just seen a name starting with C in the obituary and assumed it was Camille. It was the kind of mistake I shouldn't have made. I assured her I'd take care of it.

'What happened to Rachel's mother?' I asked, wondering if Mrs Parker would answer, or just tell me that it was none of my business. She surprised me by actually answering my question.

'She died a few years ago,' Mrs Parker said. I waited to see if there would be more of an explanation, but she launched back into her bad relationship with Rachel. 'I tried my best to step in and take her mother's place, but you saw how she was when you were helping with her vows. Whatever I said was poison. When I implied that something seemed a little strange with Luke, she went nuts.' Mrs Parker looked directly at me. 'Luke is a good-looking man with a lot of charm. I saw with my own eyes how women seem to flock to him. Rachel was cute, but not a beauty, though she came with a lot of perks. And the way he insisted on keeping the job as a bartender after Mr Parker offered to bring him into the family business seemed off to me.'

I didn't know what to say. It turned out not to be a problem. Mrs Parker looked at her watch and then got up abruptly and I got the message that we were done. As she walked me to the door, I brought up getting a story from her. She thought it over for a moment. 'My daughters and I put on a bridal shower for her; maybe put something about that in the book.'

'Could you give me some details?' I said.

'You're a writer. Just make something up. We just care that it sounds good,' she said. 'I'll be in touch to check on your progress.' As soon as I stepped into the hall, she closed the door behind me.

I checked the sky when I got outside. The day hadn't brightened any, but it still felt good to be outside, now that I didn't have to carry the bag of albums. The dance class didn't start for a while and I wasn't picking up Rocky until later. I had a lot to digest after finding out that Camille was the second Mrs Parker.

I liked to walk when I had a lot of thinking to do, so when I reached Michigan Avenue I headed north. The background blurred in my consciousness and I got lost in the rhythm of my steps. I had no sense of passing shops and food places or the wide street clogged with traffic. How could I have missed the name Candace in the obituary? It was hardly professional. Mrs Parker could have fired me on the spot. It took several blocks before I calmed myself, realizing that other than vowing to be more careful in the future there was nothing I could do, and I forced myself to let it go.

My breath came out in a gush as I stopped berating myself. My thoughts jumped to processing that Camille Parker wasn't Rachel's mother. Of course now it all made sense. It wasn't a strained mother-daughter relationship at all. It was a stepmother-stepdaughter situation. So Rachel's mother had died, as mine had. I was pretty sure I'd been younger than Rachel, but the end result was the same – feeling abandoned. I suddenly felt more of a connection to Rachel.

I suppose I was lucky that my father didn't remarry. He had some 'friends' but he kept them separate from me. Most of his time was taken up with his job teaching and his job trying to finish bringing me up. I shuddered to think what it would have

been like if he'd married someone like Camille. The wicked
stepmothers of fairy tales came to mind.

I wondered how Mr Parker had handled his wife's death. I
wondered how he was dealing with Rachel's death. I'd never met
him and only seen him once briefly. I'd gone to the wedding to
hear them say the vows I'd helped with. He'd walked Rachel
down the church aisle and stood to the side during the ceremony.
Even at a distance, he seemed a little stiff, and I knew there
wasn't a chance in the world that he and Rachel would break
into some elaborate choreography during their first dance like so
many YouTube videos showed.

The wind hit me and turned my hair into a crazy salad as I
crossed the bridge the spanning river. It blew the flap of my
trench coat open. I struggled to pull it shut and buttoned it so it
would stay closed. Below the water was a murky greenish color
and the Architectural Tour boat was just beginning to load. I
wondered how Sally would respond to my note from Evan. I'd
made a point to call their last meeting a date. Calling it a
date made his intentions clear. I hadn't said anything about it to
Evan, but I was thinking that if she truly wasn't interested in
him, it would be better to find out now. I was rooting for him,
but I also didn't want him to get his hopes up if she just viewed
him as a friend.

I continued walking when I got to the other side of the bridge.
I hadn't thought of a destination, but when I looked up and saw
the Bellingham Hotel, it seemed as if my unconscious had
brought me there. All Mrs Parker's talk about Luke and his job
had made me curious about the bar.

The Bellingham was a historic building that had been updated
to keep up with the times without losing its charm. The upper
portion of the building was dark brick with the kind of decorative features nobody bothered with anymore. The entrance was
quite grand with an arched hood that offered protection from
the elements. Gold-colored metal with an embossed design
framed the doorway.

Evan had called the bar The Top of the Town which I imagined
meant it was on the top floor, but I checked with the concierge
anyway. He directed me to an elevator that went directly to the
small structure on the roof of the hotel. Crossing the lobby, it

suddenly occurred to me that Sally and Evan both worked here. I didn't really want to bump into either of them. It would be so awkward.

The elevator had once had an attendant, but now was automated with a button to be pushed for top-floor bar. The elevator door opened into an entrance area and as I stepped out, I looked directly into the bar. I did a quick survey of the place. Everything about it said elegant oasis. The stone floor had an inlaid design which went back to another time. Lime-colored upholstered chairs were arranged around low tables. The actual bar was small. The seats running along the counter were more like chairs on stilts than stools. French doors looked out on a small terrace area and beyond the street was visible. By today's standards, the hotel wasn't very tall, but the position of the building still gave the top floor a nice view of Michigan Avenue.

I stepped closer to look outside. There were potted trees with a few leaves still hanging on the branches. Planters with yellow chrysanthemums added some color.

'That area is closed,' a male voice said in a friendly tone.

I turned and saw it was Luke. He was surprised to realize it was me and greeted me with a smile. 'The patio is closed for the season,' he said, 'but there's plenty of seating inside.' He gestured toward the empty tables and chairs. 'We don't officially open for ten minutes, but if you're really in need of something, I can bend the rules for you.'

I chuckled at the thought of me being in such need of drink as if I was some sort of alcoholic. 'No, thanks,' I said. It couldn't have been further from the truth. It must have been something in my body chemistry, but even a half a glass of wine made me feel uncomfortable, as if there was velvet stuffed in my head.

I decided to get right to the point and told him I'd just been at the Parkers. 'I had no idea she wasn't Rachel's mother,' I said.

'Oh.' He sounded surprised. 'I didn't realize you didn't know.' He'd gone behind the bar and pointed to the row of empty seats, inviting me to take one. 'I know you drink coffee from the other day. It's a fresh pot.'

'That sounds good,' I said, sitting down. He was certainly more hospitable than Camille Parker had been.

'I'm assuming Camille wanted to see you about the book you're making.' He poured a cup of coffee for both of us and pushed mine across the shiny black surface of the bar.

'I could have sent her an email with what I had, but she wanted a meeting.'

He gave me a knowing nod. 'It's a power trip.'

'That's for sure. She doesn't really care about what I put together as long as it keeps to the image they want to project. She told me she didn't care if I made stuff up.' I shook my head.

'She doesn't want my input. I was only there the other day for window dressing. At least she's consistent. She's never been a fan,' he said.

'She was pretty spare on details about what happened to Rachel's mother,' I said, hoping he'd have some details.

'She died before I'd met Rachel.' He paused to take a sip of his coffee. 'Rachel said it was an accidental overdose.' He looked at me directly. 'There's no reason you shouldn't have the whole story. Rachel wasn't so sure it was accidental. Candace was rather a fragile princess and, well, if she thought she was about to lose her husband to another woman . . .'

'Was the other woman Camille?' I asked and he nodded.

'I got all of this from Rachel, but Camille was Richard Parker's assistant. In other words, his "work-wife." Rachel thought there might have been more wifely duties than just keeping his schedule straight. They barely waited six months after Candace's death to tie the knot.'

I let it sink in. It made it seem even clearer why Rachel would have had bad feeling toward her stepmother.

'It was hard for Rachel. She wanted to be part of the philan-thropic endeavors the family business was involved with, but Camille was always trying to push Rachel off to the side and bring her daughters into the middle of things. They were brides-maids at our wedding.' He shook his head. 'Rachel only agreed to it because her father pushed her to do it.'

'Was Rachel close with her father?' I asked.

Luke shrugged. 'He's always been all about work and I gather was never particularly involved with her growing up. Except to let her know he wasn't happy with her choices of work or, well, of me. I might have been marginally acceptable if I'd accepted his offer. He wanted me to take some job in the shipping business. They're expanding into passenger cruise ships on the Great Lakes. If it had been working on a ship, I might have considered it. I like working directly with people, not administrative paper pushing. He didn't take it well when I wanted to continue on here. You can imagine he insisted I sign a prenuptial agreement. And they're really sticking to it. The boat and the apartment were gifts to her only. That's what you get for not reading the small print,' he said with a mirthless laugh.

It was interesting that he spoke without anger about the Parkers and the way they treated him. He seemed like the kind of person who let whatever happened just roll off of him.

He took another sip of his coffee and set down the cup. 'To change the subject . . . I've been thinking about what you said about wanting a story from me.' He gestured toward a seat down the bar from me. 'This is where Rachel and I met.'

Some patrons came in and he excused himself and went to help the couple. He greeted them by name and followed as they took a pair of seats around one of the low tables. When he came back to the bar, he picked up a phone and I heard him placing a food order. As soon as he was done, he began work on their drinks which turned out to be just wine. He delivered them and stood for a moment talking to them.

'Special customers?' I said when he returned.

'They're all special,' he said with a smile. 'We have a lot of regulars who live around here. I'm good at sensing what they need. I like to think of this almost like a private club for them. Sorry for the interruption.'

'Of course,' I said. 'I don't want to interfere with your work.'

'To get back to what I was saying.' He pointed to the seat and repeated that it was where he and Rachel had met. 'And it was all about a special pink squirrel.'

'What's a pink squirrel?' I asked, trying not to wrinkle my nose, imagining it was some weird delicacy.

'It's a drink,' he said, 'very pink and girly. And the one she wanted was alcohol free. I'd heard of the alcohol version. It was popular a long time ago, but we don't even stock some of the ingredients anymore. She insisted she'd gotten it at the bar before and had me check the recipe file. Apparently, the bartender at the time had created the special version for her. She apologized for being so much trouble, but said it was her birthday. She explained it was a special drink she'd gotten when she and her mother stopped at the bar after shopping. Her mother always had a martini with two olives, and she had the pink drink. She was very friendly and I was glad to make the drink for her.'

While he was talking, he pulled out some bottles and began pouring things into a shaker. 'I asked her if her mother was meeting her and her smile faded as she explained that her mother had died a year ago. I always get along with our patrons, but something about Rachel touched me.' He added some ice to the shaker.

'She came in a few more times,' he said, now giving the concoction a shake. 'By the third time I made her the drink without her even asking. She said it had been a happy time for her when she'd come to the bar with her mother and when she'd had a rough day, having the pink squirrel reminded her of that time and was somehow comforting. She mentioned dreading some affair she had to attend. It came out that she didn't have an escort and I offered to go with her. I had no idea who her family was or what kind of event it was.' He poured the drink in a cocktail glass and pushed it across the bar. He smiled thinking back. 'Everybody was in tuxedos but me. We sat at a table with the mayor and a lot of CEO types. The dinner was honoring her father for the donation he'd made for a new library for Wright University.'

I looked at the drink in front of me. It was indeed pink and frothy. 'No alcohol, right?' I said, before explaining that it made me uncomfortable. He nodded and I took a sip. A wow went off in my head – it was like a delicious milkshake. He showed me the recipe card and I saw that it was made from almond syrup, clear chocolate syrup, heavy cream, grenadine and ice.

More people had come in and I realized I was keeping him from his work. I'd also realized he was much more than just the bartender. He was clearly in charge of the place.

'Thanks for the story and the drink. Now that I've tasted it, it will be easier to write about.' I drained the last of the rich drink. 'By the way, I located the dance gym that Rachel went to. It morphed into a job for me. I hope it doesn't bother you,' I said.

'No problem. I'm sure Rachel would be happy.'

'I'm going back there to take another class and to see if I can get something else for the book. You were right, she had some friends there,' I said and told him about Kat and Kelly and the story Kat had told me. I also mentioned that they'd said that Rachel hadn't looked well.

Luke's expression darkened and he leaned in close. 'Don't include that last part in the book. Nothing that would imply it was anything other than an accident. Don't look into anything about Rachel too much either. You wouldn't want to do anything to cross Camille Parker.'

The way he said it gave me goosebumps. It almost sounded like a warning.

THIRTEEN

Time had flown by and I had to speed walk back to the dance gym. I got there just as the class was about to start. Darcy was behind the reception counter and gave me a wave. She looked down at my shoes. 'You know it's a ballet class,' she said. I nodded and then I understood her point. I might have gotten away with street shoes for the tap class, but they wouldn't do for ballet.

I noticed she had a selection of dance wear and shoes near the counter. She handed me a pair of pink ballet slippers and I gave her my credit card. 'That's Debbie Alcoa,' she said, pointing to the teacher. 'She's the dance coordinator and my partner in this place.'

I realized she'd been the teacher for the tap class. I'd been so intent on trying to follow the steps that I hadn't noticed anything beyond her feet. Now that I knew who she was, I regarded her with new interest. Debbie had the muscular, graceful body of a dancer and her dark hair was pulled back into a low bun. She seemed completely comfortable in her dance wear and her ballet slippers seemed well-worn. I made a mental note to talk with her after class. There was certainly no time now.

I barely had time to hang up my jacket and shove my valuables in one of the cubbies before the music started. This time everyone was standing at one of the bars running along each of the side walls. I went for the one with the smaller group.

I had actually taken some ballet classes when I was very young, while my mother was still alive, so it wasn't as foreign to me as the tap had been. I checked out the others at the bar, thinking about what I would write about the class for the publicity piece.

Everyone was in leotards, some with dance skirts and leg warmers. As I watched them, I got it. They'd probably had ballet lessons when they were kids and had dreams of being in Swan Lake someday. They were reliving the fantasy even though we were just doing the basic steps. Maybe I'd write something like *another chance to get your ballerina on.*

When the class ended, I went to get my notebook before I approached Debbie.

'Hey, New Girl,' Kelly said, catching up with me.

I smiled at the nickname. 'You don't remember my name, do you? It's Veronica Blackstone.'

'Sorry, I'm terrible with names,' she said. 'OK, then, Veronica Blackstone, how'd you like the class?'

'I liked it, but I'm really here so I can write about it.'

'Tap is fun, ballet builds grace.' She did a move with her arms to demonstrate.

'I like that,' I said. 'Could I quote you for the piece I'm writing?'

'For sure,' she said, brightening and apologizing again for not remembering my name. 'And I know you're looking for stuff about Ray. I thought of something. She was always on time for class.'

I thanked Kelly, but explained I was looking for something a little more emotional. She shrugged it off and walked on ahead. I rushed to grab my notebook. When I approached Debbie, she had already changed into her street shoes and appeared about to leave.

I quickly introduced myself and explained what I was doing. She seemed surprised. 'Didn't Darcy tell you about me and what I was going to do for Dance with Me?' I asked.

'No, but she's the bigger partner and she handles the business end of the place. She does stuff without checking with me all the time.' Debbie dismissed it with a smile. 'But then I make all the decisions about the dance classes.'

'I was hoping to get some background information about you. The big appeal of a place like this is that it isn't corporate and part of a big chain. It's owned and run by two women with a love of dance.' I started to ask her about Rachel, but she cut me off.

'Married with two kids,' she said. 'I'm a professional dancer and have been in a lot of local shows.' She kept glancing toward the door, and I sensed she was impatient to go.

'Oh,' I said with interest. 'It would be great to include the names of some of them.'

She let out a quick breath and turned to me. 'Could we finish this another time? I have to be somewhere.' I barely had time to nod before she was on her way out the door.

Well, there was always next time.

I went to get the rest of my things feeling only slightly less sore than I'd been the day before. And now to get the cat.

Suddenly not sure what I'd gotten myself into, I felt a wave of trepidation as I went into the pet store. I'd never had a pet besides a goldfish, and it hadn't turned out well. Melissa had a cardboard carrier ready to load the big cat in, along with a shopping bag with some cans of food. There was no way I could manage all that on the train, so I decided to spring for an Uber to get us home. Melissa helped me out with the carrier and shopping bag to the car waiting at the curb.

It turned out that Rocky didn't care for the car ride and spent it banging against the sides of the carrier and making the most terrible yowling noises. I noticed the driver checking the rearview mirror from time to time to keep an eye on what was going on.

'The cat can't get out of that box, can it?' he asked nervously. I could see his point. The carrier did seem to be rocking around and there was loud scratching coming from inside.

He pulled up in front of my building and barely gave me time to step away from the car before driving away. I could feel the cat shifting his weight around in the box. I switched from using the handle on the carrier to holding it from the bottom, afraid the cardboard handle would break. I had my tote bag, my purse and the shopping bag of food to manage as well. I made it up the stone stairs outside and went into the small vestibule. I struggled to push open the outer door noticing at the last minute that someone was standing in the door's path.

'Sorry,' I said, trying to see over the top of the carrier. I was surprised to see that the someone was Ben.

'You're not here for the writing group, already?' I said. I strained to check my watch, juggling my load so I didn't drop everything. I'd been pretty occupied and lost track of the time.

'No. You know that I usually have dinner at my sister's first?' he began. I knew very well that he did. She'd tried on numerous occasions to get me to join them. 'It turns out Sara's not home.

I got a text just now that Mikey stubbed his toe or something and she went rushing to urgent care.' He noticed my concerned expression. 'I'm sure it's nothing. She overreacts in case you haven't noticed.' He turned his attention to the carrier in my arms.

'What's that?' Rocky let out a yowl and the box moved in my arms. 'I guess I mean who's that?' he said, moving closer and I struggled to keep my grip on Rocky's box. 'Let me help you,' he said, taking the box from me. He seemed a little surprised at the weight of it. 'I'm guessing it's not a loud kitten.'

'Right,' I said with a relieved smile. 'Thanks for the help.' I shook my arms, glad to be able to move them freely. I unlocked the inner door and we walked inside.

'Looks like that's for you,' Ben said, indicating a padded envelope sitting on the newel post at the bottom of the stairway. He grabbed it and led the way up the stairs. As we went up to the third floor, I told him the story of the cat.

'And you just went and adopted him?' he asked. 'No preparations or anything.'

I shrugged. 'The manager gave me some cat food and I have a bowl I can use for water. I always heard that cats were pretty independent.'

His usual flat expression broke into a smile. 'Did you consider that the food and water are going to go through him and need to exit?'

I thought for a moment. 'The manager said something about a box?'

He shook his head in a scolding matter. 'That's right. Cats need a box with sand or litter,' he said.

'I'll just take care of that tomorrow,' I said, putting my key in my door. 'In the meantime, I can take him for a walk outside.'

'You don't know much about cats, do you?' he said, shaking his head. 'He needs a box now.'

I opened my door and he followed me in. 'Of course, you're right.' I looked around. 'I probably have a shoe box and maybe I could put in some shredded paper.'

He put the envelope on the coffee table and set the carrier down on the floor before opening the top. Rocky popped his head out and then leapt over the side. He stayed put for a moment and then cautiously began to look around.

'No problem. I'll go get what you need now,' Ben said. He looked at Rocky. 'Wow, he's big boy.'

'Let me give you some money,' I said.

'Even if you have it kind of wrong, you're doing a nice thing. Consider it my contribution.' He left before I could thank him.

I dropped my things and took off my jacket. Rocky had begun to move toward the long hall, and I followed him to see what he would do. He checked out every room on the way back to the kitchen. I set up a bowl of water and another bowl for food. He checked them out and then followed me as I went back to the front. We'd just finished making the tour of the place when the doorbell rang, and Ben announced himself through the intercom. He'd gotten more cans of cat food, a bag of dry food and several bags of litter along with a cat box, and a cardboard scratching pad. He helped me set everything up. 'You might have figured that, unlike you, I've had pets.' He opened one of the cans of cat food and spooned some in one of the bowls and had me get another bowl for the dry food as Rocky observed.

As soon as Ben stepped away Rocky went straight to the wet food and began noisily eating.

I glanced up at the clock and saw that there was still an hour before the group would be arriving. 'I should really feed you after Sara dropped the ball and all you've done for me. How about the place on the corner – my treat?'

'The place is fine, but it's on me.'

He had the serious expression, but I couldn't help but say, 'Is all this some play for me to go easier on you when we discuss your work?'

He cracked another rare smile. 'The thought had crossed my mind.'

We left Rocky to get used to his new home and went across the street to the coffee shop on the corner. 'Their burgers are supposed to be great,' he said, as we walked in.

The place was a neighborhood fixture and had been there forever. It was frequented by students, neighborhood people and cops.

'That's the word on the street,' I began. I considered leaving it at that, but if I didn't order a burger, I felt like I owed him some explanation. 'I'm a vegetarian, so I've never tried them,' I said.

I hoped he would let it go and not give me the usual grilling about what I ate if I didn't eat meat. How about everything but meat, fish or fowl. Then it usually turned to 'so you eat a lot of tofu?' I got ready for the onslaught, but he just shrugged and said, 'Whatever floats your boat.'

We took a booth with a window that looked out on the street. The Metra station was just down the way and there was a constant flow of foot traffic as people came home from work. I ended up ordering a Greek omelet. I noticed him looking at it with interest and offered him some. He gratefully cut off a piece and put it on his plate. 'Good choice,' he said after tasting it. It felt a little weird sharing food with him when he'd always been so distant.

Silence hung over the table after that, making me nervous. I knew from the mystery I'd written that cops used the silence to get suspects to talk. I wasn't a suspect, but I felt obliged to say something. Or ask him something. I thought back to what now seemed like a long time ago when I'd been at the bar with Luke and he'd told me about Rachel's mother. 'Since you're a cop, you probably know this. If a family has a lot of clout, can they influence the coroner to rule something as an accidental overdose?'

'It's not supposed to work that way,' he said. Before he could elaborate, the door *whooshed* open and Sara came in with Mikey. The toddler saw Ben and pushed away from his mother and ran to the booth we were sitting in. He climbed next to his uncle and hugged his arm. Sara arrived a moment later. She looked at the table and smiled at me. 'We don't want to interrupt,' she said, going to grab Mikey, who started to protest.

'Nonsense,' Ben said. 'Sit, join us.'

I'd watched Ben's face as Mikey climbed in next to him. His expression softened as they playfully wrestled, making me believe there might be some life underneath that flat tone of voice and blank expression.

I was glad for the company, and it took the burden of trying to make conversation off of me.

'How'd this come about?' Sara asked, looking back and forth between us. I knew what she was thinking, that all her efforts at matchmaking had paid off and we'd suddenly discovered each other. I hated to poke a hole in her balloon of hope, but it was never going to happen.

'I adopted a cat and Ben helped me get some supplies,' I said. 'And since you weren't home, we decided to come here and grab dinner.' I left off the part about me wanting it to be my treat for his helping, but he wanted it to be his treat like giving the teacher an apple. She'd read way more into it than there was. She ordered some food for Mikey and herself and the conversation turned to Mikey's trip to urgent care.

'I overreacted,' Sara said. She reached over to give Mikey a snuggle.

'I figured,' Ben said. He'd eaten his burger in a couple of bites and noticed me watching him. 'You get used to eating in a hurry when you never know when a radio call will interrupt your meal.' He crumpled his napkin and put it on the plate.

Mikey lost interest in sitting as soon as he'd finished his grilled cheese sandwich. Sara was anxious to get home so Mikey could unwind before bedtime and they took off.

I looked at my watch. 'It's almost time for the writing group.' I signaled the server and got the rest of my meal packed to go. 'I still have to set up.'

'Right,' he said, taking the check and putting his credit card on it. 'I suppose I can stop at my sisters to kill time. Maybe I could read Mikey a story or something, even though Sara complains I make them sound too exciting and then he can't go to sleep.' He shrugged. 'Or I could just sit in my car until it's time for the group.'

The hints were too obvious, and he had helped me with the cat. There was no choice but to invite Ben to my place to wait until the others arrived. This was going to be awkward.

FOURTEEN

I usually closed the doors to my office and the bedrooms to wall off my personal space on the nights the group met. They all knew to go right to the dining room.

But everything had changed with Rocky's arrival. I didn't want to shut him in or out of any room, so I left all the doors open. I didn't know what to do with Ben. It seemed cold to send him back to the dining room to wait, and he'd been all over my apartment when he helped set up everything for the black-and-white cat. I invited him into the living room and offered him coffee.

It might have seemed like the right thing to do, but that didn't mean I was comfortable with it. I was clumsy and almost spilled coffee on him as I handed him the mug.

What was wrong with me? I was used to dealing with all different kinds of people. Why was this so uncomfortable? I blamed it on him and his closed-up personality. He'd broken his monotone a couple of times, but then he'd gone back to the dry tone, devoid of emotion.

I was relieved when the doorbell announced the next arrival. Tizzy whirled in, living up to her name. She wore a black shawl over a red-print kimono and all of it fluttered as she talked, gesturing with her hands. She was all excited about being allowed behind the scenes at the Museum of Science and Industry.

'Yesterday's Main Street is the perfect spot for my character to time transition,' she said, stopping inside the door for a moment. 'It has an authentic cobblestone street and shop windows featuring period dresses and high-buttoned shoes. I can't wait for the group to see my pages describing it.' She went back to the dining room and I doubt even noticed that Ben was in the living room. He took her arrival as a cue and followed her back to our meeting place. They all knew that he had dinner at his sisters before our get-together, so she wouldn't think there was anything strange about him suddenly appearing like that.

Ed and Daryl arrived together. It was obviously pure coincidence that they had shown up at the same time. Aside from the fact that he seemed surprisingly happily married, I couldn't imagine the very trendily dressed Daryl being interested in a cantankerous man in track pants. As soon as they sat down, we got down to business.

Tizzy closed her eyes and listened as Ed read her piece describing her character standing under an old-fashioned streetlight on the cobblestone road. He read it without too much enthusiasm. We discussed it afterwards, which meant that I gave my comments and the rest of them nodded in agreement while Tizzy scribbled down notes.

She had done a masterful job of describing the street inside the museum. I'd been going there my whole life and Old-Fashioned Street, as I called it, had always been one of my favorite spots. There was something magical about turning a corner and going from the hubbub of the museum to a dark cobblestone street made to look like the turn of the last century. It was the perfect spot for someone to time travel.

Daryl read Ben's work. It was very much like him, buttoned up. We saw what the detective did and saw, but nothing of how he felt. The sentences were short and to the point with very few adjectives. Daryl was the most self-absorbed in the group and really only cared about her own work. She read his pages in a lackadaisical manner which made his work seem funny. Even so, none of us cracked a smile. It was unwritten rule, unless something was supposed to be a comedy, we never laughed.

Ben read Ed's weekly dose of his fantasies of a man who seemed like a younger version of himself surrounded by a bevy of famous women on a TV dating show. As usual, the man ended up in the Getting to Know You Suite. We'd kind of gotten him to use more euphemisms but his descriptions were still pretty graphic. Ben as usual read it in a monotone like it was a police report. When he was done, Ed looked at all of us. 'I just wanted you to check it for punctuation and spelling. I've been following a fan fiction website for *The Singleton* and I'm going to submit this encounter to them. Fingers crossed they'll put it up. I know what you people think, but you're not my audience.' Everyone wished him good luck.

Tizzy got stuck reading Daryl's work. Every paragraph or so, Tizzy would look up with a worried eye to see Daryl's reaction to her reading. More than once Daryl corrected her by telling her she wasn't putting the emphasis on the right words. When it came time for me to comment, I took the coward's way out. Daryl was so thin-skinned, so, I just said her story seemed to be coming along. The rest of them nodded in agreement.

We usually had our small talk at the beginning but for some reason, this time it was at the end. Rocky made a momentary appearance and then disappeared. I told them all about my new resident and explained how I'd come to adopt him.

'It sounds like you wrote too good a piece,' Tizzy said. She turned out to have a lot of information about cats and readily shared it. 'But what about that other thing you were working on? It seemed like you thought there was more to the story and you were going to investigate. Did you find out anything new?'

Had I really said I was going to investigate what happened to Rachel?

There was so much to tell them, though I wondered what I could say. I gave it a moment's thought and decided it seemed okay to talk about what I'd found out as long as I was vague on details of who the people involved were.

I began by describing how I'd decided to do the book. 'The search for anecdote led me to the school where she taught and then to a dance gym.' They all wanted to know what a dance gym was and thought it was cool that I was doing work for it now, too. I mentioned that a number of people had said that Rachel seemed different recently. I described the wedding picture versus the one I'd seen on Luke's phone. 'It turns out the woman I thought was Rachel's mother is really her stepmother and she has two daughters of her own. And before that she was her current husband's assistant.' They let out a collective *oooh*. 'And there's more: I found out that Rachel's mother died of an accidental overdose, but it was probably covered up just the way it seems Rachel's death has been.'

Ben seemed to be listening intently, but said nothing. Tizzy immediately started to conjecture that the stepmother might have been involved in Rachel's mother's death.

Daryl threw a bucket of cold water on all of it.

'What's the difference whether it was suicide or an accident with this Rachel or her mother?' Daryl asked. 'It doesn't change anything. She's dead. What's it to you, anyway?'

I thought a moment. What was it exactly that made me want to find out more about what had happened to Rachel? 'It's curiosity. What makes someone tick? What makes someone change so much? And I feel a little guilty, as if maybe I could have made a difference.'

'How exactly did she change?' Tizzy asked.

'Aside from losing her smile, it seems like she lost her confidence and I get the impression that she was worried about losing her grip.'

'Wow,' Tizzy said. 'What about her husband?'

'It turns out he's a bartender at a hotel bar.' I shared the story of my virgin pink squirrel. As expected, I got a lot of quizzical looks, except from Tizzy who explained that the cocktail dated from the 1950s and had originated at a bar in Milwaukee, Wisconsin. She knew the ingredients as well. The Crème de Noyaux was bright red and made from peach pits which naturally contained a tiny amount of cyanide. Then it was just crème de cacao, heavy cream and ice.

'No buzz in mine, but it sure was delicious.'

By then it was after ten and they were all ready to call it a night. Despite what Daryl said, I promised to keep them in the loop if I found anything out and the group broke up. I walked them all to the front. It had been a long day and I was glad to shut the door and have the place to myself, or almost to myself, as I remembered I had a cat housemate.

The cat carrier was still sitting in the living room. I went to retrieve it and saw the padded envelope sitting on the dark wood coffee table in front of the black leather couch. I recalled that Ben brought it up from the post downstairs. It was a common practice if anyone saw mail left in the vestibule, they brought it inside the locked glass door. I glanced at it and saw that it was addressed to me, but there was no stamp or return address. I pulled it open and found an unmarked CD in a clear plastic case inside. It seemed strange to say the least. I felt a little uneasy as I took it into my office and put it into the computer, not sure what to expect. Was it a video or an audio recording?

I waited until a dialogue box appeared on the screen asking me what I wanted to do with it. I hit play and waited. A picture flashed on the screen as plaintiff piano music began. It was Rachel in her wedding dress, but the photo was from a distance. I barely had a chance to make note of the dress that I'd thought so lovely before it faded. The next picture was of her walking on the street carrying shopping bags. The music continued as the image morphed into her at Dance with Me. The angle suggested that it had been taken by someone on the outside looking in. She was wearing a leotard and had her hair tied up in a topknot. She appeared to be talking to Debbie Alcoa. There were more photos of Rachel all taken from a distance. Then there was one that had a closer view of her as she faced the camera. My breath caught when I saw how thin she'd become and the haunted look in her eyes. It melted into a picture of a balcony and across the bottom of the screen it said: *Money can't buy you happiness or love. The only way out.*

And then it repeated over and over. As I watched it again I tried to pay more attention to the background and where the photos had been taken, but without much luck. Finally, I hit stop and sat back in my chair. What was this supposed to be and who had sent it? There had been no note in the envelope or return address. It hadn't been mailed, so someone had to have delivered it. I felt unnerved by the whole thing and sat there until the screen went dark. It took numerous cups of chamomile tea before I finally fell asleep. And even then, it was far from peaceful.

FIFTEEN

I t was strange waking up to find out that I wasn't alone in bed. Sometime during the night, Rocky had joined me. He'd taken up a position on a pillow behind my head and he didn't stir when I got up. I was glad he'd made an appearance. Other than his initial walk through the apartment and his brief appearance when the group was there, he'd stayed hidden. Ben had made a point to remind me that the cat was there as he was leaving.

Tizzy'd had a number of cats and said he was probably just getting acclimated and might be so glad to have a real home that he might be worried about being taken back. Later I noted the food I'd left out for him was gone, so it seemed as if she might be right. Tizzy had advised me just to let him find his own way.

With his water, bowl with dry food and cat box, all Rocky's needs seemed attended to and I felt OK leaving him. Another day, another dance class. The schedule called it Serendipity 1, but there was no description of what it was. The leggings and a loose shirt were becoming my dance uniform and I figured they would work. I put on a long cream-colored sweater over the shirt to make it a little dressier for the street. I chuckled thinking of what Tizzy had said about the way people used to dress when they went downtown. Women wore hats with little veils and white gloves. Those ladies would be shocked to see me, I thought, as I pulled on a pair of black boots. I stowed my sneakers and the ballet slippers in the tote bag, sure that one of them would be right for the class.

I was getting ready to leave when the phone rang. I didn't even get out a hello before Evan spoke. He didn't identify himself either. Lucky for him I excelled at recognizing people by their voice.

'You have to do something,' he said. He explained that he'd left a copy of the note I'd written for him, along with a boat on

Sally's desk as we'd discussed. 'She hasn't said yes, or no, or even maybe. She hasn't said anything and it's already Wednesday and I invited her for a cruise on Sunday. Why hasn't she said anything?'

'I don't know,' I said. It did seem kind of strange. Sally didn't seem like the kind of person to not give an answer. The only thing I could figure was that she might be waiting, trying to find a way to say no while staying on good terms since he was the one who helped her with her computer.

'You have to find out,' he said. He sounded a little frantic then apologized. 'I mean, can you do something?'

This was outside what I considered my responsibility and I was stumped. 'What do you want me to do?'

'I don't know.' He sounded befuddled. 'What would Hugh Grant do?'

This I could answer. 'He'd probably duck his head, looking adorable and just ask her if she wanted to go on the cruise.'

'I can't do that. I mean, I could duck my head and look sheepish, but I don't think it would be all that adorable.' I wanted to tell him that the very fact that he didn't think he was adorable probably meant he would appear that way, but I didn't think he'd believe me.

'How about you find a reason to see her. Say you heard her computer was malfunctioning.'

I heard him sigh. 'That would be lying, and she would know it because her computer would be working fine.' I wanted to explain that she would probably also understand that it was an excuse to see her and be flattered – unless it made her feel cornered. But I understood that he wasn't going to deal with her directly.

'I hope you realize this isn't what I do, but I'll figure out something. I'm going downtown for a dance class. Maybe a grand plan will pop into my mind.'

'Will you call me as soon as you know anything?' he said, sounding a little less frantic.

'Do you want me to run whatever plan I come up with by you first?' I asked.

'No. Just do it. Whatever it is. I trust you.' And after a goodbye, he hung up.

What had I just agreed to?

His phone call had delayed me enough that I barely made the train. I grabbed a seat on the side that offered a view of the lake. I just wanted to forget about everything and look out the window. For now, the sun was shining and the lake seemed placid, though the weather report had said something about rain.

I thought I'd managed to clear my mind, but somehow the water made me think of the strange DVD I'd gotten. It was disturbing. I hadn't a clue who'd sent it. Or why? Did they mean for me to somehow use it in the book?

I'd have to see if I could find out without asking anyone directly. Maybe how to do that would magically appear during the dance class, too.

When I got to the gym, a group was waiting for the start of the class. They were just standing around in no particular formation and the clothes were everything from dance wear to street clothes. Nobody was wearing ballet slippers, so I opted for the sneakers. I made a mental note that there should be something in the description of each class explaining what to wear. I left my bags and boots with my jacket and stuck my valuables in one of the cubbies.

I looked around for somebody to ask about the class. I'd only talked to women so far, so when I saw a man about my age wearing leggings and a red bandana on his head, I decided he'd be the one.

'Hey,' I said with a friendly nod. 'Have you come to this class before? I'm working on class descriptions and publicity material for the gym.' It was as if I was a news reporter and had turned my microphone on him. His face lit up as he began to talk.

'You haven't lived until you've taken a Serendipity class,' he said. 'Fun, fun, fun and always a surprise.' He struck a pose.

'Do you think you could be more specific,' I said, smiling at his antics.

'It's mostly folk dancing. The hora, the mizerlou, and like that. But sometimes they bring in a caller and it's square dancing. Once we did the hokey-pokey, but once we knew what it was all about, it got a little boring. Can you believe they called it an American folk dance? I suggested that Irish dance where everybody holds the top of their body kind of rigid and it's all in the feet. But so far, no go.' More people had come in and I saw Debbie Alcoa fiddling with the sound system and talking to someone I assumed was the teacher. I debated trying to talk to her before the class, but she seemed busy and she might be annoyed by the intrusion, so I stayed talking to my dance mate.

'There was a woman who used to come here. She went by Ray or Rachel,' I said. 'Did you know her?'

'I thought you wanted to interview me about the class,' he said, as his expression drooped. He let out his breath and took a moment to think. 'Was she kind of curvy with brown hair?'

'Yes,' I said, looking at him expectantly.

'I didn't *know her* know her, if you know what I mean. Like, I might have said hi, but that's all. She was, like, here all the time. I think she was getting some kind of private lessons.' He stopped for a moment before continuing. 'The last time I remember seeing her was at a tap class. She got mixed up in the routine and there was a bunch of drama about it. She started crying and said something about losing her mind before she took off. I mean, it's just an exercise class.'

I was trying to process what he'd said and ask for more details, but he'd gone back to talking about the class. 'I'd be happy to tell you about the other classes. I've taken them all. Do you need my name? You know, if you want to quote me.'

I sensed he wanted to give it to me and who knew, maybe I'd use it. I went to my bag and got out my notebook and wrote as he spelled out 'Talmadge Edwards' for me. Really? What were his parents thinking?

The class turned out to be devoted to folk dances. I hadn't caught the names of all of them, but the pattern was the same. We'd learn the steps and then do the dance in a circle or sometimes a line. The dances were all easy to pick up and fun. By the time I was walking out with the rest of the people everyone seemed to be in good spirits. I planned to come back to Dance with Me in the afternoon to observe Serendipity 2. I only had it in me to participate in one dance class a day. I also hoped to get a chance to talk to Debbie Alcoa. I'd missed her again, but I had come up with a plan to deal with Sally. I wouldn't call it a great plan, but I thought it would get the job done. In the time between the classes I figured I could go to the Bellingham and talk to Sally with the excuse that I was planning an event. I'd bring up Evan and see where it went from there.

I came up with more details as I walked to the hotel. A strong wind was blowing out of the north and as it blasted me in the face it literally took my breath away. I had to turn and face the other way just so I could take in some air. I would tell Sally I wanted to put on a birthday party for my aunt who was turning sixty. I decided to call her Julia and came up with a back story. There was a touch of truth to it. I did have an aunt and she was probably close to sixty. She was my mother's sister and lived in Seattle. She'd married someone the family hated and cut herself off from everyone after that. I'd never even met her or knew her name. All I'd heard her called was 'the one who married that jerk.'

The wind died down for a moment and I took the opportunity to unwind the scarf that the blasting air had kept plastered against my face. What had I gotten myself into? I was making up stories about fake relatives to find out if Evan had a chance with Sally. Someday maybe I'd learn not to get so involved with my clients' lives.

I cared too much about the booklet for Rachel. I regretted the whole idea of gathering stories from people who'd known her, now wondering if I'd have enough. I certainly couldn't use what Talmadge told me. The wind whipped up again as I crossed the river. I heard a couple talking as they walked behind me. The woman commented on the wind and the man reminded her that Chicago was called 'the windy city.' I chuckled to myself thinking what Tizzy would do if she was with me. She'd turn and tell them that was not why Chicago had the moniker, and that it referred to the hot air bellowing from politicians.

The couple quickly got to know something else about Chicago. The weather was fickle. There was a saying that if you didn't like the weather, wait five minutes and it would change. The sun had disappeared behind heavy gray clouds. The wind had come to a dead stop and it began to rain. I pulled out the umbrella I'd stashed in my bag and walked faster.

It was really coming down by the time I reached the Bellingham.

I was glad to step under the overhang while I collapsed my umbrella. I went inside hoping for the best.

I asked the desk clerk for the location of Sally's office, prepared to give him my birthday story. But he simply pointed me in the direction of the other side of the lobby. 'Though I just saw her going up to The Top of the Town,' he added.

I headed to the elevator, wondering what she was doing up there. Hanging out with Luke? Poor Evan if it was true.

Not wanting to be seen, I borrowed from the playbook of Derek Streeter and edged against the wall when I got off the elevator and peeked into the bar. Luke was behind the counter, talking to a woman. I leaned a little closer to see if it was Sally and was relieved to see it wasn't her. I felt even better when I saw that Sally was standing near the windows talking to an older woman. I slipped inside the bar and stepped behind a decorative drape that hung across the windows where I could watch and eavesdrop.

Luke was too busy at the bar to notice. What I'd thought was one woman was actually two and I noticed they had that polish of wealth about them. He was certainly being cordial and appeared to be listening with interest to whatever they were saying. The women seemed to eat it up and were offering him seductive smiles over their wine glasses.

I turned my attention to Sally. 'We need a place for an intimate breakfast,' the older woman said to her. She was dressed in 'expensive casual': fancy jeans and designer heels. She didn't seem very happy about whatever she was planning. The woman shifted her weight a few times and glanced around at the room. 'I might just as well level with you. My daughter is insisting on getting married next to Buckingham Fountain in the park. She didn't think it through. They're shutting off the water for the winter. That's why the rush.' She shook her head with dismay. 'It's only going to be family and a few friends, but I want to at least offer them a nice brunch after standing around outside. This seems perfect.' She glanced at a plaque on the wall I hadn't noticed before. It read: Candace's Refuge. 'Good name for the place,' she said. 'It will certainly be a refuge after standing outside getting sprayed by a fountain.'

Sally had a tablet and been swiping at the screen and taking notes. 'We could certainly do that here even with such short notice. Depending on the time, you could have the whole space.' She eyed the patio. 'And if your daughter changes her mind, we could have the wedding out there. It's officially closed for the winter, but we could make an exception.' The woman followed her gaze and then stepped closer to the windows to look outside.

'I'll certainly mention it to her, though I don't know that she'll listen.' The woman rolled her eyes. 'I suppose I should be glad she doesn't want a really big affair considering who she's marrying. You'd think by thirty he'd have a job.'

'We can do something very nice,' Sally said reassuringly. 'Let's go down to my office and I'll put together a proposal for you.'

'I'll have to talk to my daughter first,' the woman said. 'When's the latest I could let you know?'

The event planner closed the cover on her tablet and flinched. What a job she had. The woman was talking about the upcoming weekend. As they went to the elevator, I watched to see if she'd make any contact with Luke, but she never looked his way. So did they know each other or not?

SIXTEEN

waited until the elevator door closed before I came out from behind the drape. I was hoping to slip out unnoticed, but Luke looked up just then and when he saw it was me offered a friendly smile. Even though he wasn't my type, I could see how he would have appealed to Rachel and, apparently, other women as well. He was looking at me as if I was the most important woman in the world.

'Becoming a regular,' he said with a lift of his eyebrows. 'At the bar or at a table?'

'The bar is fine,' I said, sliding onto one of the comfortable upholstered seats. He'd caught me and I couldn't very well leave without an explanation. The easiest thing to do was to sit. Besides, Sally was still busy with her potential client. I glanced at the two women out of the corner of my eye and they didn't seem happy that I'd taken Luke's attention away.

'As I recall you're not into alcohol,' he said.

I was going to say it was a little early for it, anyway, but I realized the two women sipping wine might hear me and take it personally. 'Maybe some juice. I just came from the dance gym.'

'Ah,' he said with understanding as he took a pitcher of fresh squeezed orange juice and poured some in a wine glass. 'Did you take a class?'

'I'm trying them all so I can write up descriptions. The tap and ballet were pretty much what I expected, but this morning's was folk dancing. Well, actually the class is called Serendipity One and it was a lot of fun. I'm going back this afternoon, but this time I'm just going to watch.'

He seemed puzzled. 'Fun? Wow, I never got that impression from Rachel. She always came home seeming worried.'

'Really?' I said, surprised. Then I remembered what Talmadge had said about her trying to get private lessons. 'I think she might have been concerned about getting the steps wrong.' I thought about what Luke had said the last time I'd seen him. It had seemed like a warning. I asked him about it.

'I just meant that as much as you seem to care about doing a good job with the booklet you're putting together, it might be better to stick to pleasing Camille Parker and just skim the surface. Put in a few heartwarming stories and that's it. You could change the story I told you and just make the pink squirrel the focus. She's like a lioness when it comes to protecting Richard Parker. I think he's considering getting into politics. I suppose that's another reason they want Rachel's death ruled an accident.' He was slicing a lemon as he talked to me. 'I think it's great what you want to do with the memory book and how you are delving into what was going on in Rachel's life, but I think it might cause you problems in the end.'

The tone was softer this time, but it still seemed like a warning.

Just then my phone began to ring. I pulled it out of my bag and looked at the screen. It was Evan. 'Excuse me,' I said with a smile. 'I have to take this.' Luke nodded and went to check on the two women.

'Have you found out what happened yet?' Evan asked. He sounded like he was pacing, and I felt for him. And I worried that he was trying for something that wasn't going to happen. I had a way with words, but it could go only so far.

'I'm working on it,' I said, not wanting to say too much. I didn't want to tell him where I was or how close I was to seeing Sally.

'Call me as soon as you know anything,' he said. 'And anything you could do to put in a good word for me would help.'

I promised I would and clicked off. Luke came back to my section of the bar just as I put the phone on the counter.

He looked at my almost empty glass. I hadn't meant to drink it so fast, but it was delicious. 'Would you like another?'

'I'm good,' I said, thinking about the price of the juice. 'Just the check, please.' He slid a folder holding it toward me. I almost choked when I saw the bill. I put my credit card in the folder with it and said I'd be right back. I pulled out the tiny purse inside my tote bag and left everything else there. 'And now where is . . .?' I glanced around and he figured out I was looking for the ladies' room and pointed to the other side of the elevator.

The powder room was old-school elegant. It was pink with soft lighting designed to make everyone look great. Well, almost everyone. I caught a look at myself in the mirror. I'd rushed out of the dance gym and never thought about what the class and the wind had done to my appearance. I understood now why a lot of people pulled their hair back into some kind of top knot or ponytail. My shoulder-length brown hair had managed to get snarled in the back. I combed it with my fingers but it could only do so much. The exercise and outdoor air had left me with a nice glow, but I still added a little lipstick to give me some color.

When I returned, I passed the plaque that the woman and Sally had looked at.

'I thought this place was called The Top of the Town,' I said, pointing toward the plaque.

'The new owners decided to call it The Top of the Town,' he said. 'Before that it was named after Rachel's mother.'

'What?' I said surprised. 'Why would a bar be named after her mother?'

'Her family used to own the Bellingham. She helped design the bar as a quiet place to get away from it all.'

'So, that explains why she stopped here so often with Rachel,' I said processing the information. 'And why Rachel came here after her mother was gone. It was a family place.'

He nodded. 'She told me it was always comforting for her to come here. Particularly after her father married Camille. She had a very hard time dealing with her stepmother, who apparently is nothing like her mother. So much for the idea that people are attracted to the same kind of person over and over again.'

'You seem to know a lot about psychology,' I said.

He nodded with a knowing look. 'You learn a lot being a bartender. You'd be amazed at the things that people tell me. It's true that people who come in here alone often just want someone to talk to. It's part of the service.' He dropped his voice as he took another lemon and began to slice it with precision. 'As I told you, Candace died before I met Rachel, but Rachel talked about her a lot. Her mother had a lot of emotional issues. Rachel never gave a name to her mother's problems, but what she described sounded as if she went through periods when she

just fell into the kind of deep depression where she was unreach-
able. But when she wasn't that way, she was warm and fun.'

I was a little surprised by the way he talked about Rachel.
'You seem to be doing OK,' I said. I was trying to be diplomatic,
but I was actually a little surprised at how well he was handling
Rachel's death.

'There was no choice for me to get it together and keep going,'
he said. 'The Parkers didn't wait a beat before they started pushing
me to sell the boat and asking when I could move out of the
condo.' There was a touch of anger in his voice.

'Luke, we need some refills here,' one of the women at the
end of the bar called. When I looked in their direction, they both
shot me looks of displeasure, apparently unhappy that I'd taken
over his attention.

'Time to go,' I said, draining the last of the orange juice. I
figured that by now Sally ought to be free and there was the
dance class I had to get to. The folder with the bill and my credit
card was still there and I pushed it toward him. He turned away
so no one could see him and tore up the check before handing
me my credit card.

'The prices here are ridiculous,' he said with a friendly smile.
'Remember what I said. Stick to the heartwarming and most of
all, nothing that makes it seem like she was losing her mind.'

It wasn't until I was riding down in the elevator that I remembered the DVD. I'd meant to ask if Luke knew anything about
it. It was too late now, and I had to focus to Evan's problem,
anyway. When I reached the lobby, I remembered the clerk's
direction and went looking for Sally's office. I found a sign that
said *Event Planning* and looked inside the open door. The small
office was empty.

I thought back to when I'd written the mystery and wondered
what I would have had my detective Derek Streeter do in this
circumstance. He was a fearless detective, so of course he would
have looked around. I'd followed his lead at the bar, and it
had worked, so why not continue. The door *was* open after all,
and Sally's desk was easily accessible. I took a quick look around
me to make sure there was no one watching and went inside. I
expected she'd be back any minute, so I got busy.

I glanced over the top of her desk which was perfectly arranged.

Even the papers in her in basket were in absolute alignment. There weren't any stray sticky notes or paper clips lying around. I wasn't even sure what I was looking for. Derek Streeter might have had nerves of steel, but I didn't. I suddenly had cold feet and wanted to get out of there. In my haste, I dropped my tote bag and of course the contents spilled. I was on the floor trying to grab everything quickly and managed to send my favorite pen rolling under her desk. As I went to retrieve it, I saw a piece of paper under there. I reached for it and saw that it was Evan's note.

I threw everything back in my bag and slapped the paper on Sally's desk. I considered making a run for it, but I heard someone coming down the hall. I slid into one of the seats and tried to act nonchalant as Sally came into the office. She looked at me with surprise.

'You're Evan's neighbor, Veronica,' she said. 'What can I do for you?'

In my head I was thinking fall in love with Evan so he hires me to write his proposal and then probably write his part of your wedding vows and then who knows – baby announcements, but out loud I said, 'Sorry for just coming in, but the door was open. I understand you're the person to talk to about arranging parties here.'

She shut the door behind her, and it created a *whoosh* of air and the paper I'd just put on her desk sailed off and landed on the floor. I held in a laugh as I realized why Evan hadn't gotten an answer.

'Let me get that for you,' I said, diving to the floor and then putting it on her desk.

She glanced at the paper. 'What a coincidence, it's a note from Evan.' She stopped to read it over and then got a puzzled expression. I felt my stomach clench, worried that the next thing she was going to say was that she wasn't interested in him in that way and then ask me if maybe I could break the news to him, since I seemed to be his friend. But then she smiled and pulled open one of the drawers and produced the toy boat. 'Now it makes sense. I wondered why somebody left a boat on my desk. Funny that the note just showed up now, though,' she said. She showed it to me and I read it over, even though I knew exactly what it said.

'Sounds like a nice afternoon. Cute touch with the boat, but then you know Evan – he's just full of fun,' I added with a friendly smile. 'Maybe he sent the boat first to fire up your curiosity.' I watched her face to see if I could get a hint of what her answer would be. At least I knew why she hadn't said anything. She hadn't seen the note. Suddenly she looked up at me and I thought, *Here it comes.*

But she smiled and said, 'So what kind of event was it you wanted to discuss?'

SEVENTEEN

'Did you come to the morning Serendipity class?' Darcy asked. She was behind the reception counter greeting people as they swiped their cards to check in.

'Yes, and that's why I'm only going to be observing now. One class a day is all I can handle.'

'What did you think of the class? Different, huh?' she said.

'Definitely different. And fun.' I moved aside as more people came in.

Darcy pulled out a small bench and offered it to me. 'You might as well be comfortable,' she said. 'Did you go home and come back downtown?'

'No, actually, I stopped by the Bellingham Hotel about something else I'm working on,' I said. 'It's all about romance.'

'For you or someone else?' she asked.

'It was for a client,' I said with a smile. 'No romance for me right now.' I didn't mean to, but I told her about my divorce and how it had left me gun-shy about anything serious. 'And it's hard to meet someone when you spend most of your time alone with your computer.'

'Maybe you'll meet someone here.' We both looked out at the crowd which was mostly women and then she rolled her eyes. 'Or maybe not.'

'But I do like the social aspect of this place. I'm going to include that in what I write. I'll make it clear that it's more about friendship than romance.'

Debbie went to the front of the room and announced that today's class was golden oldies with music and dances from the past. She led them through a brief warm-up before turning on the music. Everyone watched as she did a demo of the different dances. There was a lot of laughter as some of the steps were pretty funny. She turned up the volume and had everyone join in.

'What a great idea,' I said, as the group began to jitterbug. From there they moved onto the twist, the mashed potato, the monkey, the swim and finally the stroll.

'We keep switching things around. Next time they'll be doing the Macarena and the hustle with some cha-cha-cha thrown in,' Darcy said. She'd joined me on the bench, and I had fun talking to her while we watched the class. Unfortunately we got so involved in our conversation, Debbie had grabbed her bag and was on her way out the door before I could catch her. I'd talk to her next time for sure.

Even though I'd only watched the class, I was glad when it was over, and I could head home. It had been a long day.

My cell phone rang just as the train was pulling out of the dark of the covered Randolph Street Station into the cloudy late afternoon.

'Did you talk to her? What did she say? How did she seem?' Evan asked. He sounded like a machine gun, shooting out words, and I pictured him pacing again. He was probably running his hand through his hair at the same time. 'Well?' he demanded. 'What happened? I know she said no, and you don't want to tell me. It's OK. I can take it. I'm ready.'

I waited for him to take a breath before I tried to speak. He stopped at last. 'First things first,' I said. 'She didn't answer you because she didn't see the note. It had fallen under the desk. But I made sure she got it this time.'

'And?' he said, sounding like he was holding his breath.

'I know that you don't want her to know that I'm the behind the scenes person, so I couldn't be too obvious, but I tried to put in a good word for you. She seemed upbeat when she read the note. I think you'll be hearing from her soon,' I added. I heard him let his breath out.

'Then she didn't say no,' he said in a cheery voice. 'Thank you for going undercover like that. Otherwise she never would have seen the note and I would have assumed she didn't care enough even to say that she didn't want to go.' The train pulled to a rough stop at Roosevelt Road and I lurched forward and then back against the seat with an *oomph*.

'Are you OK?'

'I'm on the train,' I explained.

'What should I do if I don't hear from her by tomorrow?' he asked sounding worried again.

'I know this is a cliché but I'm going to use it anyway. Why don't we cross that bridge when we come to it, or if we come to it,' I added, thinking that somehow made it less a cliché. Evan seemed to care less about whether what I said was original or not, but he got the point and agreed.

'I hope you can relax now,' I said.

'A little bit,' he said. 'Thank you.'

It had started to rain again by the time I got off the train at 57th and I dug the umbrella out of my bag. The Bellingham was so classy the doorman had given me a bag to keep my wet umbrella in so that it didn't drip over everything in my tote bag. Back on ground level, a group of U of C students jogged by me, seeming unconcerned about the weather. I considered stopping at the coffee shop on my corner for a bowl of soup. It was homemade and delicious, but I opted to go home instead. As I was going up the stairs, Sara's door opened, and she stuck her head out. She had that bedraggled mom look – hair pulled into a scrunchie, T-shirt smeared with something that looked like chocolate and a pair of jeans that were clearly all about comfort.

'I'm glad it's you,' she said. 'I hope you're up for some company. I need some girl talk time.' She let out her breath. 'I love Mikey to pieces, but I need some time to be me for a little while. I'm a mom, but I'm still a person.'

'Sure, of course,' I said quickly. She stuck her head back in and called to her husband that she was going to my place.

'One good thing about him working crazy hours is that he's sometimes home during the day when I really need to get away for a while.' She started to follow me up the stairs, going on how happy she was that I'd finally gotten home. 'I opened the door when I heard someone on the stairs hoping it was you, but it was just someone from the management office there to show the condo.' She let out a sigh as we reached the landing. 'And I want to meet that cat,' she said when I opened my front door. We both looked down, expecting the black-and-white feline to be waiting by the door, but there was no greeting kitty.

'I guess it's only dogs that hang out at the door,' she said, as we went inside.

'He's still getting used to being here,' I said. 'He only came out of hiding after I'd gone to bed and then took over one of my pillows.'

'I'll wait until he comes out on his own then. Now tell me what you're working on. I need to hear about what adults are doing. Why is it that kids like to hear things over and over and over? I've read *Louis the Caboose on the Loose* so many times I started to dream about it.'

I hung up my coat and took my tote bag into my office with Sara on my heels. I pulled out my notebook and laid it next to the computer. 'There's Evan and the illusive Sally,' I began. 'I'm not sure how that's going to turn out, but they are both really nice people. I hope I manage to express Evan's personality enough in the notes, so she sees past his plain exterior – you know, slicked-down hair and blah clothes.'

I did a little twirl. 'I'm doing work for a dance gym and it's turning out to be great. It's fun, the people are nice and I'm getting some much-needed exercise. To think that it all came about because I went there looking for a story for the celebration of life booklet I'm working on.' I looked at Sara to see if she remembered.

'Yes, for the woman who went off the balcony,' Sara said. Her words reminded me of the DVD I'd left in my computer.

'You have to see what somebody sent me. I guess they wanted me to use some of the photos in the book.'

I turned on the computer and ran the DVD. Sara was standing next to me watching the screen as I waited for the first shot of Rachel to come up.

'That can't be,' I said, leaning in close to the screen. The image was of a basket full of kittens. I fast forwarded it thinking it must be further up ahead. But there were only more cat pictures scrolling past to upbeat music. 'That's crazy,' I said. 'Last night there were just shots of Rachel.' I showed Sara the envelope. 'Your brother is the one who noticed it on the post downstairs.'

'Maybe we should play it again. Could it be somewhere else on the DVD?' Sara suggested. We played it three times and it was still only cats.

'That wasn't what I saw last night,' I said, feeling uneasy. I looked around the desk to see if there was another disk.

I finally shut off the DVD and showed her a screen with the photographs I'd scanned into the computer. She stared at the picture of Rachel in her wedding dress.

'You said it was last night. Maybe you didn't really watch it. You just unpacked the DVD and then dreamt that you watched it.' She mentioned that she'd dreamt she was riding on Louis the Caboose more than once. 'And maybe the place where you got the cat gave it to you, like a "welcome to being a feline friend" or something. You said you were carrying a lot of stuff. It could have fallen out of something and landed on the post,' she offered.

Everything she said made sense and could have happened, but I didn't think so. There had to be a logical explanation.

She was happy to drop the subject and as I expected went right to talking about meeting Ben and me at the coffee shop. 'It looked like you two were hitting it off,' she said.

I choked back a laugh. 'He helped me with the cat, and we grabbed dinner. In case you didn't notice, you and Mikey did most the talking.'

'I know my brother and I could tell by his face that he was having a good time.'

'Then you must be a mind reader. He had the same lack of expression he always does.'

'There's something beneath that,' she said. 'He's like that Evan you were talking about. His outside doesn't really tell what his inside is.'

'But Evan at least gives hints. Ben is like a statue. You should hear him read Ed's ridiculous sex scenes. He doesn't break his monotone once. It's actually very funny and the rest of us, except for Ed of course, find it hard not to laugh. Does your brother even know how to laugh? Does he have any sense of humor?' I asked with a smile.

'Of course he does. Doesn't everyone? I'll give him some jokes to tell next time I see him.'

I almost laughed out loud thinking of him repeating a joke in that matter-of-fact voice of his.

Rocky finally made his appearance. He rubbed against my legs and then Sara's before sitting down and looking at both of us.

'Wow, he's a big cat,' she said. 'But he has such soulful eyes.' I looked at his yellowish eyes and had to admit she was right.

'Look at his face. The black marking makes it look like he has a crooked moustache.'

We retreated to the kitchen and I gave him some cat food, before making some tea for us. It was the brightest room in the apartment. The windows looked down on our building's small yard and beyond to the large yards of the houses on the block behind us. The shortcoming was that it was most exposed to the sun and the wind, making it hot in the summer and cold in the winter. In October though, it was just fine.

She was on her second cup when her phone pinged with a message. 'I know,' she predicted, before she'd even looked. 'Something happened downstairs and I have to go.' She read the text. 'I was right.' She sounded triumphant and weary at the same time. 'Why doesn't anyone tell you how exhausting a toddler can be?'

When she'd left, I put the dishes in the sink and went back to my office. I pushed play again on the DVD, somehow expecting it to be different, but it was just the cat pictures again.

I was sure of what I'd seen the night before, wasn't I? But Sara's explanation made sense. Could I have dreamt it? What was going on?

EIGHTEEN

I kept thinking about the DVD and the more I did the more confused I felt. I went over the whole chain of events again and again. It became like a word you looked at too long and it ceased to make sense. I felt confused and uneasy. The only thing to do was to put the DVD back in its case and forget about it.

I tried to get my thoughts off of it by doing some work. I began with the dance gym. I read through my notes and came up with descriptions for all the classes I'd taken so far, using quotes from Talmadge and Kelly.

Part of me didn't want to deal with anything about Rachel after the whole DVD thing, but I couldn't put it off. What I'd shown Camille had a lot of placeholders and I started filling them in. When I got to the spot I'd marked *story from Mrs Parker*, I stopped. She was probably serious when she told me to make something up. I felt uneasy about doing it, concerned that she wouldn't be pleased. But I also had no choice.

I took the few facts that I knew about Camille arranging a wedding shower and created a warm moment between them I knew never would have happened in a million years. She'd mentioned her daughters had been part of it, so I made something up about them too. Though I had to refer to them as sister 1 and sister 2 since I didn't know their names.

When I sat back and read it over, I worried how she would react to it. Had I made it too sweet and emotional?

Next, I wrote up Luke's story about meeting Rachel because of a pink squirrel. I kept the part about the drink being a link to time with her mother light. I reread the story about the wedding shower. I decided to show it to Luke before I gave it to Mrs Parker. And he'd know the names of the sisters.

I thought briefly about Mr Parker. It seemed incomplete not to have something from him. But Camille Parker had said an emphatic no.

There was nothing left to do for Evan but keep my fingers

crossed that Sally said yes. Satisfied that it was all good for the moment, I left the computer.

With everything going on, I had forgotten about eating. All I'd had all day was the glass of orange juice. My stomach rumbled to remind me it was dinner time. Some people who lived alone survived on frozen entrees and peanut butter sandwiches. I admit I occasionally went that way, but most of the time I made a meal for myself and sat down at the table.

I went into the kitchen to see what I could create. I found some pasta which I cooked in the microwave and then mixed it with garlic oil, cheese and some leftover mixed vegetables. I made a quick salad out of some baby lettuces, cucumbers, tomatoes and green onions. The dressing was always the same. I added some olive oil and seasoning before tossing it. I poured on some balsamic vinegar and tossed it again.

I brought my plate into the dining room. Most of the other residents had turned the room into a den, but I'd kept it set up for its original purpose. It was a large room completely separated from the butler's pantry and kitchen with a swinging door. I wasn't sure why the short hallway with cabinets and some counter space was called the butler's pantry since I doubted that anyone actually had butlers, but I liked the name. As I sat in there, I imagined someone sitting at the head of the table stepping on the button in the wood floor that summoned the maid. The button was still there, but whatever it connected to was long gone.

I cleared everything off the table when the writing group met, but the rest of the time it served as a place for me to eat with a place mat, a tray with condiments with a decorative bowl as a centerpiece. The sideboard was filled with stuff I didn't use, like tablecloths and candles. A tall bookcase on the opposite wall had shelves of books mixed with decorative glassware and pretty things that I'd collected. The furnishings were finished off with a couch and a TV set.

The windows were covered with half curtains to block out the view of the next building. The apartments were laid out in a similar arrangement to mine which meant that my dining room looked into theirs. The tops of the windows were uncovered and there was enough exposure to the sky that it was bright during the morning and early afternoon, but then the light faded. Right now, all I could see was a strip of the night sky.

The cooking smells had awakened my hunger and I dove into the plate of food. I even had seconds on the pasta.

Since there wasn't anyone to have after-dinner conversation with, I cleared the table as soon as I was done.

I brewed myself some coffee and took it down the long hallway into the living room. The feeling of this room was totally different than the dining room. The bay windows looked out over the street and to the buildings on the other side. They were all brick and the same height as my building and probably close to as old. They all had balconies similar to mine and the same types of decorative features that nobody bothered with anymore.

I put down the coffee and turned on the TV. I was a little surprised when Rocky came in from wherever he'd been hiding and jumped up on the couch beside me. I was still getting used to the idea that I had a feline housemate. It had to be an adjustment for him, too. But it was certainly better than being in a cage at the pet shop. I didn't want to think about what his future would have been if he hadn't found a home.

Melissa had told me that he'd been an indoor cat. I was a little conflicted about that. It seemed unfair to cut him off from the outside, but the thought of him wandering on the street worried me, particularly since there were so many ambulances rushing by on 57th Street on the way to the university hospital complex. The balcony didn't seem an option. What if he saw a bird in the tree out front and tried to leap onto the branches? I thought that once he was acclimated, I would try walking him on a leash.

I needed a dose of laughter and turned the channel to a half hour comedy. I'd already seen the episode about several generations of a family living together, but it didn't matter. If anything it was funnier because I was laughing in anticipation of what was coming next. I usually drank my coffee black but sometimes at night I liked it with some cream. I went back to the kitchen to get a small pitcher of it.

I came back to the living room and poured it into the cup until the coffee was the right shade of beige. Some shouting came from the TV and when I looked up at the screen, I was surprised to see a night shot of cops surrounding a house. Before it could really register, they'd started shooting with loud bangs. I grabbed the remote control and hit the guide. It showed the TV was set to a totally different channel than I'd been watching. Thinking I must have somehow pushed it when I got up, I changed it back to the comedy show. I drank some of my coffee and picked up the bag with one of my crochet projects. I was working on a square with a heart motif in the middle. The outer area was purple and the heart, of course, was red. It involved carrying over the colors when I changed from purple to red and back to purple, so I had to pay attention. It was only when the purple ball fell off the couch and rolled across the floor that I thought about Rocky. Didn't cats love to play with yarn? I looked at him, expecting him to pounce on the rolling ball.

Instead, he lifted his head momentarily, checked it out, but then put his head back down and closed his eyes. 'Well, that's a relief,' I said, retrieving the ball and reaching in the bag for the ball of red yarn. Once I'd settled in, I glanced up at the TV and was surprised to see two cars racing on a highway. *What?* I reached for the remote control. The guide showed the TV tuned to another channel again.

Instinctively I looked around to see if there was someone else in the room. The only faces were from the paintings on the wall. I shot the cat a look. 'Did you do this?' He didn't stir, but that had to be it. I once again tuned it to my comedy show and this time, I put the remote control on the coffee table where there was no chance the cat could touch it, or I could lean on it.

I stared at the TV not taking my eyes away from it and it seemed OK. Just as I was about to relax and go back to my crocheting, out of nowhere the image changed to a basketball game. I looked at the remote control still on the table. Nothing had touched it. 'OK, this is getting creepy,' I said. I picked up the remote and turned the TV off.

I crocheted for a few minutes, until I started to feel a bit calmer. I took a couple of deep breaths and began to relax. And then the TV came on all by itself with the volume turned way up.

'That's it,' I said, getting up and unplugging it from the wall. I looked at the dark screen and this time nothing happened.

I grabbed my phone and called Sara. 'Is something weird going on with your TV?' I asked.

'Nothing here. Why? What's going on up there?' After the business with the DVD, I didn't want to tell her the TV was changing channels on its own and turning itself back on by itself. She'd really think I'd lost it.

'It's nothing. It's probably just my TV telling me it's time to replace it,' I said, hoping she wouldn't push for more details.

'Ben's here for a makeup dinner since he missed it last night. I'm sure he'd be glad to come up and have a look at your TV,' she said. I could hear whispering in the background and assumed it was him trying to stop her. I knew she was matchmaking and I was sure he'd figured it out as well. He was a cop after all.

'No, no,' I said quickly. 'It's nothing really. Let him enjoy his dinner and time with Mikey.'

'Then maybe you want to come downstairs if you're having trouble with your TV. You can watch your program here.'

'It's already over. Don't worry about it. Forget I called,' I said, chuckling at her persistence. She finally gave in and we both hung up.

But once I was off the phone the uneasy feeling returned. Something was going on.

NINETEEN

My mind longed for normalcy and I didn't want to believe anything weird was going on. So by morning, I'd brushed it all aside. The TV thing probably had just been some sort of fluke malfunction. When I'd gotten up, I'd plugged it back in and watched the morning news without a problem. And the DVD probably was as Sara had suggested – I'd just thought I watched it, though that still didn't explain who had sent it.

It was back downtown for another dance class. I had started looking forward to them. Even after just a couple of days, I could feel my body getting into shape. It was easy to get dressed. Once again, I just put on some leggings and a loose T-shirt, throwing a long sweater over it. I wore the boots again and carried a pair of sneakers.

When I got to the class, I noticed that a lot of the others were in bare feet tying scarves with dangling metal discs on them around their hips. 'What's with the wardrobe and lack of foot-wear?' I asked Darcy, realizing I hadn't paid attention to the name of the class.

She smiled. 'Some of the people find it easier to dance without shoes. And the scarves make it more . . .' She stopped searching for the right words. 'Interesting. But you don't have to do either. I did tell you that it's a belly dancing class, right?'

I shook my head. 'My mistake, I should have checked. I think I should put something in all the class descriptions to suggest what to wear.'

I glanced over the room. 'Where's Debbie?' I asked.

'Her day off. Carmen teaches belly dancing.' Darcy noticed I seemed disappointed. 'Carmen's a great teacher. I'm sure you'll be happy with her.'

'I'm sure I will be. I was just hoping to talk to Debbie to get more for the About Us part of what I'm putting together for you.' It was easy with Darcy since we'd spent enough time together that I'd picked up interesting tidbits here and there to include.

'You seem a little frazzled. Is everything OK?' Darcy asked.

I let out a sigh. 'I didn't realize that it showed,' I said. 'It's the reason I came in here in the first place to see if I could get something about Rachel.' I sighed again. 'I think I might have taken on too much when I decided to give the essence of who she was through anecdotes.'

Darcy nodded sympathetically. 'Been there, done that. I'm sure you'll figure it out.'

'I'm sure I will, too,' I said. 'Rachel's husband had been a big help. He's a good guy. He's the one who told me about this place.'

'Really?' Darcy said. 'I wonder if I ever met him.'

'I don't think so. He didn't even know the exact location of Dance with Me. I'm just glad I have him to look over some of what I've put together.' I left it at that, not wanting to say anything negative about Rachel's stepmother. 'I'm afraid it isn't the most efficient way of working, but it seems like the writing is only part of what I do. I spend a lot of time gathering information, which gets me in the middle of things.'

'I see your point. Not everybody would actually take all the classes they're going to write up. But I'm sure that's what makes you better at what you do.' She glanced across the room. 'Speaking of that, you probably should get some background on Carmen. It would be good to have something about all of our instructors in the material.'

Darcy pointed to the woman who was jangling as she walked in. 'That's Carmen. You better get ready for the class.' She looked down at my boots.

I did the usual dropping off of my stuff and changed from boots to bare feet. I found a spot in the midst of the others. This class was all women.

Carmen introduced herself and said the class was a chance to be seductive, sensuous and have fun. She offered triangular scarves fringed with those metal discs to anyone who wanted to borrow one. I grabbed one and tied it on. Then she demonstrated the basic moves and told everyone to follow along with what she did. There was a lot of hip wiggling and jangling from the scarves. Each song she played had a different routine and at the end there was free dance which was fun and a little crazy. A few of the women really had the moves down, but the rest of us were whirling around the room, making up our own dance. I glanced toward the front window thinking we must be attracting a crowd. Most people walked by without looking in. There was just one well-dressed woman who seemed to be getting her laugh of the day.

We were all laughing and worn out when the music stopped. After Darcy's request, I immediately grabbed my notebook and approached Carmen before she could leave. I dropped the scarf in a bag next to her. I began by thanking her for the class and explaining what I was doing for the dance gym. 'I want to put in some background information for each of the instructors,' I said.

Close up, I got a better look at her. Her appearance was very different to Debbie Alcoa. Instead of having her hair pulled back, she wore dark wiry hair loose and it just brushed her shoulders. She seemed heavy into eye make-up which made her seem exotic. And instead of trying to hide her shape under loose clothing, her leotard showed off her curvy hips. The jangling scarf only accentuated them.

She enthusiastically told me she'd taken belly dancing up in college and when she wasn't teaching, she danced at a local Middle Eastern restaurant. As we talked several other members came by and hugged her. I noticed that she seemed to know them all. When she finished telling me that she was married with a four-year-old daughter, I asked her if she'd known Rachel.

When she nodded, I broke the news of what had happened to her and what I was doing. The enthusiasm went out of her face and she let out a heavy sigh.

'Oh, dear.' Carmen seemed distressed. 'I wonder if it would have helped if I'd talked to her again.' Although I'd said that Rachel had fallen off the balcony in an accident, Carmen like the others didn't seem to buy it. I got the impression she was quite upset and I waited, assuming she would explain on her own. 'I know this place is about exercise and getting in shape through dance, but I believe in acceptance. Accepting who you are, how you are. When she first started coming to class, she came up to me afterwards and wanted to know how many calories the class burned. I sensed she was upset with her shape and I told her that curves were essential to be a good belly dancer. I said she was a natural, thinking it might make her feel more comfortable. I thought that since I obviously have the same kind of shape, it wouldn't upset her. But she didn't seem to take it well and I think making the point that she was curvy made her self-conscious. She didn't come back to the class. I saw her around here a few times and she kept getting skinnier. I wondered who she was trying to please.' She shook her head. 'We come in all shapes and sizes and we need to see the beauty in that instead of all trying to be a size zero.'

I wanted to give her a round of applause and told her I totally agreed with her philosophy. She'd had plenty to say about Rachel, but unfortunately nothing I could use.

When I'd retrieved my things, I saw that there was a message from Evan on my cell phone. I called him as soon as I got outside. I braced myself to hear he'd gotten bad news from Sally, but it turned out there was no need. 'She said yes,' he said with a happy lift in his voice. 'But I need to talk to you and show you something.'

I tried to get details and to do it over the phone, but he was adamant it had to be in person. 'Please meet for coffee. I need your opinion on something. Everything you've done has worked so far.'

I'd already masqueraded as his neighbor to make contact with Sally and even snuck inside her office, looking for hints as to why she hadn't responded to him. I was way beyond just writing notes for him. I had a real problem keeping my clients at a professional distance. I couldn't help getting way too involved. Look at what I'd done with the cat. And Evan'd gotten up my curiosity about what he wanted to show me.

'OK,' I said. 'I'm already downtown anyway.' I didn't mention that I was already planning to stop by the bar to show Luke what I'd done so far and see if he could add anything. It was none of Evan's concern so why even bring it up. We agreed to meet at a coffee place down the street from the hotel.

Once I hung up the phone, I went outside. It was still early, and the sidewalks were relatively empty since the lunch crowd was still working. The rain had cleaned the air and it felt fresh.

It was always a pleasure to walk on Michigan Avenue. There was a reason they called this section the Magnificent Mile. The street was lined with high-end shops, hotels and fancy restaurants. It didn't take long for my surroundings to slip into the background though. I did some of my best brain work when I was walking.

I thought back to when I was writing the first mystery. I'd made the detective Derek Streeter a Sherlock Holmes wannabe. He wasn't as clever as Sherlock, but he investigated by deducing things like if someone had a sunburn, it didn't track that they'd been inside all day. I transferred the concept to Rachel. What could I infer from what I knew about her?

The teachers had noticed a change when she came back to school in the fall. So something must have happened during the summer months. It was over the summer that she joined the dance gym and was most intense about the classes. Was that out of enthusiasm or something else? I'd heard from a number of people that she'd been obsessed about losing weight. I had to wonder why since when I'd met her before her wedding, while she thought she could lose a few pounds, she seemed accepting of her body.

Everything I'd heard about her from recent times painted a different picture than the person I'd dealt with. The teachers had remarked how different she'd seemed when the fall term started. Luke had said something about texts he'd gotten that she had no memory of sending. And there'd been packages delivered with things that she insisted she hadn't ordered.

What could have caused all the changes? Camille Parker seemed to view Rachel as a problem and who knows what she could have said to her. Mr Parker was a mystery. Then there was the obvious. She was newly married. Maybe it wasn't turning out as she'd expected. I knew that she was absolutely in love with Luke when we were working on the vows. But what if things had changed after the ceremony?

I thought of my own brief marriage. I shook my head with regret thinking how stupid I'd been with my romance-novel view of happily ever after. I'd definitely thought that once we were married, we'd be companions sharing life's adventures. Ha! I laughed out loud at the thought and a woman walking past me did a double take.

He'd just kept doing what he'd been doing which was finding all kinds of reasons not to spend time with me. I blamed myself for not seeing the truth. I was older and wiser now. I was only interested in a relationship with someone who clearly wanted one with me.

I was so deep in thought that I didn't realize I was crossing the river until a bus went by making the bridge shake. As soon as I got to the other side, I started looking for the coffee shop that Evan had chosen. There were so many coffee places around here now, it seemed like there was one on every corner. Luckily Evan was very detail-oriented and had been very specific with his directions.

He'd picked a new place that wasn't part of a chain. Burlap coffee bags decorated the walls and gave off the pungent scent of the beans that had filled them. I glanced around the whole place looking for him. As usual, most of the tables had people hovering over computers or some kind of screen – even tables with two people. What had happened to conversation? I didn't recognize anyone and was about to grab a coffee and find a table of my own, when a hand waved from the back.

I had to look twice to make sure it was him. We tend to recognize people by the outline of their shape. Evan's was suddenly different.

When I got closer, I saw what he'd done and had to restrain a laugh. When we first met, his hair had been non-descript, parted on the side and slicked down. Now it was floppy on top and the part was gone. The color was lighter, but the style was definitely reminiscent of Hugh Grant.

'What do you think?' he said, noticing that I was staring at his hair.

It was definitely an improvement, but I didn't want to be too gushy because it would make it seem like he'd been a total dud before. Kind of like marveling too much about someone's weight loss, so they felt like they must have been the size of a hippopotamus.

'You look very nice,' I said. But then I started to worry. The point was for Sally to get to know the real him, not for him to try to be someone else.

'Evan,' I said finally, trying hard not to turn this into a lecture,

'I've tried to portray the real you in the notes I've written for you. I know I said she likes movies with Hugh Grant in them, but do you really want to try to be someone else, or at least have their hair style?'

Evan's mouth curved into a big smile. 'That's what's so funny,' he said. 'This is the way my hair really looks. I usually put goop in it and comb it flat. I got a trim today and told the barber to leave off the gunk.'

'OK, in that case, great,' I said, feeling foolish for what I'd said. He motioned for me to sit and I saw that there was a coffee waiting for me. 'I'm assuming that's what you wanted to show me,' I said as I took the chair.

He nodded. 'But you're kind of right. It *is* the way my hair is naturally, but I was inspired a little by Hugh Grant's style.' He ran his fingers through it and then gave it a shake. It was quite amazing what a difference it made to his appearance. Before, he'd seemed too precise somehow and on the nerdy side. Now he had a little sizzle.

'Has Sally seen it yet?' I asked, and he shook his head.

'I wanted your stamp of approval.' He opened his computer bag and showed me the tube of hair goop he had. 'If you thought it was too much, I was prepared to go back to my old look.'

'Keep it,' I said. I drank some of the coffee and thanked him for his gesture. It was strong and gave me the boost I needed. 'Was there anything else you wanted to talk about?'

'I want some advice. You were there when the zoo trip went south because she had to leave and you advised me to do the kiss on the hand. I don't want to blow this date with her. What do I do?'

'You know I am not a dating coach or anything,' I began.

'Yes, you've said that numerous times, but you seem to know more than I do.'

I laughed inside thinking again of my failed marriage and my doubts about my judgment. But there was one thing I did know for certain. 'The point is to be yourself. You don't want her to fall for some fake image of who you are, do you?'

He thought a moment. 'No, I guess not. It's just that I'm not sure that the real me is enough.'

He was so open and vulnerable, I felt tears welling up, but I forced them back. 'Just be that guy and I bet Sally will melt,' I said.

He let out a sigh. 'The trouble is that when I'm around her I freeze up. The boat tour is a good thing because I can talk about the buildings and river, but I know I need to talk about other stuff if I'm going to win her heart. That's why I'm going to need more notes from you. You know how to say who I am better than I do.'

He said he would call me after the date and give me a play by play so we could go from there. I wished him good luck and on instinct gave him a hug. I hoped Sally was worthy of him.

TWENTY

had to change gears as I walked back to the Bellingham. The man behind the registration counter looked up as I passed by. I pointed up and he nodded before I continued to the elevator.

It was convenient that Luke worked in a public place. I could casually drop by without making any arrangements. He was behind the bar organizing things for the day. By now I'd figured that the black pants and shirt were like a uniform for him, though today he'd added a taupe vest which almost matched his hair. The place was empty except for a couple seated at one of the small tables with glasses of mimosas. He looked up and seemed a little surprised to see me. 'What is it? The draw of the fresh orange juice,' he said with a friendly smile. Maybe a little too friendly. He pointed to one of the seats at the bar and grabbed a wine glass and the pitcher.

I set my bag down on the stool next to me and fished out some pages. 'Actually, this is really just business,' I said quickly. It seemed like we'd been seeing each other a lot and I didn't want him to misinterpret. 'Though the orange juice is certainly exceptional,' I added and grinned. I watched as he filled the glass and handed it to me. It was fresh-squeezed and smelled wonderful. I suddenly wondered about his easy manner and for just a moment I wondered if it was real or an act? I quickly let it go thinking nobody could be that good an actor. I took a sip of the juice and it was as delicious as it had been before.

'You know Camille Parker better than I do. I made up a story about the wedding shower she put on for Rachel, as she'd told me to do. But I wanted to run it by you before I show her, and I need the names of Camille's daughters and something about them.' I pushed the papers across the bar. 'Here, this is still just a draft, but you'll get an idea how the whole thing will look.'

I watched him as he started to look them over. The booklet opened with pictures of Rachel as she grew up. I'd created the copy out of the biographical information I'd gotten about where she was born, went to school and college, and placed photographs that illustrated key moments.

'I've never seen any of these pictures,' he said. His expression dimmed as he moved on to the more current pictures and copy. I'd included a picture one of the teachers had sent me of Rachel and her students. I had used that along with the picture of the three teachers that I'd taken. The copy told the story about her generosity to the kids and the staff. I'd made sure to mention how important the job was to her and how beloved she was by the kids.

I heard his breath catch when he skipped ahead to the wedding picture and the story he'd told me about how they'd met. He looked up at me. 'Good job. You made it sweet and a little funny.'

I pointed to the copy that preceded it. 'Here's the story about the shower.' He read it over and handed me back the sheets. 'Camille will love the story. You make her sound like a saint. The rest of it looks good too.'

He gave me Camille's daughters' names and made sure to spell them for me because both of them had a weird spelling. Kyrs and Haillee. 'As for what they're like – think about Cinderella's stepsisters,' he said with a laugh. Then he gave me something real to use. Kyrs had found the location and Haillee had arranged the food.

'That's where it ends for now. I was thinking about something from Mr Parker.'

'Didn't Camille tell you to leave him out of it?'

I nodded. 'But maybe it's a mistake. Maybe you could say something to her.' He let out a little laugh as if what I'd said was totally absurd and put his hands up defensively.

'No way am I getting involved.'

'I just thought that if they're so concerned about optics, it would look bad if there was nothing from him in the book. And then the Parkers will blame me. I guess if I heard it from him that he didn't want to be included . . .' I trailed off.

'I can probably come up with another story you can use. We went to Door County in Wisconsin over the summer and stopped in Green Bay. Rachel knew nothing about football or that the rabid Green Bay Packers fans were known to wear cheesehead

hats. When she saw the hats shaped like a piece of cheese, she
thought they were about Wisconsin being so known for their
cheese and was surprised they were so popular. I have a picture
of Rachel wearing one of them.' I scribbled down the cheesehead
hat story and he said he'd email me the photograph. Customers
had started to come in and it seemed like we were done. Once
again, he refused to let me pay for the drink.

I was glad that Luke had been OK with my imagined story,
but I was still concerned about Mr Parker. He was the only blood
family Rachel had. The book wouldn't seem complete without
something from her father and I wondered if Camille had even
brought it up to him. I intended to at least give him the opportunity, but wasn't sure how best to arrange a meeting with Mr
Parker. I doubted calling and attempting to set up an appointment
would work. It was too easy to turn me down. It was early afternoon when I left the hotel and I decided to simply go to his
office and see if I could talk my way in.

I found the address on my phone and as soon as I'd crossed
the Michigan Avenue Bridge, I turned on Wacker Drive and
continued on as it followed the river to where it split into the
north and south branches.

The elegant building was tucked into the southward curve of
the river. It was made of green glass and reflected the water.
Parker Shipping occupied the top two floors and the elevator
opened onto sort of a lobby. The spacious area had a nautical
theme. The walls were painted blue and decorated with photographs of ships and the floor was a dark wood. It was furnished
with some wooden captain's chairs and several couches with
wood frames that seemed like what you would find on a ship.

The receptionist looked up from her wooden enclosure shaped
like the bow of a boat and asked if she could help me.

'I'd like to see Mr Parker,' I said. I'd been considering what
to say the whole way there. I could say I was writing a piece on
the shipping business in Chicago and since Mr Parker was a
major player, I wanted to talk with him, but then there'd be
questions who I was writing it for and one lie would become a
whole string of them. I might omit some information, like not
telling Luke about what I was doing for Evan, but actually telling
a bunch of lies didn't work for me.

'Do you have an appointment?' she said, glancing down at something I assumed was a schedule.

'No,' I said, girding for her response.

She was polite, but dismissive when she said that it was impossible then.

'It's about his daughter,' I began. I'd remembered that Camille had worked there before becoming the second Mrs Parker and, just a guess, but I bet the staff wasn't fond of her then or now. 'I'm putting together a celebration of life book for her service.' I explained the idea of using anecdotes and personal memories to capture her spirit. 'Mrs Parker has been my only contact and didn't want me to talk to Mr Parker directly. If I didn't offer him the chance to add something, he might be very regretful.' I glanced at the woman hopefully. As expected, her expression dimmed at the mention of Camille. Now the responsibility for keeping him from having the opportunity was on her. It was just the kind of thing I'd had Derek Streeter do.

She smiled weakly as she picked up the phone. 'Let me get his assistant.'

Inside I gave myself a high five. It had worked and I'd gotten me past the first gatekeeper. A few moments later, a well-dressed man came through an interior doorway. It figured that Camille had made sure that her husband had a male assistant so there was no chance Mr Parker would find another work-wife.

'I'm Andrew Carlson, Mr Parker's assistant. What can I do for you?'

He seemed very formal and I'm sure a good part of his job was protecting his boss from people Mr Parker didn't want to be bothered with. In other words, people like me. My only chance to get any further was by making the point that if Mr Parker regretted not being part of the memory book and found out that his assistant had run interference and kept me away, he'd get the blame. The receptionist had thrown in the towel relatively easily, but I knew he'd be a harder sell.

I explained what I was doing and again mentioned that all my dealing had been with Mrs Parker. I paused for a breath and saw that he like the receptionist gave a hint that he wasn't a big fan of Camille's. This time I put more emotion into my appeal.

'Despite what Mrs Parker said, I didn't feel what I'm putting together would be complete without some input from Mr Parker. She was his only child. At the very least, I wanted to make sure that he had the opportunity to add something.'

Andrew grimaced slightly and I knew I'd succeeded. Much as he wanted to turn me away, he didn't want to take the responsibility to do it on the chance that Mr Parker would later regret not adding something to the booklet and look for someone to blame.

'Let me check,' the assistant said. 'He might have a few minutes right now.'

He went back through the interior doorway and returned moments later inviting me to follow.

He led me to a private elevator that let us off into another reception area. He knocked briefly at a door and then brought me into the office.

A wall of windows had a glorious view of the river below. The bridge was just going up to let a barge pass through. Richard Parker glanced up from his desk. He was heavyset and not particularly attractive, but there was an aura of power about him. He was formally dressed in a suit and white shirt along with a dark tie.

There were two captain's chairs in front of the desk, and he invited me to sit.

'What exactly can I do for you?' he said. His tone seemed distant. 'I understood that my wife was dealing with all the preparations for the memorial service,' he said.

I knew I only had a short time, so I quickly explained what I was doing and showed him what I had.

'I know you're very busy and Mrs Parker suggested I not bother you, but I thought you ought to have the opportunity to add something personal to what I'm doing.'

He thumbed through the pages. When he looked up, he seemed uncomfortable. 'My daughter was a disappointment,' he began. 'I'd hoped that she would come into the family business. When she said she wanted to be a teacher, I'd thought she would work in a prestigious private school instead of that inner city school she chose. When she was getting married, I made her fiancé an offer to work in our business I thought he wouldn't refuse. But he decided it was better to make drinks for a bunch of high-end alcoholics than work for me.' He leaned forward and hammered the desk. 'You better believe I insisted he sign a prenup about everything relating to Rachel's share of my business.' He shook his head with consternation.

'But I couldn't do anything about the money that came from her mother's side.' He realized I might not understand what he was talking about. 'Her mother's family owned the Bellingham Hotels. When they sold, she was given a trust fund with her share of the proceeds. Now it's his trust fund,' he finished with disgust.

'I don't know what happened to her to push her to the edge, but I blame him. He was there with her every day. He should have done something.' He let out a heavy sigh. 'We managed to keep her mother's death quiet. And we'll manage to keep Rachel's as accidental, but people will still put two and two together. It's not my fault. This business is my life. Times are changing and I've been finding ways to change with it. We've started a whole new division of small cruise ships going through the Great Lakes. Why should people go to foreign countries when they can have the experience here?' I noticed photographs of the type of ships he was talking about behind him.

I'd let him talk. He rambled a bit and then went back to Luke and how angry he was that Luke had been at the bar when it happened. 'He should have seen what was going on and not left her alone.'

I nodded to show I was listening. So far there wasn't anything I could include and I was expecting any moment he was going to end our meeting. But then he took a framed photograph that was facing him and turned it around to show me. He was standing with a little girl, holding her hand, and they were on the deck of a ship as a crane was loading something on it. Both of them were smiling.

'She used to come to work with me on Saturdays. We'd go to a diner down the street and have pancakes. She loved going on the ships. She told me that boats were in her blood.'

I tried to keep my professional distance, but talking to him reminded me of my own losses. I'd never really faced it, but his anger had touched a sensitive spot and I realized I was angry at my mother for dying. It wasn't rational or as if she had a choice, just the upset of a little girl losing her mother. I swallowed back my emotions before asking him if I could use both the photo-graph and the story. He nodded with a solemn, sad face. 'She was my dear little girl,' he said.

'Thank you for your time,' I said, as he handed me the picture.

'Thank you for persisting,' he said. His expression had softened with understanding. He didn't explain, but I knew what he meant. I'd ignored his wife's orders and talked my way past his gate-keepers and in the process gotten him to open up his heart.

TWENTY-ONE

As I walked back to the train, my mind was spinning from what I'd just heard. Mr Parker not liking his daughter's choice of a husband wasn't that strange. My father hadn't been too pleased with mine either. Now I wish I'd listened to him. But what jumped out at me was what Mr Parker had said about the money from his first wife's side. Luke had mentioned the prenup, but said nothing about the wealth not covered by it that he stood to inherit. I wondered if that was intentional. Mr Parker hadn't given any figures but it had to be sizeable fortune for him to be concerned.

Luke had portrayed himself as someone who didn't care about money and who was content to stay on managing the bar in the hotel. What if that was an act? What if he hadn't been so hot for her as much as for what she came with? These thoughts made me uncomfortable and I pushed them away, instead thinking about where I'd place the photo and the story from Mr Parker in the celebration of life book. Maybe when Camille realized that her husband wanted to be included, she wouldn't be upset that I'd gone around her.

I was on autopilot when I got off the train and followed some other passengers to the stairway down to the street level. But as soon as I walked out from under the viaduct my thoughts came back to the present and I remembered that it was Thursday and that I'd arranged an extra session with the writing group at a neighborhood restaurant.

My thoughts were on the assignment I'd give them as I went up the stairs to my building. Collecting my mail from the box in the vestibule, I noticed a package on the ground. I grabbed it, intending to leave it at the base of the stairs as we all did. After unlocking the glass door that led to the inner portion of the building, I was about to set the box on the newel post when I checked for the addressee. I was surprised to see my name. Unlike the padded envelope I'd received the other day, this had a return address. It was a familiar online store.

Had someone sent me a gift?

I dropped my jacket and bag as soon as I got inside my place and took the box into my office. After cutting it open, I found a black merino wool sweater inside. I pulled open the packing slip to see who'd sent it, but all I saw was my information. It made no sense. I'd admired the sweater and even put it in my wish list. But ordered it? No. I found a customer service number and called. What I found out shocked me. The sweater had been charged to my credit card and had been ordered the day before with one-day shipping. I might have gotten a little heated as I insisted that I hadn't ordered the sweater. The customer service woman was probably used to crazies and didn't react.

'However you got the sweater, if you're not happy with it you can return it and we'll credit the charge,' she said in a deliberately pleasant voice. 'It does happen that some customers have ordered items and not remembered,' she said in a more personal voice. 'You know, by accident, or even under the influence.'

The whole thing made me so uneasy, I wanted her to cancel my online account, but she insisted that I leave it open until the return was complete. 'The best I can do is to put a freeze on them taking any orders in the meantime.'

I didn't want to say anything to anybody about it. After the business with the DVD and then the TV last night, it would sound like I was losing it. Something popped into the back of my mind that made me even more uneasy. These occurrences were reminiscent of what I'd heard that Rachel had claimed had happened to her.

I left it on my desk and flopped into the burgundy wing chair. It was almost dark, and I needed to turn on the lights, but for the moment I needed to sit there and collect myself. I was feeling a little creeped out by everything.

I heard something fall in the other room and immediately tensed up. The frosted glass French door had closed behind me when I came into the room and now it shook as if someone had pushed on it. And then the door began to open, and someone came into the semi-dark room. My heart thudded and then I let my nerves out in a laugh as I saw the black-and-white cat swirl across the room.

'You're going to have to learn to announce yourself with a meow,' I said. I was also going to have to learn that I wasn't living alone anymore. I went over and gave him some strokes before turning on the lights. As I left my office, I forced myself to put all thoughts of the package and other occurrences out of my mind.

'You're probably looking for dinner,' I said, going back to the kitchen with the cat in close pursuit. I'd been told that cats self-regulated when it came to food unlike dogs who would chow down on everything in their bowl without thinking if they really wanted it or not. Because of that I had been leaving him a full bowl of dry cat food every morning. It was also insurance in the event, like now, I forgot that I had a pet. 'It'll kick in, I promise,' I said to the cat, as I added some more kibble and then put a dab of wet food on a plate for him. The last touch was to top off his big bowl of water, so he wouldn't go thirsty.

And now it was time to get ready for the writers' group which amounted to freshening up a little and grabbing my notebook. I'd chosen the Mezze because it was down the street and the coffee house restaurant had a good vibe for the writers' group.

The place was full of atmosphere. The brick walls were covered with artwork and the wood table had initials and sayings carved into them by patrons over the years. The crowd it attracted was interesting, made up of students, locals, and tourists visiting the university campus or wanting to see the neighborhood that had been home to President Obama and his wife, Michelle.

I found Ed waiting in the entrance when I came in. It was only going to be three of us since Ben and Daryl couldn't make it. I requested a table in the middle where we'd have a good view of the whole place.

As soon as Tizzy joined us, we ordered one of their fabulous pan pizzas to share. These events were part writing and part social. After all this time of sharing their writing, we'd all become friends of a sort. We talked while we ate the pizza and then got down to business.

I made up different assignments. This time I gave them five words – red, stone, languid, howl, and leap. They were to pick someone in the place to write about and include the five words. What they wanted to do was up to them, maybe flash fiction, a scene or an essay. The main thing was to be discreet, so their target wouldn't get paranoid that someone was staring at them. I'd brought along my notebook and wrote along with the pair of them. It was always good to sharpen my skills.

Afterwards, they both came back to my place and this time read their own work. As usual, I wouldn't share my piece since it would change the dynamics of the group if I acted like one of them.

Ed loved reading his own work. That way he could throw in all the innuendo he wanted. Thankfully his piece was pretty tame and about an older woman trying to pick up a much younger man. Tizzy sent the couple she chose to write about time traveling back to the 1960s when the Mezze was just a coffee house with a few food items and located in the back of a bookstore. When she was done reading, she started talking about what used to be where on 57th Street. She sat forward suddenly, remembering something. 'There's a program on the Public Broadcasting Station tonight all about the 1893 World's Fair,' Tizzy said in an excited voice. 'It's all about the Midway Plaisance.' She pointed vaguely south toward the strip of park that ran between 59th and 60th joining Jackson Park to Washington Park. During the World's Fair, it had been filled with amusements. Recently, a remnant of the Ferris wheel had been found. 'We should all watch it. It is about what was right around here,' she said. I noticed Ed's eyelids begin to droop before he said he ought to get home. Tizzy made no move to leave.

'It's just starting, and I forgot to record it. Do you mind if I watch it here?' she asked. 'Sure,' I said, 'it sounds interesting.' We walked with Ed to the front door, said our goodbyes and then went into the living room and turned on the TV.

Shots of the neighborhood as it was now showed, while the narrator gave the history of the World's Fair also known as the Columbian Exposition. There was a scene of the grassy area now and then a montage of photographs showed how it had looked like during the Fair. I heard the word belly dance and started paying more attention. Apparently, there was a 'hootchy-kootchy' version of the exotic dance in the Streets of Cairo amusement.

I told Tizzy about my belly dancing experience and stood to give her a funny demonstration. The TV suddenly got very loud, drowning out my voice and we both looked at the screen. Instead of old black-and-white photos, the screen was filled with a woman singing as a panel of judges watched.

Tizzy looked at it with confusion and turned to me. 'Why did you change the channel?'

Before I could answer, it had gone back to the show on PBS.

And then it happened again, and a cop show came on, before it flipped back to PBS.

'What's going on?' she asked.

'Then you saw it?' I said. 'You saw the channel change?'

'Of course, why?'

There was a part of me that thought I might have imagined it when it happened before. But now there was a witness.

'It must be something with your cable,' she said. 'Let's check the set in your dining room.' She was on her way down the hall before I could say anything.

She turned on the PBS show and we stood there watching the screen for a few minutes waiting for something to happen, but nothing did. 'Good,' she said. 'Maybe it's fixed.' We went back into the living room, which was more comfortable for watching TV. I turned the set back on and after a moment, it began doing the weird stuff again. This time the volume changed before going to mute and the channel switched a number of times.

'You did see what was happening, right?' I said and she nodded.

'It seems like this TV is possessed or something,' she said almost as a joke. I hesitated, wondering if I should tell her about the other things. It was a relief that Tizzy had actually witnessed the TV doing strange things and it was clearly not in my mind, but it was also upsetting because I didn't know the cause.

Finally, I told her everything – the DVD that changed and the package with something I hadn't ordered. She listened with interest and what I said seemed to have gotten her worked up and she talked really fast with a lot of gestures.

'It sounds like someone is trying to make you think you're losing it. Making you think you didn't see what you thought you did and that you're doing things and not remembering them. You know, gaslighting you.' I must have looked confused because she continued on. 'The term comes from an old movie called *Gaslight* that starred Ingrid Bergman and Charles Boyer. He messes with her mind, so she thinks she's going crazy. I just watched it on one of the classic movie channels.' She did a twirl, gazing around the living room. 'Though I don't know how someone could have pulled it off here.' She said it quickly, all in one breath.

'Let me see if I can find it for you.' She grabbed my remote control and did a fast search for the movie. 'Here it is,' she said. 'It's on again in the middle of the night.' Her fingers flew over the buttons on the remote. 'There, it's all set to record. OK, now it's my turn to head off,' she said breathlessly, going to the door. 'Watch it and you'll understand what I'm talking about.'

Both what Tizzy talked about and the speed she'd said it, on top of the rest of my day, left me wired. I made myself a mug of chamomile tea hoping it would calm my mind. It didn't really help, and I finally went to bed, falling into a fitful sleep only to awake a few hours later. As I lay in bed wondering how I could fall back asleep, I heard a voice coming from somewhere in the apartment.

TWENTY-TWO

What now? Or maybe more accurately who now? Things were supposed to happen in threes, weren't they? Well, I'd had three weird happenings. It might be a cliché, but that's what I'd always heard. Things came in threes. This was four. Didn't whoever was behind all this know the rules? Now I was angry and looked for a weapon. Rocky was sound asleep on my pillow and barely stirred when I quietly got up. I suddenly wished he was a dog – a big German Shepherd or even some little feisty terrier who would attack an intruder's ankles.

I grabbed the two umbrellas that hung on chair near the front door. They were the kind that folded up into a small cylinder rather than the old-fashioned curved handle ones that had pointy ends which would have made them better weapons. I followed the sound. It seemed to be coming from the back of the apartment. The voice spoke again, but although I strained, I couldn't make out the words.

Adrenalin was pumping by the time I got to the dining room and I felt like Superwoman with my weapon of two umbrellas. It was dark and I could just barely make out the table and then I heard someone speak again. The sound seemed to be coming from the corner on the other side of the room. Without thinking too much, I aimed one of the umbrellas and sent it off into the darkness. There was a thud, followed by the sound of breaking glass.

I paused for a moment and listened. There was just silence. With my free hand, I reached for the light switch. With my heart pounding, I walked around the table with the other umbrella poised ready to strike. I expected to see someone on the ground.

How about some*thing*? There was a broken dish and the cordless handset. As I got closer a warbly voice called out 'low battery.'

Really? I shook my head with disbelief. It was not some diabolical stranger, just me being careless. As I put the phone in the cradle to charge, I chided myself for the overreaction, blaming it on all of Tizzy's gaslighting talk. I cleaned up the glass and made more chamomile tea before going back to bed.

There was no problem with the battery in the morning as the four cordless phones spread around the apartment, including the one in my bedroom, rang loudly, cutting into my sleep.

Rocky had repositioned during the night and his head was resting on my forehead and I had to peel him off of me so I could answer the phone, or at least look at the caller ID to decide if it was a junk call or not. As soon as I saw Parker on the screen I reached for the phone and clicked talk.

I'd barely gotten a hello out, when Camille Parker started to lay into me. 'How dare you defy my orders. I told you not to bother my husband,' she steamed. 'I'd fire you, but I don't have time to find anybody else this late in the game. Just finish it up. I don't care what you have to do to finish it up and get it to me by Monday or . . .' She seemed to be struggling to come up with something to threaten me with but she'd already said it was too late to replace me.

At times like this, I'd found the best way to deal with the situation was to apologize. I stepped in before she could come up with something to threaten me with, and apologized profusely – with no explanation. As expected, it left her speechless. She finally made an annoyed sound and hung up the phone. Though with phones these days there was no actual hanging up, just a click, but I'm sure she would have banged the phone down if she could have.

I guess that means I can't count on her recommending my services, I thought facetiously. At least she'd given me until Monday, which left me three days to complete it.

It was a morning of crises. I'd barely made myself a cup of coffee when the phone rang again. It was Evan so upset he could barely talk.

'Take a breath and then tell me,' I said.

He followed my command and I could hear him suck in air and let it out, then he wailed, 'She cancelled.'

'I assume you mean Sally,' I said in a calm voice. 'Maybe you should give me the details so we can sort it out.'

'She called me this morning and said she couldn't go on the boat cruise.'

'Did she say why?' I asked.

'Just that she had to work. It has to be an excuse. Events are always booked way in advance.' He sounded crushed and I felt for him. And I blamed myself. I know the note was supposed to be a reflection of Evan, but I felt like I hadn't done a good enough job. Or I should have read her better when I saw her look at the note. I really had to keep myself from getting so involved with my clients. Even the dance gym. I was trying too hard to make the copy too clever when all I actually had to do was spell out what the place was and describe the classes.

'I thought I'd have another chance with her. She hasn't even seen my hair style yet.' He paused. 'There has to be something you can do.'

I felt bad for him and I was afraid that my fear was true, that Sally wasn't interested and she wasn't even going to give him a chance to show her his true self.

'I'm going to be downtown,' I said. 'Do you want to meet up and talk about it in person?'

'Yes. I know you'll think of something.' He had way more confidence in my ability than I did. We arranged a time to meet at the coffee shop again.

I left extra early so I could drop the sweater off at the shipping service center. I wanted it out of my house and on its way back where it came from as quickly as possible. Then I could forget all about it.

And then it was back to normal. It had already become a routine to catch a mid-morning train for the dance class of the day. I'd gotten to look forward to it, too. The classes were the perfect mixture of work and personal. I was getting good material for the copy, and it was a fun way to start the day. I expected to keep on going there even after I finished my work, though not as often. I was pondering what classes I'd continue to take regularly as I got off the train and walked the few blocks to the place.

An El train rumbled on the tracks above when I reached Wabash. It was odd to look up at this upper level and realize there was a whole world up there with a station and people on the platform waiting for a train, all held up by giant claw legs.

There was already a crowd gathered for the class when I went into Dance with Me. I was glad to see that it was Debbie who was teaching line dancing today. I chuckled when I saw what everyone was wearing for this class. A few people were in dance wear, but most were in jeans with boots. A few even had cowboy hats on.

The class was fun, and I picked up the steps pretty quickly and by the end of the class I was adding in my own little touches like the rest of them.

This time there were no delays. I got to Debbie while she was just turning off the music and said, 'Can we talk?'

'Sure,' she said. I hoped she might stop what she was doing, but she continued to finish things up for the class and then started changing out of her dance shoes. She was always in a totally different mental space at the end of the class than the members were. All around us people were talking and laughing as they went to retrieve their things and grab their coats. It was a fun hour well spent and now it was off to whatever else they had in their day.

She seemed less animated and maybe a little tired. We stood talking as she watched the retreating figures of the students, waving back at few who had waved at her.

'I'm happy arranging all the classes and teaching them, but there's nothing like being on stage.'

It was the perfect entry to asking about the shows she'd been in. She was glad to answer, and the list was extensive. 'But just in the chorus,' she said. 'I still go on auditions, so maybe someday I'll be out front.'

'That's great,' I said. 'I'll make a point that you are currently a professional dancer.' After that she talked a bit about hoping to get another level of classes that were beyond the basic. 'They'd still be drop-in classes, but I'd come up with more elaborate routines and maybe add some props for the tap class. Think top hats and canes.' She smiled at the thought. By now, she'd gotten her street shoes on and packed everything back in her gym bag. 'Too much to do, too little time.' She hoisted the bag on her shoulder clearly ready to go.

As an afterthought, I asked her about Rachel. Debbie let out a sigh. 'She was too worried about getting the steps right.' She adjusted the strap of the bag. 'Do you have what you need?'

'I'll write it up and if there's any holes, I'll ask you next time.'

She was on her way to the door as I finished the sentence. I understood. Like she said, *Too much to do, too little time.*

I walked up Michigan Avenue delighting in the fact there was no wind. My hair didn't blow in my face and my trench coat didn't flap around. As usual, I used the walking time to think. I went back to the phone call from Camille Parker. I'd thought she might say something about my talking to her husband, but I figured it would be something mild since it turned out that Richard Parker had appreciated my efforts and wanted to be included in the book. I certainly hadn't expected her to explode.

I'd done a little research on her since finding out that she wasn't Rachel's mother. She'd been a widow when she was Richard Parker's work-wife. Her husband had been a podiatrist and they were comfortable, but hardly rich, though I had the feeling she'd always been a snob.

She clearly loved her position now and, I thought, would do whatever she had to hang onto it.

I was at the coffee shop before I knew it and turned my thoughts to Evan's situation. As I went in the door, I remembered something. And it was something that hopefully would get Evan to calm down.

He was at the same table he'd sat at before. His hair looked even better now that it didn't have the just-styled look. His slacks and striped dress shirt suited him. He was not a jeans and T-shirt sort of guy.

There was a cup of coffee waiting for me once again and I thanked him. Poor Evan looked like a wreck as I slid into the seat across from him. I couldn't make him wait while we made small talk, so I went right to it. 'I know you think that Sally was just giving you another excuse, but she was telling the truth. A few days ago I saw her showing a woman the bar area with the idea of using it for an intimate wedding reception. It had to be the coming weekend. The woman left saying she needed to talk to her daughter before she committed.'

Evan just stared at me.

'Don't you see? The daughter probably agreed and it's all very last minute.'

Evan's face relaxed and his lips curved into a hopeful smile.

'I'm sure you're right. Thank you.' He let out a big sigh of relief.

'So, what you should do is offer her a raincheck. Invite her for Saturday.'

'Oh,' he said as his face brightened. 'I didn't think about that.' He grabbed my hand and then didn't know what to do with it, so he shook it. 'Thank heavens for you. I'm so bad at this romance stuff. You have to write something. It has to be special and cute.'

'What if I wrote it in verse?'

'That's perfect.' He looked at me expectantly. 'It's already Friday, so you need to do it now.'

Sometimes pressure works for me and sometimes it paralyzes me. Luckily this time it was an incentive and, in a few minutes, I wrote:

Dear Sally,
If you can't come on Sunday, I have an offer of another way.
Is your Saturday free, to come away with me?
We'll sail without fail down the river Chicago,
And see buildings and bridges just like we ought to.
I hope you can come, and I promise you fun.
Fingers crossed the day will be warm and there will be sun.

'That's brilliant,' he said, reading over what I'd written.

'I wouldn't call it brilliant, but I think it'll do,' I said, and suggested that he sign it affectionately.

'We have to get it to her now,' he said. There was some discussion on what form to send it to her in. Handwritten was more intimate than typed. He copied down what I'd written, since we agreed it should be in his handwriting. When we parted company, he rushed back to the hotel to leave it on her desk. This time under a paperweight.

I didn't stop in at the bar this time. I was afraid it might seem as if I had an ulterior motive if I showed up too often. Anyway, I was glad to go home early. After my previous night of interrupted sleep, I was worn out. I was looking forward to going home and relaxing. The last thing I expected was to be dealing with the police.

TWENTY-THREE

When I turned the corner onto my street, I was surprised to see a cop car in front of my building. And more surprised to see Tizzy out front talking to one of the cops. She was definitely living up to her nickname. Her clothes were fluttering from the broad gestures of her hands and body as she spoke to the officer.

I stopped next to her. 'What's going on?' I asked.

Her very straight chin-length brown hair swung wildly as she turned to me. 'I thought the police should know about what's going on with you.'

'You called the cops,' I squealed.

'No,' she said. 'I saw him leaving the coffee shop on the way to his car and I stopped him.' She turned back to the cop. 'She's the one I was telling you about. Her television seemed like it had been taken over by demons. The channels switched around and the volume went up and down. There's more – she got a sweater she's sure she never bought, and a DVD that had one thing on it at first and then something else the next day. I'm telling you someone is gaslighting her – you know, trying to make it seem like she's losing it.' I was stunned as Tizzy made a circular motion next to her head, the thing we used to do as kids to imply someone was nuts.

'Then you witnessed all this?' the cop asked, seeming confused.

'Only the TV,' Tizzy said, getting more worked up. 'You should have seen it. I'm telling you it was like it was possessed.' She glanced in my direction and then back to the cop. 'She told me about the rest of it.'

The cop listened with a patient expression at first, then I saw a subtle shift and he eyed her with disbelief. I couldn't blame him. Tizzy was making it sound like we'd both lost it.

Naturally we were attracting the attention of people passing by, but luckily no one had stopped. Then I noticed a man in my peripheral vision make a stop. I turned to get a better look and my shoulders dropped as I realized it was Ben.

His gaze moved from Tizzy and me to the cop, taking in the situation. He gave the two of us a nod of recognition before directing his attention to the cop. He pulled out his badge and introduced himself. It had never occurred to me that he always had the badge on him and probably a gun, too. 'I know these ladies. What's the problem?'

I wasn't so sure about being referred to as a lady, but I guess it was better than calling us females. Best might have been if he'd said 'these two people'.

The officer looked back and forth between me and Tizzy, seeming relieved to have someone on his wavelength to talk to. He pulled Ben aside and they conversed in voices too low for us to hear.

I couldn't help myself from giving Tizzy a dirty look. I would have liked to have thrown in some words with it admonishing her for getting the police involved. Worse now Ben was in the middle of it.

The conversation between Ben and his uniformed brethren came to an end. The cop gave Ben a smile and a thumbs up before going back to his car. I could hear his radio crackling, probably with a real call for his services.

Ben rejoined us and put his hands on Tizzy's and my back as though he was rounding up a couple of errant sheep. 'I told Officer Smith that I'd handle this,' he said. He was using what I assumed must be his professional voice. I wondered if there was a special class in cop school where they were taught how to speak that way. It was full of authority and empty of emotion. 'How about we take this inside?' And he steered us all move toward the gray stone stairs that led to the building entrance.

He dropped his hands as soon as we started up the short stairway. I led the way up to my place and the three of us stopped once we reached my living room.

Tizzy started before I could stop her. 'Someone's gaslighting Veronica. She wasn't going to do anything about it, but I was worried for her.' She peered at Ben. 'You do know what gaslighting is? That other police person didn't seem to.' Without giving him a chance to answer, she moved on to talking about the movie.

He put his hand up to stop her. 'How about you tell me exactly what happened.' By now he was looking straight at me.

I felt highly embarrassed, both because he was my student and because it made me sound a little crazy – as if I was seeing plots where there weren't really any. As Tizzy liked to say, we writers had active imaginations.

He kept his gaze on me and I got the message that I couldn't simply dismiss the whole thing. I was stuck giving him all the details.

Tizzy abruptly looked down at her smart watch which was vibrating on her wrist. 'Oh, it's a text from Theo,' she said, referring to her husband. 'I forgot we're having company for dinner.' She looked between Ben and me.

'It's okay, you can go,' I said. 'I can take it from here.'

Tizzy looked relieved as she rushed to the door. Just before she went out, she turned back. 'Be sure to tell him about all three things.'

I let out a sigh when she had gone. 'I'm afraid Tizzy made a big deal out of what's probably nothing.'

'Why don't you just tell me the whole story.' Even though he was wearing jeans and a gray hoodie instead of a uniform, he was definitely in cop mode. It had been different when he helped me with Rocky. This time it felt like we were the teacher and the cop in a standoff, which sounded like a situation in a romance novel.

I just wanted to be done with an explanation, but I also felt an obligation to be cordial and offered him a seat and some sparkling water. He hesitated and I got it – as long as he stood with no refreshments, he could hold onto his role as a cop. He seemed as if he did some inner considering and he agreed to both.

He glanced around the seating arrangement in the living room. His gaze stopped on the two chairs with a table in between near the bay window, but he dismissed it, looking back into the alcove near the entrance hall. His eye went from the blanket made of crochet squares in different designs on the wall that had hung in my father's office to the black leather couch below. 'How about there?' he said pointing and I nodded. He maneuvered around the coffee table in front of the sofa and took a seat in the middle of it.

I brought in the drinks and prepared to go over all the three incidents quickly, since Tizzy had made sure to mention that there were three, then he could go downstairs to his sister's.

I excused myself and went down the long hall to the kitchen to set up the drinks. As I loaded up a tray with glasses and the bottle of berry-flavored sparkling water, I tried to collect my thoughts and figure out what to say so I wouldn't sound crazy. This was all very awkward. As a last-minute thought, I added a bowl of ice cubes.

He'd already set out some coasters on the coffee table by the time I returned. I stalled a little longer offering him ice, which he accepted. I poured him a glass, then poured myself a half a glass straight. I could feel his eyes on me as I did it and I felt an obligation to explain. 'I like my drinks at room temperature,' I said.

'So you're a vegetarian who doesn't like cold drinks,' he said. I took my glass and sat in an adjacent soft gray wing chair.

'It sounds like you're keeping a profile on me,' I said. I meant it as a light comment, but he didn't even crack a smile.

He glanced around the living room as if he was studying it with a fresh eye and then up at the wall hanging behind him. 'That's very nice. It adds a lot of color to the room.'

'Thank you. I made it. What I mean is I crocheted all the squares.' Talking about crocheting was easy and I elaborated. 'People crochet all kinds of different things, but I seem to have settled on squares.' I pointed out all the different stitch patterns. I considered whether I should mention that most of the squares had a story connected to them. What was going on in my life when I'd made it or how I'd gotten the particular yarn. I decided it opened too big a door to my personal life and let it be. I did pull out the bag I kept in the old straw sewing box next to the couch and took the half-done purple square out of the bag to show him. 'It's a pretty basic pattern.'

'Yarn and a cat,' he said. 'That's going to be tricky.' Rocky had just sauntered in and was considering where to go.

'It turns out he's not really interested in yarn. I think he's mostly just happy to have a home. He seems to hide a lot. Maybe he's worried about going back to the pet shop.' The large black-and-white cat jumped up on the couch and settled next to Ben as if he remembered that he'd been the one to rush out and get him his cat essentials. Ben responded by giving the cat a stroke from his head to his tail.

'Relax, buddy,' he said to the cat. 'I'm sure she's going to let you stay.'

I nodded in agreement still feeling keyed up. 'I don't want to keep you from your time with Sara and her family. I'm assuming you were on your way there for the dinner.' Maybe the drinks and the small talk had made him forget about why he'd come, and he could leave without me having to explain anything.

Or maybe not. My hopes dropped when he said he'd text his sister that he was at my place. When he looked up from his cell phone, he went into interrogation mode. 'How about you tell me what Tizzy was so worried about.'

There didn't seem to be any other choice, so I took a breath and began. 'As Tizzy said, there were three incidents.' I still had the small bag with the square in progress on my lap and started working on it as I talked. It somehow made it easier. 'I guess the best way to do it is to start with the first one. You remember you saw that padded envelope when you were helping with the cat?' I glanced at him and he nodded. 'There was a DVD in a box with no label. When I played it that night, it had photographs of the client I told the group about. Then the next day, Sara came upstairs and she asked me about what I was working on and I went to show her the DVD. But it had somehow changed to a bunch of cat pictures. Of course, that would be impossible. The more I thought about it the more I began to doubt myself. Did I really watch it the first time or maybe I'd dreamt it? I've had that client on my mind a lot and I had a bunch of pictures her family had given me. I could have somehow put it all together in my sleep.' I'd stopped crocheting as I talked and began to move the hook through the yarn again.

'And now for number two,' I said, trying to keep a light tone. 'The other night I was watching TV and the set started to do weird things. The channel would change to something else, and then change back. It was very quick, and I began to wonder if

I'd really seen what I thought I had. It made no sense. How could the TV do that? The volume had appeared to get louder and softer, too.' I glanced up at him to see how he was reacting to what I was saying. I expected something like what the cop out front had done. I thought Ben might be rolling his eyes or something, but he had the same expression or lack of that he always had.

'And lastly, there's number three. I received a package with a sweater I don't remember ordering. It was paid for with my credit card, but not the one I usually use for online shopping.' I stopped to take a breath. I'd given him the facts, now I would explain how Tizzy was involved.

'I was just going to let all of it go, but Tizzy stayed after the group outing the other night.' I glanced at him and made sure he knew what I was talking about. He muttered an apology for missing it, but said he'd had to work.

'Tizzy had forgotten to record some program on PBS and was going to miss it, so we started to watch it on my TV.' I gestured toward the dark screen across the room. 'Once again, the channel flipped back and forth, but this time she saw it too, so there was no question that it wasn't real. I told her about the other two incidents and she got all wound up, saying that they were the kinds of things someone would do if they wanted to gaslight you.' I checked to see if his face showed any recognition of the term. It didn't and I continued. 'The term comes from an old movie. Tizzy was insistent that I should watch it and then I'd understand what she was talking about. She even set it to record in the middle of the night.'

There was a moment of dead air as I waited for him to say something about what I'd told him. 'So the movie explains it?' he said, and I nodded. There was more dead air which was making me nervous, so I rushed to say something to fill it.

'I probably should watch it since Tizzy was so worked up about it. I don't suppose you'd like to see it?' I said, hoping he'd refuse.

'After what you said I'm curious. I would like to see it. Is it available now?'

'Well, yes, but are you sure you want to see it now? What about your dinner downstairs?'

He shrugged. 'I'm sure she'd be glad to give me a raincheck.' He was already writing a text to her as he spoke. I heard a *ping* as she replied, and he looked uncomfortable as he read her answer. 'Like I thought, no problem making our dinner another night.'

'OK,' I said, wondering what I'd gotten myself into. He offered to go to the restaurant across the street and get some food to go for us. 'You got it last time. I can make something as long as you don't mind that there's no meat,' I said, 'and it's nothing fancy.'

'I'm not fussy. I live on take-out fast food and frozen stuff. I'll help.' I wanted to say no, but he was on his feet before I could stop him.

When we got in the kitchen he looked around with interest. 'It's a lot different than my sister's,' he said. 'No offense.'

'None taken,' I said. 'Mine is pretty close to what it was like when this building was new. We replaced the sink, but there's no dishwasher or modern cabinets,' I said pointing at the bare walls. He wandered into the butler's pantry and looked up at the glass doors that covered shelves going all the way to the ceiling.

'I like the old stuff,' he said.

I used a small table in the middle of the room for food preparation and to hold appliances. There was a small pantry that had been for food storage but I, like almost everyone in the building, had turned it into a laundry area with a small washer and dryer that hung over it. He glanced at the former maid's room. I'd had shelves built in there and used it for storage.

I put some tomato soup on to heat and melted some butter for the grilled cheese sandwiches. Ben took over watching them, while I made some salad of Persian cucumbers, green onions, grape tomatoes and avocado. I added some seasoning and a sprinkle of balsamic vinegar.

I made conversation about the writing group as I poured the soup into bowls. 'I don't know how you manage to read Ed's work without any reaction,' I said.

Ben's face softened and he almost smiled. 'It's a little secret I have. I simply read the words without thinking about their meaning.' The sandwiches were nicely browned and the cheese oozing. He took them out of the pan and put them on the plates I'd set out.

'All I can say is thank heavens you're in the group. I don't think any of the rest of us could manage to read out loud "his throbbing tool" without embarrassed laughter.'

'You deserve an award with how you handle Daryl. I can only speak for myself, but I never want to say anything to her.' I could see his point. Daryl put us all in a difficult position. She over-reacted to anything that sounded like criticism, but if everyone just nodded and said 'good work,' she got upset, too, saying that wasn't helpful to her.

'It's all in how you say it,' I said. 'I stick to things like "don't you think it would be better if . . ."' I finished setting up the plates and put them on trays. We each grabbed one and went back to the living room. After depositing the trays on the table, we resumed our seats.

It was the most conversation I'd ever had with Ben and while he still seemed a stiff, he had loosened a bit. 'I'm glad to see there's another side to you. You've seemed pretty uptight in the group. I understand. It's hard to have your work read in front of a group.' I doubted that was the only reason he spoke in the monotone and seemed so closed up, but it seemed easier to give him an excuse.

He arranged his napkin on his lap and pulled the tray a little closer to him and I wanted to start the movie, but it seemed like he had something on his mind.

He smiled and tilted his head in agreement. 'She mentioned it. She thought it was something we had in common.'

'It looks like what we really have in common is that neither of us wants to go forward with her suggestion,' I said carefully.

I watched him take a deep breath and then let it out. His whole body seemed to relax. 'That's a relief.' He dipped the tip of his sandwich in the soup. 'I like your company, and of course the rest of the group's. The writing group is doing what Sara hoped it would – it gets me to be with people who aren't cops or suspects.' When he looked up, I saw he was smiling to let me know that was supposed to be a joke. So, he did have a sense of humor after all.

'Problem solved,' I said. 'We can be friends with no benefits.' I smiled to let him know it was a joke too. 'Let's watch the movie.'

I hit a few buttons on the remote and *Gaslight* began. It was in black and white and the sets looked artificial compared to movies now. It was also a little melodramatic, but it still got my attention and soon I forgot all about eating. The story was simple – a charming man played by Charles Boyer married a vulnerable woman played by Ingrid Bergman and he attempts to convince her she's going insane by making her believe she is seeing things that aren't there and that her memory isn't working right.

'Well, now I understand what Tizzy was talking about,' I said as I turned off the set when it finished, almost disappointed that the TV hadn't acted up. 'But the difference is someone was telling Ingrid Bergman's character that she was losing her mind while making things happen to reinforce what he was saying. I've just had weird occurrences.'

Ben ate the last of his food. 'The obvious fact is that unless you have a ghost, someone would have had to come into your place to switch the DVD.' He didn't say it, but I knew he meant that if it was real.

'There was no sign of anyone breaking in. I was gone a lot of that day,' I said with a shrug.

'Does anyone have keys to your place?' he asked.

'Your sister does,' I said.

TWENTY-FOUR

'You might have noticed that my sister has been trying to push us together. Giving me the birthday present of the writing classes and then her comments in the coffee shop.' He paused and glanced down at his phone, obviously thinking of the return text she'd just sent him. I was glad he didn't read it to me as I was sure she'd probably said something embarrassing.

I nodded. 'It's hard to miss.'

'Yes, she's not known for her subtly,' he said. 'I don't want you to take it personally that I haven't followed through.' He stopped and seemed to measure his words. 'I don't know how much she told you about me. She probably told you I was divorced.'

'She might have mentioned it,' I said. If I'd been uncomfortable telling him about the changing DVD, the mystery package and the crazy TV, it was nothing compared to how I felt about this line of conversation. I had no idea where it was headed.

'What did she say?'

I felt on the spot. I didn't want to admit that Sara had gone into a lot of detail. 'She just said that it had been hard on you.' This was getting uncomfortably personal. I had the TV remote in my hand and was tempted to flip on the set and just go to the movie.

'I'm supposed to be able to read people as part of my job. Figure out if someone is lying or going to be violent. I didn't have a clue that Marcy was unhappy until she left. Sara keeps pushing me to get back on the . . .' He stopped himself. 'I am not going to say "get back on the horse" even if she did. I remember what you said about clichés. Maybe "back out there" sounds better. Anyway, I'm not ready.'

'I understand. I'm really in the same place myself. The "not looking for a relationship" part. I'm sure Sara mentioned I was divorced too.'

He smiled and tilted his head in agreement. 'She mentioned it. She thought it was something we had in common.'

'It looks like what we really have in common is that neither of us wants to go forward with her suggestion,' I said carefully.

I watched him take a deep breath and then let it out. His whole body seemed to relax. 'That's a relief.' He dipped the tip of his sandwich in the soup. 'I like your company, and of course the rest of the group's. The writing group is doing what Sara hoped it would – it gets me to be with people who aren't cops or suspects.' When he looked up, I saw he was smiling to let me know that was supposed to be a joke. So, he did have a sense of humor after all.

'Problem solved,' I said. 'We can be friends with no benefits.' I smiled to let him know it was a joke too. 'Let's watch the movie.'

I hit a few buttons on the remote and *Gaslight* began. It was in black and white and the sets looked artificial compared to movies now. It was also a little melodramatic, but it still got my attention and soon I forgot all about eating. The story was simple – a charming man played by Charles Boyer married a vulnerable woman played by Ingrid Bergman and he attempts to convince her she's going insane by making her believe she is seeing things that aren't there and that her memory isn't working right.

'Well, now I understand what Tizzy was talking about,' I said as I turned off the set when it finished, almost disappointed that the TV hadn't acted up. 'But the difference is someone was telling Ingrid Bergman's character that she was losing her mind while making things happen to reinforce what he was saying. I've just had weird occurrences.'

Ben ate the last of his food. 'The obvious fact is that unless you have a ghost, someone would have had to come into your place to switch the DVD.' He didn't say it, but I knew he meant that if it was real.

'There was no sign of anyone breaking in. I was gone a lot of that day,' I said with a shrug.

'Does anyone have keys to your place?' he asked.

'Your sister does,' I said.

'Well then, we should talk to her.' He was already getting up from the couch.

I grabbed my keys and shut the door behind us. The light was on in the hallway and when I looked up through the skylight, I saw the moon in the night sky. We went down to the second floor and he knocked at the door, calling out that it was him.

When Sara saw that it was both of us, she got a knowing smile. 'You're together,' she said, sounding surprised and pleased. 'Come in, come.' Her smile had turned smug and I knew what she was thinking. All her efforts to match us up were working. First, we'd been together at the coffee shop and now here we were together again. Before she could say anything embarrassing, Ben gave her a severe look and a quick shake of his head.

'Veronica said that you have keys to her place. Have you let anybody in there in the last couple of days? Maybe somebody claimed to be a plumber or the pest control guy.'

Her smiled faded. 'What's going on?'

'You remember that DVD that I showed you?'

She shrugged. 'You mean the one that didn't have what you thought on it?'

'Yes, that one,' I said, and then gestured to Ben. 'I was telling him about it. And we were trying to figure out how the DVD could have been switched.'

Ben broke in. 'Someone would have had to have gone into her place to switch it. Did you let anyone up there and maybe forget to tell Veronica?'

She appeared shocked at the question. 'Of course not. The keys are for an emergency or if Veronica gets locked out. I wouldn't let anybody in her apartment and if I had, I'd have told Veronica.' She seemed upset with her brother. 'You know me better than that.'

'I'm sorry, but I had to ask. We were looking for a logical explanation.' She repeated that he should know her better than to think she'd be careless with my keys and he apologized again. I was still getting used to the change in him. I suppose he'd always been more relaxed with his sister, but he was suddenly like a new person to me. As they spoke, I felt like I was looking at him for the first time. I'd never noticed that his dark hair had a hint of a wave in it that probably would become curls if he didn't keep his hair cut so short. His brown eyes had always seemed flat, but now there was some life in them. His formerly expressionless mouth had actually gone into a smile before. The kind of smile that went all the way up his face and made crinkles around his eyes. He'd dropped the monotone and sounded like a regular person.

While they were having their brother-and-sister moment, I remembered something from the other day. I turned to Sara. 'Sorry to interrupt, but didn't you say you saw someone in the hall?' I said.

Sara thought it over and muttered something about how quiet it had been, then her face lit up with a memory. 'That's right. I did see a woman on the stairs. She introduced herself as Penny Clark, explaining she worked for the real estate company that manages the building and handles selling the condos. She seemed a little nervous, explaining that she was new at the job. She had someone who was interested in the unit across the hall from you.' She turned to her brother. 'The condo has been for sale for a while. You should look at it. Then you could see Mikey all the time.' She made just the slightest gesture toward me, then said, 'I'm afraid I was a little needy for adult company that day. She kept trying get away. She wanted to check the apartment to make sure it was presentable before she brought over the client. I told her the place was empty and tried to give her some information about the building, but she barely listened.'

'Thanks for the tip about the condo,' he said clearly filing it in the forget-about-it file in his mind. 'Did you see the prospective buyer?'

Sara shook her head. 'We went to the playground. They must have come while we were gone.'

'It doesn't matter anyway,' I said. 'It's not like she would have had keys to my place.'

A little voice started calling 'Mommy, Mommy,' or the toddler version of it, as something crashed in the other room. Sara looked panicked. 'Oh, no. I gotta go,' she said. 'Why don't you go back upstairs and put your heads together some more.' I had the feeling she didn't mean it like brainstorming either. I think she was hoping for something a little more literal. She rushed down the hall and we let ourselves out.

He hesitated at the landing and I thought he was going to say goodbye, but then he pointed toward the third floor. 'I left my jacket.' He followed me up to the next floor and glanced at the door to the apartment across the hall while I unlocked my door. 'Could the woman from the management company have had a master key?'

I shook my head. 'Everybody has their own locks.'

We went back into my living room and he looked at the trays on the coffee table. 'Let me help you clean up,' he said.

I let him carry his tray back to the kitchen and then we walked back down the hall toward the living room. 'It seems like we reached a dead end,' I said, as we passed through the entrance hall. I looked at my front door. 'Unless there's a way someone could have managed to pass through a solid wood door, I can't figure out how they could have come in here. I think I'll have to accept that I didn't really watch the DVD the first time. I was tired and I had pictures of that client I'd scanned into my computer. It probably all got mixed up in a dream.'

'Fine, maybe you did imagine it, but that doesn't mean you're losing your mind.'

'Right,' I said.

He thanked me for dinner and the movie. I thanked him for rescuing Tizzy and me from the cop before he decided we were both nut cases.

He grabbed his jacket off the end of the couch, and I opened the door. There was a moment of awkwardness of how to end the evening. When he was there for the writers' group, he just went out the door like the others with a quick goodbye. This time he stood in the doorway.

'Thanks for being so understanding about what I said. I didn't want you to take it personally.'

'I know. You said that,' I said. 'Don't worry, I didn't.' I smiled thinking of Sara. 'You know she's probably going to step up her campaign after seeing us together the last couple of days.'

He shook his head with mock regret. 'You're right.'

It seemed like there had to be some kind of gesture between us now that we were no longer just teacher and student. A hug was too much, but a handshake seemed weird. Rather than just thinking about it, I brought it up to him. 'It seems like a gesture should go along with our goodbye,' I said.

He smiled. 'How about an arm pat?'

'Arm pat, or upper arm squeeze?' I said, returning his smile.

'OK, how about this – on the count of three, we give each other an arm whatever,' he offered.

'Sounds like a plan,' I said.

We counted three together and I gave him an arm pat and he gave me an upper arm squeeze, then we both laughed and said goodnight.

Even if we'd reached a dead end on the mystery of the changing DVD, it had been quite an evening. It was as if the robot had come to life.

I had no idea that something was going to happen that would change everything.

TWENTY-FIVE

I felt at loose ends after Ben left. It had all been a little surreal. How he happened to visit and the visit itself. But I had things to do, so I pushed it out of my mind.

I left the dishes until later, made myself a strong cup of tea and went into my office determined to get some work done. But then I just sat, drinking my tea and looking around the room, stalling. I often wondered what this space had been designed for when the building was first built. It was separated from the living room by a pair of French doors, while another pair of French doors opened onto the entrance hall. There was a closet which made it seem like it was supposed to be a bedroom. Another door led to the shaving closet as it was called. The tiny space had a marble sink and a white tiled floor and opened onto the next bedroom as well.

Outside, the weather had changed and I could hear rain pelting loudly against the window. Instead of feeling cozy to be inside, I felt on edge.

I usually smiled when I used the square with a sunflower in the middle as a coaster. It was one of the first squares I'd crocheted that had a motif in the middle and I was really proud of it. Tonight I barely noticed. After Camille's phone call, I knew I had to work on Rachel's book first. I wrote up Mr Parker's story and positioned the photograph of Rachel on the boat. Since the booklet was still on the light side for copy, I sent an email to the teachers asking if they had anything else. I googled for clip art to sprinkle through the copy and found some nice boats, ballet slippers and a little schoolhouse. I started to look through a book of quotations but closed it after a few minutes.

My mind had wandered back to the evening with Ben. It was a little unsettling to see him as an emotionally functioning human. He even looked different since he'd dropped the brick wall he'd seemed to have had around him. I remembered giving him the

once-over when he'd come to the first session. My impression
was nice features, but no heat.

Personality wise, I'd tagged him as distant and cold and then
really hadn't thought much about him. Until now, though I
suppose it had started when he helped with the cat. I had to
recalculate my impression of him. He was actually OK, maybe
a little better than OK. I hadn't been totally honest when I said
I wasn't interested in a relationship. I wasn't averse to something
with the right person, but certainly not with him since he'd made
it so clear he had issues.

I thought about how I would describe Ben now. Nice guy with
nice features, could be heat. Details to follow as they become
known. It was easier with the rest of them. They'd been more
open from the start. Ed was the old guy with sex on the brain
who was basically a good guy and very helpful if I needed advice
on something that needed fixing in my place. His job was in
maintenance and he knew how everything worked, or why it
didn't, and he was generous with the information. Whenever I
thought about Daryl all I could think of was a minefield. It felt
like we were all walking through one when we discussed her
work. I often wondered why she kept coming to the group since
she was so upset with what anyone said. She stood out because,
unlike the rest of us, she was always dressed in the latest style
thanks to her job as manager of a trendy clothing store.

Tizzy was a whirlwind of enthusiasm, though there was more
of a comfort level with her than with the others since she lived
down the street and I'd known her before she'd joined the group.
Like Ed, she was generous about sharing. And injecting herself
in the middle of things. I thought back to the afternoon and what
she'd started with all her talk about gaslighting.

There was that word again. As soon as I even thought about
it, everything started to swirl around in my mind. What was real
and what wasn't. I thought about how I'd overreacted to the low
battery on the phone. How real was the concept of gaslighting?
Or was it something that Tizzy had grabbed onto and made more
of than it was? Was it even an actual term? I did what I always
did when I had a question about something – I researched it.
The first step was checking my paper dictionary. I pulled out
the heavy hard-bound book and thumbed through the almost

tissue-thin pages. Old habits die hard. I chided myself for thinking in clichés. The trouble was that they got the message across in a few words. I considered what other words I could use that had the same meaning. *It was my habit and it was hard to break.* It took more words and didn't have the same zing that the cliché had.

There was no entry for gaslighting. The closet word was gaslight and it referred to lights that were powered by gas.

I put the book back on the shelf and got more contemporary. I typed the word into my browser to see what would come up. I was surprised to see a whole list of information. It started with a definition from an online dictionary followed by a long list of articles and subheadings.

I clicked on the definition first and read that gaslighting was a transitive verb meaning to control a person by undermining their sense of reality by denying facts, denying the environment around them or denying their feelings.

Next I clicked on one of the entries about the movie. Along with a description that said *Husband manipulates his adoring wife into believing she can no longer trust her own perception of reality*, there were stills from the movie. Just seeing a picture of the Charles Boyer character with his sinister charm gave me the creeps. I moved on to the articles and read until my eyes were spinning. They all confirmed each other. Someone with bad intent manipulates someone else so that the person doubts their own perception. The likely perpetrators were spouses, even parents, bosses or co-workers and finally cult leaders.

It seemed the point of someone doing it was to get control over another person. It didn't quite fit in with what was going on with me since there was no person connected with the three strange incidents. But then I thought of Rachel. When I'd helped with her vows, she'd seemed confident and happy much like the Ingrid Bergman character at the beginning of the movie. But from what I'd heard from everyone I'd talked to recently, she'd become confused, forgetful and frantic like the Ingrid Bergman character when she was under the spell of the Charles Boyer character.

All along I'd been wondering what had happened to make her change. Now I began to think it was more a case of *who* had caused her to change. Could someone have pushed her so far to the edge that she felt there was no way out but to die? Made her so confused she didn't know what was real anymore? And the unsent text saying she needed help had been her way of saying she was giving up. She must have felt hopeless.

It was a crime to push someone to suicide, if that is what had happened. The question was who and how could it possibly be proven.

The rain had picked up in intensity and the wind had started to blow. The weather coupled with what I'd been thinking about left me feeling more on edge. I tried to brush it all aside and picked up the notes from the dance gym. Maybe if I typed them up, I'd get my mind on something else. I looked over the notes on belly dancing, but I couldn't concentrate on them. The more I tried the tenser I got. The drumming sound of the rain only made it worse. The best thing to do was walk away from my work for a while.

I emptied the undrunk strong tea into the sink and put the kettle back on. I pulled out a chamomile tea bag and put it in the mug. When the kettle whistled, I poured in the steaming water. The sweet floral scent of the tea was already beginning to calm me as I carried the mug back to the living room. The bag of crochet things was still sitting out from when I'd shown it to Ben. I picked up the hook and partially done square and began to crochet. Rocky came out from wherever he'd been hiding and joined me on the couch, as the storm really let loose. The wind was making the windows rattle and suddenly I felt a rush of cold wet air and saw that the door to the balcony had blown open.

I rushed to close it, making sure to click the lock. As I looked at the torrent of rain hit the dark balcony, I suddenly realized how someone could have come into my place.

TWENTY-SIX

The storm was forgotten by morning, but not what it had showed me. I took my coffee to the living room and stood looking out of the glass insert on the door to the balcony. I saw how easily someone could have come from the apartment across the hall. The divider between the two sides of the balcony would have been easy to slip over. It was barely waist high. And I'd left the door unlocked, so there would have been no problem getting into my place.

I had mixed feelings. A logical explanation meant that I hadn't imagined the pictures of Rachel, but it was disturbing to think someone had gone into my place with the intent to make me think my mind was going. Who could have done it?

And then I remembered Sara's story about the woman in the hall who was going to show the apartment across the hall to a potential buyer. I'd dismissed it when Sara had said it since there didn't seem to be a way into my place. But now I knew different and was suddenly very curious about who'd been next door.

After a quick shower I put on my gym uniform of a pair of black leggings and a loose black T-shirt. I added the boots and stowed my sneakers in a plastic bag.

I was glad to be getting close to the end of the different classes. I found them interesting and I needed the exercise, but they'd also become unrelenting. Just one class next week and I would have experienced them all.

It was lucky that I'd left a sticky note on my front door to remind myself to make sure the cat had food and water because I was so preoccupied by the time I left, I would have forgotten otherwise.

I was already thinking ahead to my stop at the management company that handled our building, to see if I could connect with the Penny person Sara had talked about. They were only open for a half a day on Saturdays and I'd stop on my way to the

train. I concocted a story that I hoped would get her to disclose
the identity of whomever she'd shown it to.

The receptionist was on the phone when I came in. She gestured
with her finger that she'd be off in a moment. I tried to see inside
the place, but there was a partition blocking off my view of the
desks. When she finally hung up, I told her I was looking for
someone named Penny.

'Sorry, she's not here. Can I help you with something?' she
said. This was not what I'd hoped for, but I was determined to
make the best of it. I had to come up with a new story on the
spot. One thing I'd learned when I'd written my mystery was
that detectives didn't have to tell the truth.

'She showed a perspective buyer my condo on Thursday, and
they left something at my place. I wanted to get it back to them,'
I said. The receptionist seemed disinterested and suggested I
leave a note for Penny. I realized I had to make it seem urgent.
'It was a bottle of medication. They probably didn't realize where
they dropped it. I only found it this morning, but what if it's
something life or death?' I said. 'I've tried calling Penny's cell
and texted her with no response, so I'm just trying to cover every
base. Maybe she has an appointment schedule in her desk,' I
offered.

The woman hesitated, but I could tell that she was weighing
what I'd said. Finally, she got up from the reception counter
and I stuck close to her as she went back into the office. All
the desks were empty. 'This is hers,' she said, pointing at one
near the wall. The top was clear and there were a few pieces
of paper in the inbox. The receptionist seemed uneasy, but
opened the top drawer and riffled through it. 'I don't see
anything.'

I sensed she was giving up and was going to show me the
door. I'd made my detective Derek Streeter persistent and I was
going to be the same. 'Do you have some kind of master list of
appointments?' I asked.

'I didn't think of that, but you're right.' She was hesitating
again. 'I'm not really supposed to do this, but since it sounds
like it could be an emergency.' We went back to the front and
she turned on her computer screen and started scrolling through
something. 'You said Thursday and where?' she asked, and I

nodded before giving the address. 'Here it is.' She read off the time and the location.

'What's the name?' I asked quickly.

'F. Poppins,' she said, looking again. 'And there's a phone number. I can't give you the number, you know, security. But I'll call them for you.' I was disappointed that the name meant nothing to me, but let her make the call. A moment later, I heard her ask for F. Poppins. There was a pause before she hung up and turned to me. 'It was a hotel and they didn't have anyone by that name registered. They were probably in town looking for a place and left.'

I didn't know what to think. What the receptionist said could be true, or it could be a fake name and a fake number. I really wished I could talk to Penny and get a description of the person. As it was, I didn't even know if it was a man or woman.

There was no choice but to give up for now. I thanked her and left, hurrying for the train station.

I ended up on a local train that took forever to get downtown and I rushed the few blocks to Dance with Me. I just had time to leave my things and change my shoes before the hip-hop class started. The teacher introduced herself as Lola and said she was a substitute. She did the usual pitch that the class was meant to be fun. Like all the other classes, it started with a warm-up and then moved on to the dance moves. I did my best to follow along. We did some upward arm moves. There were more arm moves that I thought of as the hip-hop hula. We added feet with a running move and then squatting and rolling our hips around. Lola kept saying it was all about putting attitude into your moves.

'What did you think of the class?' Darcy asked, as I went past the reception counter. She was busy putting away a new shipment of ballet slippers.

'I'm trying to think how to describe it,' I said. 'Maybe get your groove with attitude.' I pulled out my notebook and was ready to write something down.

'You look a little stressed? Is everything all right?' Darcy asked.

'Oh, no, does it show?' I said feeling self-conscious. She seemed genuinely concerned and I considered telling her about my week, but she was also a client. I never wanted to give the impression that I was overburdened. I mentally went over the stress causers in my life. Let's see . . . I'd adopted an adult cat – the first pet of my life; my relationship with one of my students had changed and was confusing; somebody might be trying to make me think I was losing my mind; I had a deadline to finish Rachel's memory book with an impossible person to please; I had to create the publicity material for the dance gym from the notes I'd taken; and I had to see what was next with Evan. I parred it down and just told her about Rocky and making sure to reassure her that I was on top of the publicity project for the gym.

'I should have it all for you next week. I'm still working on the bio for Debbie. We never seem to have time to talk. She's a busy lady, always on her way out of the door. I need more about her background and her philosophy.'

'I'll tell her you want to talk to her on Monday and make sure she doesn't leave,' Darcy said. 'Enjoy your weekend.'

'You too,' I said as I made my way out the door.

Evan hadn't called me to let me know if my invitation in verse had worked. I didn't want to call him in case the news was bad, but I was also really curious. I knew what time Evan had booked the tour, so decided to do a little spying.

The storm had left the air cool and fresh. The sky was an electric blue and contrasted nicely with the golden and red leaves on the trees that lined the wide street. I walked quickly and stopped when I got to the middle of the Michigan Avenue Bridge. Down below a crowd was waiting to board the architectural cruise. I looked through the people with my fingers crossed that I'd see Sally and Evan. The cruises only ran for a couple more weeks before it got too cold. I shivered thinking of how the river iced over during the winter.

I didn't realize I'd been holding my breath until I finally picked them out of the crowd, and I let it out in a gush of relief. Evan grabbed her hand and led her to the entrance. I couldn't see her expression to tell if she liked the contact, but he looked super happy and cute with his floppy hair. I knew I'd hear from him afterwards. What would he want me to do next?

I continued over the bridge to the Bellingham Hotel. I'd brought the piece I'd written for Richard Parker and was going to use it as an excuse for seeing Luke. I'd ask his opinion and by the way mention the money I'd heard he stood to inherit. I was curious what he'd say. When I got to the bar, someone else was working it. 'Where's Luke?' I asked the dark-haired man.

'Everybody loves Luke,' he said with a smile. 'Nobody comes in when he's working and asks for me. The name's Jax,' he said offering his hand. 'Are you a friend or one of his many regulars?'

'Neither exactly. I'm Veronica Blackstone and I've been working on a celebration of life book for his wife.' I shrugged. 'But I've gotten to know him, so I suppose that makes me a friend.' He offered me a seat at the bar. 'I was hoping to show him something I'd gotten for the book.'

'What can I get for you?' he asked. The walk had left me thirsty and I asked for a sparkling water with a twist of lime. He gave me the drink and I went to check the messages on my phone. I laughed when I saw that Evan had sent me a selfie of him and Sally. The wind was blowing her hair into her face making it hard to tell if she was smiling or grimacing. Evan appeared thrilled.

I looked over the clientele. There were a few single men, drinking and looking at their cell phones. A woman sat alone at the end of the bar with an almost empty wine glass. She had the melted look of someone who'd drunk too much. The bartender stopped in front of her and swiped her phone off the counter as he did. He moved down the bar and I saw him doing something with it.

He saw me watching him and as soon as he laid the phone back down came over to me. 'I wasn't doing anything nefarious. We have an understanding that we'll use a patron's phone to arrange a ride for them when they'd had too much to drink.'

A few minutes later, the woman's phone began to vibrate, and the bartender grabbed it and pointed something out to the woman. She gave him a boozy smile as he helped her to the elevator. 'She even said thank you,' Jax said to me on his way back, showing off a twenty-dollar bill.

'I don't suppose you have a nice story about Luke's wife I could put in the book I'm doing,' I said.

'Only that the poor guy seemed devastated when she died. Of course, he kept it all under wraps here. He looks at his job as far more than making drinks. That's why he's the manager and so well liked. He always looks after all our patrons.'

And one of them had become his wife. It made me wonder about his relationships with the others.

'And you fill in when he has time off,' I said, thinking back to when I'd stopped at the bar in the middle of the day. I knew that whoever had been next door to my place had been there in the late afternoon. 'What about last Thursday? Did you take over for Luke?'

He shook his head. 'As far as I know he was here all day.'

I made myself a late lunch when I got home and thought over my day so far. I'd completed one more dance class, Evan had gone on his date, and I was wondering about Luke. Was he really as he appeared to be? When I'd worked on their vows, he'd seemed easygoing. He wasn't controlling or demanding. He'd seemed supportive of Rachel's wishes. I'd gotten to know him more in the last couple of weeks and all I could say about him was that he'd been nice. The bartender's explanation of why Luke hadn't appeared so devastated made sense. He hid it behind the front he kept up for the public. You could say that Luke was perfect. But I was always suspicious of perfection.

I went into my office ready to get down to work. Between the storm and my nerves, I'd basically wasted the time the night before.

The deadline for the celebration of life book was looming and I had to get it together to give to Camille Parker in just two days. She'd turned into the worst kind of client. She was probably impossible to please and she seemed to take pleasure in making me feel lesser than. Even so, I wanted to do the best I could for Rachel's memory.

I checked my email, hoping there would be something back from the teachers. There was a note from the pet shop asking me to come in and meet a terrier named Reginald who was another hard-to-adopt. No details on why, but I was already getting worried for the dog's future. I looked at Rocky and wondered if he'd end up with a dog roommate. Under that, there was an email from one of the teachers, who had sent some more photographs of Rachel and her students. I decided to expand the section about her teaching and to make it more emotional. I added onto the stories about Rachel's generosity and wrote that Rachel could have taught anywhere, but she'd chosen a school where she could make a difference. I illustrated it with the photographs I'd just gotten of Rachel standing with the kids all hugging her.

There was also an email from Luke with the photo of Rachel in the cheesehead hat. The picture was silly and made me smile. I wrote up the story Luke had told me about their trip to Wisconsin and included the picture. I looked over everything and when I got to the end of the copy, I made up my own quote and put it in. *Never gone when you leave love behind.* I played around with it until I got it in a font I liked and added some clip art of a heart and some flowers.

I sat back and looked at the screen. I'd worked non-stop with no sense of time. Now I would let it sit overnight and give it a last polish on Sunday.

I felt on a roll, so I moved on to write up what I had for Dance with Me. My notebook had plenty beyond just the descriptions of the classes. I had their mission statement and the fact they were a single place rather than a chain. There were scribbled down sentences that I hoped captured the personality of the place. For now, I set all of that aside, determined to work on the piece about Debbie Alcoa, so I could see what was missing and get it from her on Monday. I wrote up a draft and saw the holes in the piece. Grabbing my notebook, I wrote down that I needed to know when she started dancing and where she'd studied and something about her philosophy of dance and exercise. It was then that I saw that I left myself a note to ask her about Rachel, hoping she'd have something I could use. But now I realized it would be too late.

I was about to start on a description of the hip-hop class since it was fresh in my mind when I got a call from Ed. He was so excited he could barely talk. He'd sent in one of his fictional dating show stories to a website devoted to a fictional dating program called *Finding the Right Mate*. They'd posted his piece and it had gotten a lot of likes. Now they'd asked for more. He had something ready, but wanted me to give it another look before he submitted it. I agreed to let him come by later, hoping he didn't expect me to read his work out loud.

TWENTY-SEVEN

I looked around as I hung up the phone from the call with Ed and was surprised to see that it had gotten dark. I'd completely lost the sense of time when I'd been working. It was commonly referred to as being in the flow and was a writer's dream.

My cell phone pinged announcing a text. Sara had some leftovers from dinner and was offering them to me. I gratefully accepted since I'd suddenly noticed I was hungry. I'd barely hit send and there was a knock at the door. I opened it expecting to see my neighbor, but instead it was Ben.

'Oh,' I said surprised as I reached for the plate, hoping to thank him and then shut the door.

'I have orders to watch you eat it,' he said. 'She wants to know what you think of the dish, or so that's what she said.' There would be no peace from Sara unless I let him follow her orders.

'C'mon in,' I said stepping aside so he could enter. He had the blank expression again and I wondered if he'd gone back to his old self.

'This was another makeup dinner from the missed one on Tuesday. As soon as she heard I had the day off, she said Mikey was asking for me.' He looked at the plate I was holding. 'It's really good. Pasta with vegetables. Ours had meatballs mixed in.' He stopped and smiled. 'Fine detective I'd make. It wasn't until now that I realized she'd planned these "leftovers." She had to set aside some of the pasta and vegetables before she added the meatballs.' There was some light in his eyes and intonation in his voice now and he was back to being the new and improved Ben.

'Very crafty of Sara,' I said, smiling too. 'But I'm glad she did. It's better than whatever I could come up with from my refrigerator. It's pretty bare.'

'I think that's my fault,' he said with a guilty look, referring to the dinner I'd given him the night before.

'That's OK and, even if it was, you made up for it with this.' I held up the plate before glancing around the living room. 'I guess I could eat it in here, so you'll be freed of your duty quickly.' I grinned to make sure he understood I was joking and offered him a drink.

'Don't go to any trouble,' he said.

'I have coffee, tea or more sparkling water.' He seemed disappointed and probably thought I meant beer or something alcoholic. 'I have wine,' I said quickly, remembering the bottle I kept for cooking. 'All I can tell you about it though is that it's red and adds a nice taste to my vegetable stew.'

'Sounds good to me,' he said. I went back to the kitchen and got him a glass of the wine and myself one of sparkling water.

When we were finally seated, Rocky came in. He walked to the balcony door and looked at it with interest.

'What's that about?' Ben asked, watching the cat. I'd been so focused on getting to my work, I'd forgotten all about the storm the night before and how the door had blown open and I'd realized how somebody could have come in. It was embarrassing and I wondered if I really wanted to tell Ben about it. Now that I'd taken care of the problem, it wouldn't happen again anyway. But I also felt I owed him since he'd tried to help me figure out how someone could have come into my place.

'The door blew open last night during the storm and he probably got a whole feast of outdoor smells and wants them again.' I gathered up some of the pasta on my fork. 'And in the process, I realized that's how someone could have come in.' Ben got up and walked to the door, looking out through the glass portion.

'I must have left the door unlocked. I never really thought much about it since this is the third floor and unless somebody scaled the wall of the building or managed to climb the tree out front without breaking the branches and falling out of it, there's no way to the balcony.'

'Except from the apartment next door,' Ben said.

'I knew the people who lived there before and well, it's been empty for a while now. And I didn't think that anybody would ever try to get in.'

'You should talk to the real estate person – the one who Sara saw in the hall.'

'I already have,' I said. I was still holding the forkful of pasta and finally took a bite. It was delicious.

'And?' he said. 'You're not going to leave it at that.'

'I didn't mean to stop mid-story, but the pasta smelled so good and it was sitting on my fork.' I put the fork down while I told him about my trip to the management office. 'There's nothing to prove that F. Poppins wasn't a real potential buyer looking at the place across the hall. I'm back to thinking I did just imagine the pictures.' Before he could comment the doorbell rang. There was nothing bell-like about it. It had more of a buzzing sound. Whoever had arranged for the doorbells must have picked out the most irritating choice. The only good point was that it was impossible to miss.

'It's Ed,' I said, getting up to press the button to unlock the downstairs door for him.

Ed was just coming up to the third-floor landing as I opened the door. He was dressed in the usual track pants and a windbreaker, but his demeanor was different. He was all animated and held out a pile of papers. 'This is it,' he said. 'I'm going to be on the website again.' He paused in the entrance hall and he glanced into the living room. His gaze went right to Ben holding his glass of wine and on to the plate of food and back to me. 'Wine, food, looks pretty cozy. Am I interrupting something?'

He stared at Ben. 'You look different. You're smiling,' he said in an accusatory tone. 'Are you trying to be teacher's pet?'

I almost laughed. Ed sounded jealous that Ben might be getting secret extra writing help. 'You're the one getting the extra help,' I reminded him, pointing at the pile of pages. 'Ben was visiting his sister and she sent him up with a plate of leftovers.'

Ed sniffed the air. 'Looks tasty,' he said, taking a seat to the side of the couch. I saw him looking at Ben's wine and I offered him a glass with the same qualifier that I used it for cooking.

'I'll take it,' he said, seeming unconcerned about the quality. I left them and went in the back to get him his drink. I had to search for another wine glass. I really needed to be more prepared for company.

He'd taken the glass and was already sipping it before I'd even sat down. This time I avoided the middle and sat on the far side from him.

'So if he's not getting extra writing help, why's he here?' Ed said to me. 'He could have just given you the plate of food. It is Saturday night. Maybe there's a little romance in the air between you two, huh?'

'Not at all,' I said quickly. 'Actually, Ben and I were discussing some weird stuff that's been going on with me.'

'Kinky weird stuff,' Ed said, his eyes getting brighter.

'Hardly. Do you know the movie called *Gaslight*?'

'The old black-and-white film with Charles Boyer and Ingrid Bergman, sure,' he said with a shrug.

I told him about the changing DVD and the other two happenings. 'Tizzy thought that someone was trying to gaslight me and Ben was trying to help me figure how someone could have gotten in here and switched the DVD.'

'Why didn't you talk to me?' he said, sounding hurt. 'I'm good at figuring things out. You forget, I'm a maintenance engineer at the university and deal with bizarre situations all the time.'

'It's not too late,' I said.

He asked for more details about the TV and I told him the channel had switched back and forth and the volume changed. 'Tizzy was here when it happened the second time,' I said.

'Tizzy was here watching TV with you?' he said almost pouting.

'It was the other night after the group outing. She forgot to record a program and was going to miss it. She told you about it, but you said you had to get home.' I couldn't believe the fuss he was making.

'Oh, OK,' he said. He got up and looked around the living room and then went to the window. 'I think I have an answer,' he said, and then asked for the remote. He did some fiddling with it and then started to laugh.

I got up to see what was going on. I followed his gaze out the window and across the street. I could see the big-screen TV suddenly change stations. The guy watching it jumped and then looked around. 'There's your demon,' he said. Ed laughed again and he used my remote again. The channel changed and the guy got up and seemed to be examining the set. I knew exactly how he felt. 'I told you I'm good at figuring out stuff.'

'You mean it was that guy?' I peered closer. 'But he did it by accident, right?'

Ed looked across the street and thought about it. 'Naw, I think it was deliberate. You have stand in the window and aim the remote just right.'

'But I don't know him. Why would he want to bother me?'

By now Ben had joined us, looking out the window. 'Maybe it wasn't him.' He pointed at the apartment next to them. The windows were dark.

'That flat is for lease,' I said, remembering I'd seen the sign in front of the building.

Ben and I looked at each other. 'F. Poppins strikes again,' he said.

'F. Poppins?' Ed asked. To make sure he didn't feel left out, I told him about the real estate agent and the story of who had looked at the apartment across the hall from me.

I looked toward the windows. 'You know, it could have just been the TV set malfunctioning,' I said.

'Sure,' Ed said with a shrug. 'But if you don't mind, can we get down to going over my work? I'm hoping I can be a regular on the fictional dating show website. If I get enough followers, I'll even get paid.' He handed me the pages.

'Do you want Ben to read them out loud?' I asked, biting my lip so not to smile.

'No,' Ed said. 'I'm not looking for any of your suggested word changes.' He gave us both a look that made it clear of what he thought of the group's effort to get him to tone down his word choices. 'They like it just the way I write it. No hiding behind some romance novel terms like his "maleness." When Callan gets Cleopatra in their version of the Getting to Know You Suite, I'm very clear that he's talking about his—'

'We get the picture,' Ben interrupted, and then gave me a wink. I almost thought I'd imagined it. Was Ben of the flat voice and expressionless face actually being playful?

'OK, then. I just want you to make sure all the commas are in the right place,' Ed said.

I read the pages while the two men sat looking at each other. Then one of them brought up the last Bears game and all the awkwardness went away. Chicago people were true sports fans.

They loved their teams win or lose. I handed the sheets back to
Ed with a few grammatical corrections. I hoped I wasn't blushing.
All I could say was Callan and Cleopatra had quite a session,
using every inch of the Let's Do It Suite.

Ed took the sheets back and glanced over them quickly. He
didn't seem to have any issue with the corrections I'd made and
thanked me. 'I'll make you proud,' he said, getting up. 'I guess
being on the website makes me your star pupil.' He sounded like
he was gloating. I started to get up to walk him to the door. 'I
can let myself out. Then you two can get back to whatever you
weren't doing,' he said with a chuckle.

Ben watched the door close and gave it a minute for Ed to be
on his way down the stairs. 'I think the dynamic of the group
just changed. Star student – in his own mind,' he said, shaking
his head. He looked at the almost empty plate. 'I guess my work
is done. I can take a report back to Sara that you liked the food.
Any comment you want to add?'

'You can tell her it was great, and I'll get the plate back to
her tomorrow.' I waited for him to stand up, but he didn't seem
to be making a move, so I did. He followed suit and looked
around the room again.

'I know you said you're back to thinking you imagined the
photographs and the TV could have been something in the set,
but you know there might be something in that gaslighting business.' He seemed thoughtful. 'Maybe you should contact that
cop Tizzy flagged down and tell him about F. Poppins.'

'Really? And tell him what? That a mystery person might have
come into my place so they could pull what was basically a
prank.'

'What about if I talked to him cop to cop?' Ben said. Then
he thought about what he'd said. 'You're right.' It seemed to be
taking him a long time to take the few steps to the front door.
'Just make sure you keep that balcony door locked.'

When we got to the door, Ben smiled. 'I don't remember, did
you do the shoulder squeeze and I did the arm squeeze?'

There was a comedy of errors as we tried to reenact our
goodbye move from the night before. When he left, I thought
my evening was over, but there was more company to come. And
there would be a surprise revelation about the third incident.

TWENTY-EIGHT

S ara barely waited until Ben left for home before texting me that Mikey was asleep and Quentin was glued to the TV and was I up for some company. I was sure that a big part of her motivation was to find how things were going between Ben and me. I knew she was going to be disappointed, but told her to come up anyway.

'So, tell me everything,' Sara said, as she walked in. 'In fact, tell me anything that has nothing to do with Engineer Billy and his train crew. You might notice that Mikey has a thing for trains. Quentin just wants to watch sports and I need some adult conversation.' She was dressed in yoga pants and a sweatshirt. Her brown hair was pulled into a ponytail and there might have been a rogue piece of macaroni caught between the strands.

I hadn't even had time to clear up before she arrived. She came into the living room and her gaze went right to the two empty wine glasses on the coffee table.

'You drank wine with Ben,' she said, sounding surprised and excited. Before she could build it into something, I told her about Ed's visit.

'Oh, I thought you two were alone.' Her disappointment was obvious, and I figured I better clue her in on the actual situation between her brother and me.

'First of all, there is no need for Ben and me to be alone. We talked over your efforts to push us together yesterday and Ben was very clear he's off limits when it comes to a relationship, which by the way is fine with me. I'm in pretty much the same place. We're fine with being friends, and he's been helping me solve the mystery of the switching DVD,' I said in a light tone.

Her eyes went to the empty wine glasses again. 'Did they drink it all?' she asked.

'Nope, you want a glass?' I was already grabbing the empties when she nodded. I let her sit and enjoy the peace with being off mom duty while I took everything back to the kitchen. I washed up one of the glasses and returned with it filled with the dark red liquid.

'You know that friends thing never works,' she said, as she accepted the glass. She took a generous sip.

'Except if you're both on the same page – and we are.'

She let out a disbelieving sigh and then shrugged it off. 'You said you figured out something about that DVD.'

It was embarrassing, but I told her the whole story about the unlocked balcony door and what I'd found out about the mystery person who'd looked at the apartment across the hall. 'That person could have come into my place and switched them. I wish I could have gotten a description of them.'

'If only we hadn't gone to the park and I'd been a nosy neighbor, I might have gotten a peek at the person.' I didn't say anything, but I thought she had the nosy neighbor thing down.

She knew Ed was in the writing group and wanted to know why he'd come over.

'Sorry I asked,' Sara said, making a face when I got finished telling her about Callan and Cleopatra's adventure in the private suite being posted to a website.

'But he did serve a useful purpose,' I said. 'He figured out what could have made my TV seem possessed.'

She looked puzzled and I realized the only weird happening she knew about was the DVD. I went through the whole thing with her including the concept of gaslighting and the movie. 'But I think it's over with. You know how things come in threes?' The rule of three was really more of a superstition thing, but it felt like it was true.

'Wow, I sure feel out of the loop. There were three incidents? What's the third one?'

'That one might have actually been an accident.' I told her about the package arriving with a sweater that I was sure I didn't order. 'I had put it in my wish list. Maybe the store's app somehow opened on its own and I hit something and placed the order by mistake.'

Sara was an expert at buying things on her phone. It was easier than trying to navigate an actual store with a toddler. She asked for my phone and we checked the app. 'It might have opened on its own, but I don't see how you could have just hit something by mistake and ordered it. You would have had to at least put in your CVS code,' she said shaking her head. 'Someone must have used your phone.'

I was about to say impossible when a vision of the Bellingham bar came into my mind's eye. The bartender had used the patron's phone to order a ride for her. I thought back to when Luke had been working. I'd laid my phone on the bar and left it there when I went to the powder room. I'd left my credit card with the bill at the same time.

'What's with you?' Sara asked. 'You have the strangest look on your face. As if you'd just found the tooth fairy wasn't real.

'Or maybe that Prince Charming turned out to be a toad.'

TWENTY-NINE

I could always tell when it was Sunday. There was a special quietness. The apartment buildings on either side of the street made a canyon that funneled the noise from the street up and when any big trucks rumbled by, it seemed like they were driving in my living room. But on Sunday, there were none. Instead I heard church bells when I went to the small grocery shop around the corner to pick up the Sunday paper. I knew it made me seem like a dinosaur, but I liked the print edition.

When I got home, I put some coffee on to brew – I always drank French roast on Sunday – and I took a waffle out of the freezer. I made a batch of them from scratch the week before and then froze them to be used as needed.

When I took my breakfast into the dining room, a beam of sunlight had managed to squeeze between the brick wall of the next building and mine, bathing the table in warm light. It was the perfect Sunday morning, but I couldn't enjoy it.

All I could think about was Luke. I didn't have to be Sherlock Holmes to figure out that if he was behind the efforts to make me think I was losing touch with reality, he'd done it to Rachel, too.

Rachel had been so in love with him and trusted him. It made me look at everything in a new way. The teachers had said Rachel changed after the summer off. He must have spent the whole time playing mind games with her. He could have easily arranged for packages she didn't remember ordering and texts that she didn't remember sending.

When he told me Rachel could have used a friend, it was just a cover. Having a friend was probably the last thing he would have wanted for her. A friend would have seen what he was doing.

There had to be a dark side to him behind that easy-going charm. He was like the Charles Boyer character only worse, because Luke was real, not some character in a movie. What was his goal? Was it to make her feel so lost that there seemed no way out?

Did he already have someone on the side? I had an upsetting thought: what if it was Sally? She worked at the hotel and could know Luke. Maybe she and Luke were just waiting until every-thing was settled and then they'd come out as a couple. Oh, no, poor Evan if that was true. The big question was what could I do about it? Go to the police? I thought of the expression on the cop's face when Tizzy was telling him about the DVD and my TV. Unless I had some kind of proof, I'd seem like a nut case with a vivid imagination. And what kind of proof could there even be? It was hopeless. The best thing to do was to let it go.

I looked down at my plate. I'd eaten the waffle and drunk the coffee without even noticing. The newspaper was still folded on the table. It would have to wait until later. For now I had to get back to work and finish the memory book.

I opened up the file with the celebration of life book and started to go through it, looking at every word and image. I read the copy, making a correction here or there and rewriting an occasional sentence. I was tense the whole time. I had to please Camille Parker. Then I sighed to myself. Even if it pleased Camille Parker, she'd never say it. As I read it over again, I decided that the only part she would really care about was the section I'd made up about the shower she and her daughters had put on for Rachel. It was probably fine the way it was, but as extra insurance I added that the event had been a gift from the heart and that all the guests raved about Mrs Parker's skill at entertaining. I made sure that I included a photograph showing Camille in her best light.

I went over the piece about Mr Parker taking Rachel to work with him. It seemed to me to be perfect, though that alone was probably going to stir up Camille's ire. Then I looked at the two stories Luke had provided.

I suddenly saw their trip to Door County in a different way. They'd been away from it all. Away from everyone. He could have used the time to begin the whole process of confusing her. I wondered if I should say something to Camille about Luke. No. Assuming she even believed me, the last thing she wanted was any kind of scandal.

I read the whole thing over numerous times until the words ceased to make sense anymore. Then I printed up the pages and put them in a plastic binder. I made a title sheet with Rachel's name and dates of her birth and death, along with some flourishes before sliding it into the plastic sleeve on the cover. I also copied everything on to a thumb drive. The final thing was to pack it in my blue leather messenger bag I used as a briefcase. And I was done.

I always had a bittersweet feeling when I finished a project, but I was even more emotional and confused about this one.

When I finally looked up from the computer it was long past sunset. Rocky had come into the room unnoticed and was sitting in my reading chair. It was time to think about dinner for both of us. He got some pinky-looking fish, and it was scrambled eggs, toast and a sliced orange for me. I started to read the paper, but I was too tense. I kept thinking of all I had to do the next day. The plan was to meet Camille Parker first. I knew that once that was over with, I could relax and go to the gym to collect whatever additional information I needed and take the last class. If all went well, I was treating myself to a nice lunch. It was only when I was getting ready for bed that I realized I hadn't heard anything from Evan. I wondered what that meant.

THIRTY

Monday morning, I awoke to the sound of the garbage truck making a pickup. Rocky was asleep on my pillow behind my head again. It seemed like a good sign that he was feeling at home. I was anxious to get going on my day. I was anxious to get my meeting with Camille Parker over with. I was just anxious.

Getting dressed was tricky. It was important for me to look professional, but I also had that last gym class to take. I wore my usual black leggings paired with a long black tunic on top. It was a little dressy for the dance class, but I was sure it would be fine. I finished it off with a jean jacket and a scarf. My walking shoes would have to do for both. Just when I was about to leave, my cell phone rang.

It was Evan. 'I want to hear everything,' I said, as I grabbed the messenger bag and headed for the door. 'But I'm rushing for the train.' As soon as he heard I was going downtown, he wanted to meet me. It was important that we met in person because he had something he wanted to show me. I told him about my schedule, and he offered to meet me after class at the Starbucks near the dance gym.

I signed off just as I shut the front door. I tried to tell myself to calm down as I walked down the street, but commands and deep breaths didn't do a thing. It didn't help that I heard the train arriving just as I'd started up the stairs to the platform. I ran all the way up the stairs and rushed onto the train just as the conductor was about to close the doors.

I walked the six blocks to the Parkers' building without paying much attention to my surroundings. And then I was there being ushered in by the doorman.

'At least you're on time,' Camille said, when she opened the door. As before, there was no welcoming smile or even a good morning. I followed her into the living room and was surprised to see her daughters sitting on the couch. They appeared to be in their early twenties, and had that polish that came from expensive clothes and a lot of spa time. In other words, they were junior models of their mother. When it seemed she wasn't going to bother introducing me, I did it myself and told them I'd included them in the book. They looked at me like I was the help. I was actually glad that Camille didn't make any pretense about it being social by offering me a drink or even a seat. I just wanted to show her what I'd done and get out of there. Maybe a tiny part of me would have also liked to ask her about Luke, but I'd already dealt with the fact it was pointless.

'Let's see it,' she said, holding out her hand.

I pulled out the binder and pointed out the envelope containing the thumb drive attached on the inside. I thought the presentation was quite nice, but she didn't seem to notice. She flipped through all of the pages first and went back and started to read. I worried how she'd react when she got to the story I'd created from what Mr Parker had said, since the very fact I'd talked to him had set her off. Her face never changed as she went through the pages and it was impossible to read her reaction. She finally got to the end and I felt my heart rate kick up. This was it.

'Well?' I prompted.

She glanced at it again and pursed her lips. 'You stirred up a hornet's nest,' she said. I flinched at the cliché but wasn't going to mention it to her or offer other word choices. She hardly looked in the mood. 'Mr Parker wasn't supposed to be involved. I was trying to protect him and now he's upset with me.' She scowled and I thought back to what he'd said to me. He'd thanked me for what I'd done. He probably hadn't meant it and was angry at me, too. I just apologized again and again.

It calmed her only slightly and she said something about the book would have to do in a dismissive tone. And she handed me a check for half of the agreed amount without comment. What was I going to do, sue her?

Without even a thank-you or have a nice day, she led me to the door. And then I was in the hall. The only thing I could say was that the job was done. I went down the hall to the elevator wondering how my reduced pay was going to affect my celebration lunch. I'd probably stick to a peanut butter and jelly sandwich when I got home.

I pushed the button for the elevator and was joined by a woman with several dogs on leashes. I smiled and reached down to give their heads a pat and looked up at the woman as I stood. She looked familiar. 'Do I know you?' I asked.

She looked at me in the same manner. 'I know,' she said after a moment. 'We met at the Pet Emporium.'

'That's right, you're the dog walker,' I said remembering meeting her.

'And you're the writer,' she said.

'I guess we're both here in our professional capacities,' I said, giving the dogs a nod. I held out my messenger bag. 'I just delivered the material for a memory book,' I said, pointing down the hall.

'It's for the woman who went off the balcony, isn't it?' she said. 'Melissa said you did some work for her family.'

'That's right. And she told me that you were here the day it happened.'

The elevator arrived and we got on and it began to go down.

She nodded and then seemed to be thinking about something. 'I never put it together until now. I'd just picked up a pair of poodles I walk regularly who live next door. I noticed someone come out of that woman's apartment.' She paused to collect herself. 'And when I got downstairs, she was already on the ground.'

I was processing what she'd told me. Everyone had said that Rachel was alone when she went off the balcony, but if someone was there, well, it changed everything. At the very least, it meant they hadn't stopped her and at the very worst had urged her to do it. 'Was it a man, or a woman? What did they look like?' I asked.

'I just saw them in my peripheral vision. It could have been a woman, but I'm not sure. The poodles went wild and I was worried about corralling them before they jumped at the person. By the time I got to the elevator, there was no one there.' Her description didn't eliminate anyone.

We went our separate ways when we got downstairs. The sidewalks were more crowded now that it was midday, but I barely noticed as I wondered about the person who'd been there during Rachel's last moments.

I had to let the thoughts go when I got to Dance with Me. Besides, what could I do about anything with Rachel anyway? The job for her was over. I was hardly in the mood for a class called A Latin Beat but it was the last one I had left to experience. People were just arriving for the next class when I got to the dance gym. Darcy was at the reception counter, but the woman who subbed for her was checking people in. Debbie was in the front and just setting up. I dropped off my stuff and took out the sheet with what I'd written about her and the questions I had. I wasn't taking any chances that she'd run off before I could get the information. I'd ask her before class.

She looked up when I approached. 'Hi,' I said with a friendly smile. 'I thought we could try talking before the class.'

She didn't appear sold. 'I don't know how much better that will work. When it's time to start the class, no more questions.'

I assured her I only needed a few details and asked her a few questions about her background, which she answered in a couple of sentences. I scribbled down her answers and was about to turn to go. 'When I first came here, I was looking for stories about Rachel – I guess you knew her as Ray. Now that I have the time to ask you about her and it's too late. I'm done with that job.'

Debbie shrugged. 'I don't know what I could have told you. I really didn't know her any better than any of the other members.' She looked up at the clock. 'Sorry to cut you off, but it's time to dance.'

I quickly shoved the papers in the cubby where I'd left my things. I had one of those moments when you feel reminded of something, but you don't quite know what. And then all of a sudden it made sense. But I was still confused about Debbie's comment.

'Hey, New Girl,' Kat said, waving me over as I looked for a space to stand.

I was glad to see her and stopped between her and Kelly just as the music came up. I struggled with the class. I wasn't sure if it was that my feet wouldn't move fast enough to keep up with the steps, or that my mind was elsewhere. When the class ended, I apologized to Kat and Kelly for my clumsiness. I also told them that I'd used Kat's story in the booklet I'd done for Rachel. I was about to go grab my stuff when I had a thought and asked them about Debbie's relationship with Rachel, saying that I'd heard from several people that they were close. What Kelly told me changed everything. And now I knew what had happened to Rachel and to me. What could I do? Only in a mystery story did all the characters get together to discuss who did it, and then the guilty party calmly waited for the police.

THIRTY-ONE

A new teacher was standing in the front now getting ready for the next class. I took one look at the reception counter and pushed through the people on their way out of the dance gym and sprinted toward the stairs leading to the El tracks.

I ran up the stairs and through the station. I didn't have time to fuss with a ticket and slipped over the turnstile, hoping no one was looking. When I got to the platform there was just one person waiting for the train.

'You lied,' I said. 'When I told you I heard that Rachel was close to someone at your place, you said it had to be Debbie. You acted as if you didn't even know who Rachel was. But Debbie just told me that she didn't really know Rachel. And then one of the members told me that Rachel and you had been inseparable and that she called you DeeDee.' Darcy looked at me with surprise, then her eyes changed to cunning.

'I was afraid something like this would happen with you. I've been watching you fall apart,' she said. 'All the stress has gotten you. All your work and so much pressure. You've been getting confused. Forgetting that you ordered packages and imagining that you've seen things.' Her voice was hypnotic as she stared at me. 'You just need to take a deep breath and relax. I can help you.'

'It might have worked with Rachel Parker, but not me. I know how you did it. F. Poppins.'

She'd been moving closer until she was almost next to me. 'I don't know what you're talking about. You're just confused.'

'I know how you used a remote control on my TV from across the street, that you got in my place over the balcony to switch the DVDs and just now I realized you had access to my phone during the dance classes. You had my credit card number from the time I ordered the ballet slippers and you must have figured out how to unlock my phone when you used it to take my picture.' She stared at me. 'Why?' I asked and her face grew fierce.

'As soon as I heard you were involved in their wedding, I wanted to punish you for helping them.'

'So, then this all has to do with Luke Ross?' I said. And then I remembered that she'd said she was looking for a fresh start after a bad breakup. 'Were you and Luke a couple?'

'Bingo, you win the prize,' she said sarcastically. 'We were more than a couple. We were soulmates. He was the love of my life. But she was like the shiny new thing.'

'Then you were going together when he met her?' I asked.

'We'd broken up, but I knew we'd get back together. We would have gotten back together if it hadn't been for her.' Darcy's demeanor had changed, and it seemed like she was in the midst of a delusion. I was guessing that she thought with Rachel out of the way, she'd get him back.

'I had to do something,' she began. 'He thought giving me some money to start this gym would be enough to settle things. Ha! I started stalking her. Stupid Rachel never even noticed. And when I conveniently took the table next to her at a coffee place, she didn't suspect a thing. I struck up a conversation and since I already knew a lot about her, made it seem like we had so much in common. I made sure we ran into each other a few more times and suggested we get coffee. I've always been good at sizing people up. I figured right away that she was probably unhappy with her curves. As soon as I told her about the gym and how she could get a ballerina's body, she wanted to join. And then she was my captive audience. She admitted her insecurities and while I appeared to reassure her at first, I used them to smash her confidence a little later. I convinced her that she needed to lose weight, or her husband would lose interest. Then I played mind games with her. It was easy to grab her phone during the class and send texts and order things online.

'I kept making her doubt herself and she became more and more fragile. I convinced her that everyone was against her and that she could only trust me. Once she'd told me about what happened to her mother, that she'd had a breakdown and over-dosed, I knew what I had to do. I just had to convince Rachel that she was the same and that there was only one way out.'

'I know you were there when she went over the balcony.'

Darcy made a face at me. 'I told her that Luke had found

someone else and was going to desert her and how humiliating it would be. She was leaning against the barrier on the balcony. She looked over and then she jumped.'

'I don't believe she jumped,' I said. 'Luke told me about the unsent text on her phone that said: *I need help*. He'd taken it as referring to her mental state and that it was a suicide note. But that's not what it was, was it? She was trying to call for help because she felt threatened by you. But she never got to send the text. You pushed her, didn't you?'

'I kept on hammering at her and she started to argue. I couldn't wait any longer, so I pretended to be going to give her a hug and pushed her over the side instead.'

Darcy stared at me, locking onto my gaze. 'But then you understand, don't you? You know what it feels like to be all alone in the world. Your mother died, your father died. You can't manage a relationship. You can't manage to write another book. You're worthless, you have no reason to keep on going.' She was saying it in that hypnotic voice and much as I tried to fight it, it was feeding into all my insecurities.

I didn't realize it, but she'd been subtly changing her position which instinctively caused me to move as well. She was facing me and my back was to the edge of the platform.

'All you have to do is let yourself go. Let yourself fall. It'll be over in an instant.'

I knew she meant landing on the third rail. It carried the electric power for the El and one touch and I'd be fried. Just as I saw how precarious a spot I was in and tried move, she made a push toward me. I braced for the hit, but before she connected someone grabbed my arm and pulled me away. Darcy teetered, tried to regain her balance, and tumbled off the platform. There was a loud noise that sounded a little like thunder as she landed on the electrified rail.

I looked up to see who my savior was.

'Evan!' I said with surprise. At that moment, a voice from the other end of the platform yelled, 'Freeze.'

THIRTY-TWO

A transit cop stood poised to shoot me with a taser gun. 'You people who think you can get away without paying.' He shook his head with disgust and started to say something about arresting me just as he looked over the platform and saw Darcy laying there. Evan held up two tickets and said he'd paid for both of us. 'It looks like that's immaterial now. I'd say that's a worse problem,' the officer said as he reached for his cell phone.

Everything became a blur. There were sirens and then a herd of cops and first responders all over the platform. I felt sorry for anyone planning to take the El because everything ground to a stop while they investigated the scene. Evan and I were separated, and we each got our own cop caretaker. I lost track of him as I was taken down to ground level. A mobile command post, which was really a big RV made into a portable police station, was parked under the tracks.

I was led into a tiny windowless space with white walls and bright lights. It was unnerving to sit on a bench that had a pair of handcuffs hanging off of a bar across it. I instinctively started to massage my wrists. A detective in a suit and tie closed the door behind him and sat down across from me with a pad and paper.

'You just want a statement from me, right?' I said. I didn't wait for him to answer, but told him the simple facts that Darcy had tried to push me off the platform, but lost her balance when I was pulled out of the way and ended up falling herself.

The detective looked me in the eye. 'There must be more than that. Why don't you tell me the whole story?' I suddenly felt very uneasy. I knew from writing my mystery that that was the kind of thing cops said to suspects.

I did my best to lay it all out for him, but it sounded convoluted and I got a lot of details out of order. I tried to explain what Darcy had done to Rachel and to me. Switching DVDs, messing with the television and the sweater I never ordered. Even without using the word gaslighting, it sounded crazy.

The detective wrote it all down without comment and left. It wasn't clear if I could leave or not and I had a feeling that was intentional. The afternoon dragged on and I sat in the cubicle alone, worrying. Would they think that I had pushed Darcy? Even if Evan told them what had happened, it might not help. They could think we were in it together. Me and Evan as a gang of thugs? Really?

I began to fret that I didn't have my things. I'd run out of Dance with Me without even getting my purse. Just when I was starting to think about who I'd call with my one phone call, the detective came back in.

I closed my eyes expecting the worst. My distress must have been pretty obvious because the detective said, 'Hey, it's OK. You can go.'

I started to say, huh? but stopped myself. I didn't want to delay leaving the small space by even a second. I was out of there and on my way to the door of the command post before I could blink twice.

The afternoon had morphed into evening and the sky was a translucent blue. Evan came outside a moment later. We both looked around like astronauts who'd just dropped back on earth. I heard the squeal of a train above which meant the El was running again. The street was clogged with people on their way home from work.

'I thought they weren't going to let me go,' I said. 'And then all of a sudden they did. What did you say to them?'

Evan appeared a little drained himself, but he brightened. 'It wasn't what I said to them. It was what I showed them. Remember I wanted to meet you for coffee to show you something?' he said. I nodded. 'I wanted to show you the cruise. So you could see if you thought Sally was having a good time.' He pointed to the lapel of his jacket. 'I bought one of those little cameras.' He looked sheepish. 'In hindsight, it was probably a little creepy. Except it saved both of us from being blamed for what happened to that woman. The camera went on as soon as it sensed voices. It taped the whole thing on the El platform. The police kept it as evidence. But I guess it taped over the river cruise anyway.'

'What's done is done,' I said. 'It's water under the bridge.' I cringed at my double cliché. 'More important, you're my hero times two,' I said. 'Once for saving me from Darcy and again for saving me from being accused of pushing her.'

Evan seemed to beam. 'This is better than when you said it before. This time it really was life and death.' Then he ducked his head in his usual self-deprecating way. 'Do you think you could tell Sally? It might get me some points.'

'Don't worry, I'll make sure Sally finds out you were a superhero.' I shivered. The temperature had dropped and my jacket along with all my other things was still down the street at Dance with Me. Evan walked with me. The place was still open, though there were no students and a detective was talking to the teacher and the person on reception. Another detective started to stop me from coming in, but recognized me and got my things for me.

When we got back outside, I asked Evan how he'd ended up on the platform. 'It's simple,' he began. 'I saw you going down the street and I thought you forgot we were supposed to meet for coffee, so I went after you to remind you. I saw you go over the turnstile, so I paid for both of us.'

'That would have been the least of our problems, but thank you.' Just then I saw a bunch of news vans pulling up. Evan saw them, too. 'We better get out of here.' I thanked him again for everything and gave him a hug before we went our separate ways.

It seemed rather anticlimactic, but I joined the rest of the commuters heading for the Metra. I was operating on sheer nerve by then and when I finally got into my place, I kind of fell apart. I even considered having a shot of my cooking wine, but I had a feeling I was going to need to have my mind clear. So, I opted for a cup of coffee with cream and sugar instead.

I turned on the TV, sure that this time there wouldn't be any channel flipping. The local news was just starting. I was shocked to see what had happened to Darcy was the lead story. There were shots of the platform, the command post and the coroner's van. The reporter said that details were just coming in, but that it was a complicated story involving one of the most prominent families in the city. Suddenly I saw my face on the screen. It was a picture from my website along with information about who I was and what I did. They mentioned *The Girl with the Golden Throat* and even showed the cover of my book. Evan's picture was shown as well, and he was lauded as a hero, though he was referred to as a passerby who'd stepped in.

The reporter had reached out to the Parker family and there'd been no comment other than to say that I'd been hired to put together a celebration of life book for Rachel's memorial service.

There was a vague mention of the tape and that it had offered enough information that would likely lead to reinvestigate Rachel's death as a homicide.

It was the first time that I actually acknowledged that Darcy was dead. It felt strange and upsetting. Even though I knew she was ready to kill me with no second thoughts, the idea that I'd played a part in her death was devastating.

There wasn't much time to think about it. Both my landline and cell phone started ringing, texts came in with a burst of pings and my computer *boinged* as emails filled my inbox.

I skipped most of the calls until I saw Ben's name come up on the caller ID.

'Are you OK?' he asked. His voice was back to being monotone and I was almost going to comment on it, but he explained he was working. 'My partner and I were on our dinner break and I looked up at the TV on the wall and there you were. The sound was off, so I missed most of the details.' I started to try to tell him what happened, but by now I was a little overwrought and I heard something on his radio about a call, so we tabled it.

Sara wanted to come up, but I put her off. For now, I needed to let everything settle.

I went over the whole episode with Darcy again in my head, trying to make sense of it. It was all because Darcy couldn't let go of Luke. She'd directed her rage at Rachel, stalking her and then playing mental games to make her think she was losing her mind so she would think there was no way out. But when she couldn't convince Rachel to jump off the balcony, she pushed her. Darcy had gone after me because I'd helped with their wedding vows and maybe too because she thought I was interested in Luke. I stopped for a moment, remembering how I'd thought it was Luke doing the gaslighting. I was just grateful I hadn't said anything.

If I thought things were weird then, they were only going to get stranger. Richard Parker called me himself. He'd viewed the whole tape and wanted to thank me personally for uncovering what had really happened to his daughter. I took the opportunity to apologize to him. 'Your wife told me that you were upset that I'd contacted you. I thought I was doing the right thing. I thought you were OK with it. I'm very sorry if I created a problem. It wasn't my intention.'

He waited until I finished, and I heard him take a breath. 'I think there is a misunderstanding. I wasn't upset with you. I was upset with Camille.' He stopped and I knew he was measuring his words. 'She said she was trying to protect me, but it was a mistake. I'd like to apologize to you for her behavior. Needless to say, we'll want to change the book to reflect what really happened. I want you to deal directly with me from now on.' He paused again and seemed to clear his throat. 'She stiffed you, didn't she?' he said finally.

'Well, yes, but—'

'I'm sorry for that, too. It will be more than taken care of.' I heard someone in the background and knew the call was about to end. Before he hung up, he spoke kindly to me, almost like a father. 'Take care of yourself this evening, won't you, after all you've been through today.'

I sat holding the phone for a moment, thinking about the call. I was startled when it rang in my hands. I saw Luke Ross in the caller ID, and I answered.

'I'm sorry,' he said, before he'd even said hello. 'I don't know where to begin. I had no idea that Darcy would do anything like what she did. I never would have guessed that she'd use her skills for such evil. She used to be a therapist, she used hypnosis in her practice. She was burned out and going through a lot when we broke up, but I thought she was dealing with it. She seemed grateful for the money I gave her to try something new. I feel so terrible that I let this happen.' His voice cracked and I knew he was swallowing back tears. 'I don't know what I'm going to do.'

He'd called to make things right with me, but he needed it more than I did. I reassured him that he'd get through this. I told him about my own losses and that I'd gotten through them. I

knew it was a cliché, but I said that time healed all wounds. We
ended it agreeing that we'd talk again, maybe at the bar over
orange juice. So Darcy had been a therapist who'd gone rogue.
No wonder she'd seemed so easy to talk to. It had been her
profession. And she'd talked about exercise aiding mental health.

I'd been holding myself together through all the phone calls,
but I finally let go and this time when I fell apart, a cup of coffee
with cream and sugar couldn't help. I took a hot bath and called
it a night. It was reassuring when Rocky took his spot on the
pillow and I fell asleep listening to the rhythm of his breath.

Tuesday morning, the phone calls, emails and texts started
again. I wanted to shut down and back away from it all, but I
wouldn't let myself. Evan called first. Sally had seen the news
reports and been confused about what he was doing on the El
platform with his neighbor who wrote mysteries. He finally told
her the truth about how we knew each other and what exactly
I'd done. Instead of being upset, she'd melted at the idea that he
wanted to impress her so badly. 'I'm really sorry,' Evan said,
'but I don't think I'll need your services anymore.' He paused
for a moment. 'But maybe when it's the right time you can help
me plan a proposal.'

'I've never been so glad to lose a gig,' I said. 'Of course, if
you need help with a proposal, you know where to find me. You
know, I never did know how it was that you found me in the
first place.'

'Luke,' he said. 'He knew I liked Sally and how much trouble
I was having knowing what to say. He told me that you'd helped
with his wedding vows.'

The next call was from Debbie. She was stunned by what had
happened and said she'd closed Dance with Me for the day, but
she didn't know what she was going to do going forward. She'd
been contacted by all the news stations and magazine TV shows.
'You know about publicity,' she said, sounding hopeful. I promised I'd come down to the dance spot the next day and help her
deal with it all. There was no reason for Darcy to kill Dance
with Me, too.

And the calls and emails kept coming. I was astonished by
who was contacting me and how my life had changed in an
instant.

By evening I was ready for a little normalcy and looked forward to the writers' group. Tizzy was the first to arrive. 'Tell me everything. The news stories were incomplete. None of them said gaslighting but that's what it was, wasn't it?'

I waited for her to take a breath and sent her to the dining room saying we'd talk about it when everybody got there.

Ed came in next. There was a new self-important swagger. 'They posted it and so many comments.' He looked skyward and smiled. As an afterthought, he said, 'My wife said she saw you on the news.'

Ben came up from his sister's with a plate of food. He leaned in. 'She said it's enough to share. She's relentless.' He dropped his voice even lower. 'I hope you don't mind, but when I'm here with the group, I'll stick to cop mode.'

Daryl came in at the end. Dressed in a trendy outfit, she had her usual worried look and rushed to the back to join the others.

I let Ed tell about his triumph first. And then he waved a pile of papers. 'Everybody loves what I posted, but someone commented that it would be nice if I put in a little more relationship stuff. I'm sure you guys can help me with that.'

Tizzy turned to me. 'OK, now tell us everything.'

The news story had only told parts of it. I explained how I'd started off believing that Rachel had had some kind of a breakdown caused by something, but then began to think the breakdown was caused by someone.

'I helped,' Tizzy said, interrupting. 'I told her about gaslighting and *Gaslight* the movie.'

The rest of them told her to be quiet and let me talk. 'What really made me believe someone was behind it was when things started happening to me that were meant to throw me off balance.'

'I was there when it happened,' Tizzy said. 'I said someone was trying to gaslight her.'

'I suspected her husband first,' I said.

'He was the most likely suspect,' Tizzy said. 'Just like in the movie.'

'But when I found out that Rachel wasn't alone when she went off the balcony, everything got more sinister. When I was at that last dance class, all of a sudden I realized that someone could have accessed my phone and Rachel's at the gym. All along I'd thought that Rachel was close with the main dance teacher and that she'd barely known Darcy. It was a comment from one of my new friends there that set me right. She said that Rachel and Darcy had been, excuse the cliché, thick as thieves. It seems stupid now, but I got it in my head I had to confront Darcy. She'd just left, and I knew she took the El. It didn't occur to me that she'd try to push me onto the third rail.' I shrugged. 'Thank heavens for my guardian angel.'

'You mean the guy who was with you?' Tizzy asked. I told them all about Evan, along with his happy ending. I got to the end and hesitated.

'And?' Tizzy said. 'You made it sound like there's something more.'

This was the part I felt guilty about. 'The story has everything: romance, jealous rage, fabulously wealthy people who are well-known philanthropists, a sort of wicked stepmother, creepy manipulation and finally murder. So I've heard from all the local news shows and every national magazine-type show, wanting to interview me. A Hollywood production company is trying to buy the rights to the whole thing and in the meantime wants to buy my story. I don't know if any of you noticed but 57th Street Books put a display of my books in the window.'

'Does that mean you're not going to work with us anymore,' Daryl said, looking upset.

'No. I mean yes, I am going to keep on with the group,' I said. What I didn't say was that I'd gotten a call from the publisher asking about another book. I thought of the stack of pages on the shelf. Maybe I'd give it another shot.

As Ben said he would, he stayed in the flat tone, expression-less cop mode he'd always been in, but once when I looked in his direction, his eyes warmed for a moment and he gave me a thumbs up.

After they'd all left, I went to my computer and saw that a bunch of people had contacted me about writing projects. I took a deep breath. There was so much going on, my head was spin-ning. There was nothing to do but keep putting one foot in front of the other, taking it one step at a time, and forgive myself for thinking in clichés.

ACKNOWLEDGMENTS

I t was great working with my editor, Carl Smith. His fun comments made the editing process particularly enjoyable. This book wouldn't have happened without my agent, Jessica Faust. She helped with the concept and finding it a home.

Penny Fisher Sanborn is the one who introduced me to the Lakeshore East neighborhood where parts of the book take place. She also offered details of our old neighborhood and the building we both lived in.

I like books with lots of details about the setting. I tried to do that when writing about Veronica's neighborhood and her apartment. It was enjoyable to me because it gave me a chance to see everything with a fresh eye.

And of course, thanks to my family, Burl, Max, Samantha and Jakey.